FORGOTTEN RUIN

LAY THE HATE

JASON ANSPACH
NICK COLE

WARGATE

An imprint of Galaxy's Edge Press
PO BOX 534
Puyallup, Washington 98371
Copyright © 2021 by Galaxy's Edge, LLC
All rights reserved.

Paperback ISBN: 978-1-949731-57-6
Hardcover ISBN: 978-1-949731-58-3

www.forgottenruin.com
www.jasonanspach.com
www.nickcolebooks.com
www.wargatebooks.com

TECHNICAL ADVISORS AND CREATIVE DESTRUCTION SPECIALISTS

Ranger Vic
Ranger David
Ranger Chris

Green Beret John "Doc" Spears

Rangers lead the way!

CHAPTER ONE

THE storm began six miles off the Pillars of Hulk. The Portugonian sailors called those two massive shards of jade rock that stuck straight up out of the rough seas dividing the Endless Ocean, or what we had once called the Atlantic ten thousand years ago, and the Great Inner Sea, they called those rocks the *Pillars of Hulk*.

The pillars marked the dividing line between safe passage through these outer waters beyond the coasts of Portugon, and danger in the deep blue sea. Portugonian sailors told the Rangers this was where the deep began. Where the danger waited down there in the dark depths.

At first the wind sang in the tight cables and ropes of the lithe Portugonian trading galleys as small, almost monkey-like sailors scrabbled and climbed the rigging to set the big sails and beat before the storm. We were heading east into the Med, or rather the Great Inner Sea as it was now called on maps in the strange yet familiar tongues we once knew.

The ropes and the wind sang along with the busy sailors working quickly to gain some advantage off what we were heading into, and what was clearly a brewing storm off the starboard bow to the south. The sound in the rigging was not a good sound. "Like a witch being skinned alive," muttered Tanner darkly as we got ourselves ready for whatever came next.

The map was full of blank spaces that might as well have been darkness at midnight. The song of the sailors was more like a prayer. Something to be about while they were busy saving their lives. And ours too. We had little intel about the Rift off to our right. Or what people who work on boats call starboard. In Portugonian it's *estibordo*. We had no idea what lay in that dark and mysterious region off the north coast of Africa where once Morocco and Algiers were places on maps we took for granted. Thinking then nothing would ever change in the completely dramatic way it had. All we knew was this… things were about to get seriously weird.

The fables, myths, and fishwives' tales were the best intel we could develop in the ancient city of Portugon. And if a quarter of what they indicated was true, we were in for it big time.

The Portuguese, or as they are now known ten thousand years later, the Portugonians, always sing no matter what. That's because they always sing while they work. And they're always working. That's my takeaway from the first of the Cities of Men the Rangers went to after killing Ssruth the Cruel in the swamp-covered ruins of Tarragon.

Portugonians like music. It surrounds them all the time.

That there were songs that were to us, the Rangers, refugees out of time, almost familiar, and haunting now in their new forms, was weird, and often the Rangers made a game of trying to figure out which songs the Portugonians were singing that came from our time. Sometimes some caught the whiff of something that had once been metal or pop. Other times it was just a haunting tune none of the Rangers could place. I'd spotted a few but kept them to myself for reasons I could never figure out. The songs were once something we knew, but now in Portugonian, different in melody and tone. Sometimes more mournful, sometimes more like a chant. Or a prayer when the storm comes for you in the deep blue.

The old sailor came to me, speaking slowly but direct, as Santago always did. Sometimes he said little. Sometimes he mused to no one in particular. He did this when there was a lull in whatever it was that needed doing next to get three Portugonian trading galleys hired for the Rangers for an expedition to the south and east moving out in the ocean. He was taller than the Portuguese-Portugonians, and they themselves told me Santago was once from Navarre and not one of them, though they considered him to be because of his skill. Navarre, or what the rude map we carry calls *Further Navarre*, a forgotten province in a fading empire called Accadios, a city to the east where Rome might have been if Italy hadn't been hit by a comet apparently. There has been no governor from the great capital of Accadios for as long as anyone in Portugon can remember. And the phrase *the Legion never marches west anymore* is used almost as punctuation when speaking of such geopolitical matters here in the Ruin, and especially the docks, slums, alleys, and palaces of ancient Portugon. Santago the old sailor who runs the galleys and specifically the one we're on, is probably Spanish. Or at least he would've been Spanish ten thousand years ago.

Santago is their—the sailors of the three hired ships of Portugon—their sergeant major, basically. Or whatever the equivalent is in a naval unit, though these ships are not official Portugonian Navy. They are more armed traders and most likely smugglers of some sort. Whatever Santago is, he runs them and interacts between the sailors on board all three, including their short fiery captains and the Rangers who have booked passage into the east and the south, ultimately heading to Sûstagul to begin operations against the Saur and Sût the Undying.

"The Witch Storm has come now," muttered the old sailor in his salt-and-gutter-wine-ravaged voice. "Now is the time we must do everything we can to get east of it before it strikes us in the face. Tell your men, Talk-ir, that it will be rough now. Very rough. And there is every chance we will be lost before we go much further. The sea is not angry, not yet, but her anger is growing and so we must do our best if we are to survive the passage east and make it to your destination in that cursed port."

He doesn't need to convince me. The skies to the south look downright evil.

"That bad, huh?" I reply, trying to develop a little more info before I head back to the Ranger command team on deck and let them know what the old sailor is telling me.

I'm shaky. But that's from something else. Something before all this began this morning.

I said warts and all… but… I'm not ready. Not yet. Let's just get through this. And then I'll tell you everything. If I don't die first. Or drown out here in the deep waters the Portugonians call this area of the Great Inner Sea.

Águas Profundas.

But we, the old sailor and I, are speaking in Spanish, which Santago calls *Viejo Navarre*. Or *Old Navarre*. And some Portugonian creeps in because it's the local custom of informational exchange. My Portuguese is not pro, and the language has evolved quite a lot in the ten thousand years since we left Area 51 to try and save the world that got lost.

Or revealed. Depends who you ask.

But if you've read enough of this account to know me, then you know… I'm excited.

New language for the win!

We make communication as best we can under the circumstances. The Rangers are on deck and watching the south where a storm unlike any we've ever seen brews and bubbles like that skinned-alive witch's cauldron indeed.

The Rangers are ready. For what, none of us know. But that has never stopped the Rangers from being completely ready to kill their way out of something with as much brutality as possible.

The other two galleys, *Dançarina das Estrelas* and *Lobo Marinho*—*Dancer of Stars* and *Sea Wolf* they are translated as, or just *Dancer* and *Wolf* as the Rangers have begun to call them—rig their sails just as we have. At the same time those of *Sofia* above the heads of those on deck with me have begun to shift and rise, filling with the hot, almost acrid wind coming out of the south, and all three ships start to tack into the wind that's coming from the east, at the same time driving us south into the Atlantean Rift.

Officially among the Rangers' established comm, these ships are known as Sea Horse One Four Heavy, Two Four Heavy, and Three Four Heavy.

We knew this would be the most dangerous part of the *hop* but oh well, if you don't have the courage to sail beyond the sight of shore, you'll never know the sheer terror of being lost at sea.

So we all got that going for us right about now as the witch storm hits our sails and shifts the waves to small forming whitecaps.

Perhaps this account will be waterlogged, but it'll be warts and all. I promise you that.

As I was telling you… we knew this part would be dangerous. Our passage to the area of operations in and around Sûstagul and ultimately out into the Valley of the Lich Pharaohs where we've placed the location of our high-value Jackpot. We're crossing in front of the ravaged wide bay where "the stars fell long ago," as Vandahar has described, along the coast of North Africa where once the two continents were so close, and where the topography has changed greatly.

The fragments of the great comet that hit this area, the same comet that turned the Black Sea into a "Mordor-like," Kennedy's words not mine, desert of waste ringed by jagged mountains and boiling volcanos, and did other things to the geography of the Earth we once knew, also fragmented and smashed here into the western coast of North Africa, creating a great savage Rift that leads deep into the sands of the Sahara.

The ancient map we navigate by now calls the Sahara *No Man's Land.*

So that's not ominous or anything.

This passage is not the mission. This is the hop to the mission. The mission, or whatever, that Vandahar has convinced the captain we must do so that, as the old wizard puts it, "The Grand Confrontation against the Evils can finally begin…"

Any other time a long time ago and it would be Rangers mounting up on a Chinook in the waiting darkness and headed to the 'Y' for the walk, or the 'X' for the immediate thrills of bagging some HVI. Shrugging into their carriers and checking their Timex watches. Relentless and immune to the hardships they operated in because they had decided to be so.

Sua sponte.

Of their own accord.

Because they had decided to be. And that's a decision you only make once, and follow it always. I had learned that in my time here.

But now we find ourselves on strange ocean-going galleys that look like something out of ancient Greece more than any ship built in the thousand years before we leapt out of time. And we're getting hit by a massive and sudden storm where just ten minutes ago it was blue skies and the gentle roll of the deep sea we were heading out into.

Some of the sailors had made strange, almost holy signs when the sea birds that followed us suddenly peeled away and fled from our wakes. That is *their* intel. The sailors watch the birds to know what's going on with the sea. What's coming for us. What's waiting for us.

Point for the AAR if we survive this one… we need to learn their ways of developing intel.

But we knew this was what might happen. Or as the Ranger NCOs constantly reinforce… *an operational contingency for INFIL.* The tempest out of the south. Starboard. *Estibordo.*

A witch's interest in our business if you believe the fishwives' tales that are our only intel.

The Portugonians sing even now some hauntingly familiar song from our past, though they've turned it into some vaguely Arabic sea shanty. They call this devil wind from the south *La Desprezada.*

The Scorned Woman.

Then we see a black mass disintegrating and then coalescing swarms on the gray and boiling red horizon to the south. Noon has turned to the last of a winter's day, though really it's only fall now.

We jumped through the time gate in spring when it was wet and rainy. We fought the Army of the Dead at the end of spring and the beginning of summer. We slew the dragon at the height of summer.

Then stuff happened…

And by late fall we reached Portugon and were headed for the hit on Sût himself.

The defeat of the dragon is behind us. So are other things. Me and who we might have once been. Last of Autumn and the dream of another boat not this one.

If you are wondering why I haven't written in this journal in so long it's because… I've been busy. Or rather forcing myself to stay busy.

Trying to forget.

Santago said that to me when he dragged me from the bloodbath inside the Purple Abyss just a few hours before we boarded the galleys and made out into open waters beyond the breakwaters and coastal fishing boats, heading for the deep and danger. Or as the laconic Sergeant Chris put it as we cast off from the docks of Portugon, "Heading into the deep blue, and potentially right into Davy Jones's sure-to-be overstuffed locker at this point."

"What are you trying to forget, boy?" Santago had asked in the dawn dark of this very morning, his old sea-gnarled and calloused hand pressing the bad cut I'd been rewarded with in the desperate hours of the last of the dangerous night at a bar I never should have gone back to. Dawn in the east and the morning skies glowing red.

I was still drunk. On the liquor they served there in the place, and the vengeance I served too.

I remember thinking just eight hours ago as my mind reeled and I almost passed out from how bad the cut was, that red skies at morning were some kind of old warning.

But I was never a sailor, and I didn't know any except Santago and these Portuguese, or Portugonians now.

"What are you trying to forget, boy?" the old man's tequila-ruined voice gargled as he dragged me along through gutters and wet alleys where other murdered bodies and sleeping beggars lay, careless of the status it takes to achieve residence here at the end of yourself. In the distance the city alarms cried murder.

Guards scrambled from the towers.

Brass bells and whistles of doom.

Murder done at the Purple Abyss.

But that's another story. Not this one now.

Like I said. I've been busy since the dragon. Busy forgetting. And now the Rangers are in it again. And I'm with them. We're on the next pump, and I'm more ready than ever.

Sua sponte.

The Rangers watch the boiling southern sky fill with the harpies coming out of the south. Their screeching calls and cackles can barely be heard above the howl of the wind in the ropes and the beat of the sails trying to pull us from the clutches of the sudden storm. The Portugonian sailors are singing as they make signs to themselves and chant out their quick prayers that we might be saved and that they might return home once again to the ones who love them. Working hard and watching the wind and the waves, they are ready for the captain's command, or really Santago's command, from the helm on the low quarterdeck. It's clear they know we're in trouble. Big trouble in fact.

We know we're in trouble too.

But trouble is where Rangers live, comfortably.

The Rangers have a lot of dragon gold to hire their rides into danger. That's the way the Ruin works. Life is dangerous. Some things you must do if the gold is worth the risk. Danger is every day for everyone in the Ruin. It ain't like back where we came from. There's no safety net here. There are walls and sometimes even those aren't enough if you listen to the histories of the Cities of Men and all the places that have been overrun by monsters and other darknesses.

And then there is Santago and the old sailor says, "Some danger, like some women, Talk-ir, is worth the risk, eh?"

I look up at the sky and see the coming swarm of half-hag, half-vulture monsters and shudder. Then I see the Rangers getting ready for the killing work that must be done.

They, the Rangers, they are the spiders. And everyone, and everything else to them, is the fly.

Even *La Desprezada*. The Scorned Woman. Sultria of the Southern Citadel. Medusa and Queen of Tribes who rules the ruins of the Atlantean Rift along the Lost Coast at the End of the World. Or so say the maps.

Rangers gonna Ranger.

CHAPTER TWO

"PRIVATE Talker!" shouts Kurtz. "You worthless slag. You're on AG!"

That's Assistant Gunner for Soprano who's carrying the two-forty Lima version. Shorter, lighter, and can be fired effectively from the shoulder. The Forge cranked these new medium machine guns out because the old ones were already breaking down from the nano-plague. And there's a long hump into the North African deserts ahead of us once we reach our destination. This mission is going to require more maneuverability.

And of course, the firepower. You always need that too.

Jabba is belowdecks ready to bring more ammo up should Kurtz give the order. The ocean makes the little gob more jittery than usual.

Thirty seconds later as the storm hits in full, sending waves over the low main deck, Soprano begins to rock on the distant target as I stand and feed the belt. We trained for this in the week we spent on the docks at Portugon near the entrance to the Tagus River. The sailors, through Santiago, had told us that some ships lost to *La Desprezada* were overwhelmed by a sky filled with screeching harpies. Vengeful half-women, half-vultures.

We'd seen one of those at the battle on Ranger Alamo. It had taken out our drone.

The plan developed by the Rangers was to go kinetic on the harpies before they could reach our sails and tear them to shreds. If they did that, then we'd get dragged down into the Atlantean Rift—assuming the oars couldn't get us out of the dangerous currents, which, according to Santiago, was a fool's bargain. That would put us off course and derail the journey to the insertion point far to the east. Getting involved in the Rift was not part of the plan.

The plan was to do our best to avoid the Rift.

It was a bad place apparently. Real bad. How did I know that? Because anytime you even mentioned the place, the Portugonian sailors, all short, swarthy, mustachioed, bandy-legged males who looked perpetually angry despite their generally friendly dispositions, rolled their eyes and made signs usually reserved for warding off evil curses.

Hot brass and linkage danced out and away, and one randomly bounced off a gunwale and crawled down into my combat shirt as Soprano began to rock the incoming harpy air cav high above. Nothing I could do about that but let it burn as I was busy feeding the medium machine gun firing bursts while maintaining an appropriate dance with Soprano's position as the gunner shifted, aimed, fired for effect—lather, rinse, repeat. All of this on a Bronze Age sailing vessel while the deck rocked and pitched in the waves, the sudden storm getting angrier by the second.

But I did get to watch the show for free.

Dancer, or Sea Horse Three Four, was off to our side and running just behind *Sofia*, our ship. *Sea Wolf* was cutting behind us, driving north and stealing our wind to get away from the harpies.

The captain of the *Sea Wolf* was a known shrewd pirate whom the command team had identified as highly capable but possibly untrustworthy. Unfortunately, he was one of the few Portugonian ship captains who would take Ranger gold for the dangerous haul south and east along the Lost Coast to reach the insertion. Or what we once called North Africa. A supposedly haunted region filled with wrecks and warlike tribes of orcs and other monsters just waiting for you to have to come ashore for water, or because you were driven there.

There were giant orcs even. The Portugonians didn't know that we had done giants and orcs before in other regions. In the Ruin orcs were everywhere, and there were all kinds apparently. As the small angry sailors whispered and swore, making signs with their hands to ward off the evils, the Rangers merely shrugged at the news.

It was clear in the opening moments of our first contact with the enemy that the assessment of the pirate's nature had been correct. The plan, once *La Desprezada* began, had been to close the galleys into a wedge formation and put up as much anti-air fire as possible to drive the harpies off as they came to disable our sails. All we had to do was make it to a small island ten miles east of the Pillars of Hulk and we were supposedly safe from the powers of the Scorned Woman.

"I know not the veracity of this superstition," mused Vandahar over his long-stemmed pipe in the dockside tavern the Rangers had secured as their base of operations once inside the city, during phase one for the hop to the mission pump. Which is the planning phase. Now we were in phase two, which is movement to objective. Phase three was kill Sût. Phase four was consolidate and reorganize. Five was exfil, or beat feet. "But such superstitions are usually rooted in some fact," continued the wizard. "So it seems a good plan to use the islands as a waypoint for our escape during the journey, if that be possible."

Now it was clear from the wind and waves that that wasn't going to happen. If we were going to reach the isle, then we were going to have to fight our way there to give the sails and oars any kind of chance to fight the drag and pull of the dangerous waters of the Rift.

Tanner already had another two-forty Lima on deck as Soprano screamed, "Get some!" firing more bursts into the elevated flying hags. Rangers were firing from the deck as the wind drove the saltwater waves to whitecaps all around the three ships. The sea began to thrash the bow of our ship, creating great booms as the *Sofia* dove into the deepening troughs of sea foam and green churn while the harpies attacked and the Rangers put up a wall of air-defense fire and targeted fire for the shooters.

The boom of *Mjölnir* from the low forecastle was constant. Harpies exploded, making little bursts of artwork against the sky. Sergeant Thor's medium was a fifty-caliber high-velocity brush, and he was creating his first seascape with it. And here's an interesting thing… the M105 anti-materiel rifle hadn't broken down yet like the rest of our weapons had, needing to be replaced by the Forge.

"That's curious," Penderly the tech had noted. The Baroness, who'd remained at the FOB, gave one of her bookishly sexy enigmatic smiles behind her large glasses and asked if she could run some tests.

Sergeant Thor uttered a simple *No.*

End of discussion.

The waters around our ships were now getting darker and the sky was becoming both hot and gray. In other words, it all seemed surreal and unnatural, like the end of the world was being rolled out especially for the assistant gunner to have something to do while Soprano got his rock and roll on, switching between Ranger English and Sicilian promises of cold murder delivered promptly via the death machine that was the two-forty Lima.

I watched as some harpies exploded, or had their wings torn off and tumbled, spiraling, into the angry waves out to sea, shrieking madly as they plunged into the increasingly violent chop. Their screeching was a hell chorus that made even the mournful wind that keened and moaned in the ropes and sails seem like some calm relaxation music composed to combat stress.

More hot brass burned the linguist. Linguist listened to Kurtz bark at him to shift left or right, so Soprano could work clusters of the sky hags. Linguist do good at being AG.

I felt that shaky papery thin feeling leaving me as the gun fired in short bursts, raining brass onto the wet deck where the waves were now beginning to come across and soak our boots and the bottoms of our Crye Precision pants. The feeling of being cut badly. The feeling of what I'd done in the darkness before dawn, just hours before we boarded the galleys for the hop to the mission. Being somewhere I wasn't supposed to be, involved in something I never should have been involved in. The gunfire and action of now made that a nightmare that might have been a dream. Or maybe it was the other way around. But whatever it was, it was gone now as the fight got underway. The hot acrid wind, the cries of the Italian gunner, the blast of the gun, the smells of salt and the war cries of the harpies… I felt it all, and also the nothing I hadn't ever expected to come of what I'd done in the Purple Abyss.

Abismo Roxo.

Purple Abyss. Just that. That was the place's name. Its name in fact still unless it burned down to the ground after what had gone down there. Not *The Purple Abyss.* That would be *O Abismo Púrpura.*

Linguist doing languages in weird firefight. Never mind. It's just me doing me.

I'd expected something else then there at that place I was never supposed to be in. To *feel* something else as Santago dragged me from there. Bleeding and drunk. Bodies on the floor. I'd expected to feel something else.

But I didn't.

And that wasn't important now. It was time to *Be meaner than it, Talker,* in the words of the sergeant major who was aboard the *Sea Wolf,* or Sea Horse One Four Heavy.

The gun roaring near me as I fed the beast reminded me I was alive right now. Reminded me I was in combat and that I was both excited and scared as Soprano shot down the harpies, screaming at them as he did so. I was alive… which is combat. The living and the dead. The winners and losers. I was alive, and… that was enough of a feeling in lieu of what I had expected to find in the *Abismo Roxo.*

And hadn't.

I haven't felt much in a while even before that place. But I'd expected to finally find something. I lied to myself that I would.

I liked this now… this moment of automatic gunfire rattling and Rangers in my EarPro over the comm, working the problems like calm cool killers killing together.

Yeah, maybe once… in some other fantasy I'd had about the Cities of Men and the two of us in a boat… her smile, yeah, maybe I'd wanted that then.

But that was then… and this is now.

To the south, beyond our racing galleys, the sky was turning dark with furious harpies flapping their great vulture wings, some of them shifting in formations, others beginning to climb high above us despite the gale-force winds hitting us from off the coast of Africa, or the Atlantean Rift, call it what you will. Then they began to dive on us like witchy kamikaze bombers of old. But kamikaze bombers from the nightmares of demons in hell.

The Rangers returned fire in their ugly faces, the decks littered with expended brass and seawater coming over the rails.

They came shrill and shrieking, streaking down out of the racing clouds, great curved black nails like claws out as they raced for the wide square sails of *Dancer*, *Wolf*, and *Sofia*. Some of them had small curving bows and nocked arrows with black feathers. Others carried hatchets and crude spears. Charms of shrunken heads and bone necklaces dangled over their withered chests, flapping madly in the insane wind as they came out of the boiling clouds.

"Sergeant Kurtz!" shouted Brumm, who was acting as spotter and picking up targets with the MK48 SAW. "Three from above. One o'clock."

Even though the alert was for Kurtz I knew it was also for me. I needed to be ready for Soprano to shift fire from our left and low along the water where he'd just exploded a harpy who'd been gliding in across the whitecaps with an axe in one claw and a small jagged sword in the other. Like I said, I had a front-row view of all the carnage as the enemy dove and attacked our small fleet. I watched as the outgoing seven-six-two rounds streaked past her, some hitting water and skipping away in the wind and skirling sand.

Yeah, there was sand in the wind. So that's weird. It was stinging and scouring my exposed skin as I tried to hold the belt and keep it matched with the shaking, jumping machine gun.

Then one of the rounds smashed into her wing pinion and blew it clean off, her mouth opening in a horrible scream as she plowed into the waves and disappeared forever.

The waters here off the Atlantean Rift are shark-infested, according to the Portugonian sailors.

"Very bad," one had told me while knotting ropes as we loaded gear for the hop into the south. "Much feasting there."

I was working on my knots. Which was one of the first things I'd gotten gigged for in Kurtz's Ranger School back at FOB Hawthorn.

I told the sailor I hoped we didn't go down there in the waters outside the Rift.

"I know!" he said almost angrily. Which is how the Portugonian males respond to everything. It's not really anger. Or a challenge. It's just how they say it. Something a linguist notes. Not important to the story of Rangers versus harpies, I know. But like I said, I haven't been able to write much with Ranger School, and getting ready for the pump we were going on, and…

… and staying busy. Trying to forget.

I looked back at the sailor as we worked on ropes and knots and replied, "I know." Just like he did. It's how they communicate. He nodded like he understood that I understood and went back to furiously working on the knots he was making in the lengths of the rope.

"Reorient the gun to the four-o'clock position, Talker! Hang on!" shouted Kurtz between bursts of the machine gun. I felt the barrel of the gun climb through the feed of the belt as I scanned to spot the incoming harpies in that direction, Soprano swearing in Italian, promising to murder all of them. We'd need a new belt in the next few seconds at this rate. At almost the same moment, I acquired the three sister vultures Kurtz had identified, diving out of the storm-covered daylight, as Soprano, satisfied with range and elevation, began to fire on them.

One halted, fluttering her ugly, black, dirty wings in a sort of braking gesture. She pulled back on her small recurve bow, preparing to fire, and Soprano shifted fire and sent his first burst right into her, since she was going to oblige and give him an easy target.

I had no idea where the round hit her because it looked like she just exploded into nothing but black feathers and then her limp body began to spiral and fall end over end into the storm-tossed waters below.

The other two pinned their wings and shrieked in faster. Soprano, who wasn't tall, raised up, lowering the barrel down toward the horizon, and raked both. One lost its mishappen, huge, jawed head, the body literally getting carried away as the round, moving at just over twenty-four hundred feet per second, smashed into her, spraying dark blood that the wind carried away. The other continued down toward us. She swooped in and cut a savage line in the cloth anchoring one of the corners of the sails. The huge sheet began to flap as the harpy streaked off, cackling maniacally and spreading her vulture's wings, gliding out of our firing arc.

Kurtz swore and Soprano shifted the gun as a huge front of screaming harridans made their attack en masse. Farther down the deck Tanner was going high-cycle, with Jabba acting as the AG.

The look on the little gob's face was pure misery.

"All guns!" shouted Kurtz over the blare of the two-forty, his thundering bark cutting through the comm and obliterating the drone operator's message that she was losing the drone. "Shift fire to my target."

Kurtz's carbine went full auto on a sudden phalanx of winged vultures streaking in for a massed attack. He had tracers in the mix just to show us where he wanted the mass of fire and what he wanted dead right now. All guns shifted fire and executed what is affectionately known in a weapons squad as a "mad minute" with guns going at a cyclic rate of fire inducing as much damage as possible as fast as possible. Some of the harpies died. But not enough.

Now, I'm no expert, but things looked pretty dire already. Our ships were out of formation. We were losing drone coverage. And with my arms and shoulders shaking and my exposed skin getting all kinds of hot brass burns, including another one down the front of my chest, there was no way I could get to my cold brew in my canteen.

I don't want to say that's a crisis. But it is. If I was gonna die by harpy then I wanted to make sure I had a mouth full of coffee. But that's true if I was gonna die by anything and on all days that end in 'y' generally.

The next mass wave of harpies came in toward *Sofia* and *Dancer*, suddenly blotting out the thin daylight of the noonday sun the storm was obscuring. Everywhere all around us was a madhouse of shriek-screaming and black feathers. Hectoring relentless shrill calls on a sonic sea of insanity as the harpies cackled and chattered amongst themselves in their headache-inducing language.

And then died because Rangers gonna Ranger despite your noise.

Just because you do something stupid like go ahead and attack a Ranger-laden smugglers' galley in the middle of the Great Inner Sea with some sort of magically controlled storm as an ally, didn't mean things were going to go well for you. In fact, the Rangers just went full Viking immediately as the harpies got dumb enough to get close.

At the same time Kurtz directed Brumm to employ the Carl G using airburst HE on the swarms that were massed close enough for it to be super effective. This scattered great clusters and allowed the gunners and shooters to work them over.

One of Brumm's first shots exploded inside a dense cluster of these sky hags and sent body parts in every direction raining down into the choppy seas around our beleaguered ships.

"Carl G provides!" shouted Tanner as the triangular fins of ravenous and frenzied sharks instantly shot toward the bloody carnage like fast-moving self-guided torpedoes.

A lot of the harpies died by high-cycle violent gunfire at close range as they climbed the rails and landed on the decks of both ships. *Sea Wolf* seemed to be free of the attack and getting farther out to sea and away from the Rift. Some of the harpies were even crawling into the rigging now. It was like blinking your eyes from normal to a glimpse of hell. One second it was our ship. Then they were everywhere. Yeah, the two-forties were in dire need of a barrel change. But the other Rangers on deck in the command team, which had taken Kurtz's weapon squad and the rest of First Platoon with it, were engaging from every available space where they didn't interrupt the Portugonian sailors trying to get our ship out of harm's way as best as possible.

To their credit, the Portugonians were all business despite the madness and probably just as brave as the Rangers even with their swearing and scowling and continual sign-making as they did their sailing work. This was their ship, and they were damned if they were gonna end up just another marker of a lost-at-sea ship near the Portugon Sailors' Hall back on the Street of Sorrows beneath the dark smoke of looming nearby temples and all their strange gods and monsters. They cut and hacked at the vulture women with their sailors' knives. Driving them away from the rigging and sails where they could.

When we first came to Portugon, I wondered if we could trust these guys. The Portugonian sailors. Portugon itself even. It was a beautiful city. A dark, almost medieval city. But it was a violent city in which knives were out on every street. Beautiful and mysterious women. Short angry men.

Everyone always about something.

They were humans just like us though. Not elves and dwarves and other… strange and wonderful creatures. Sometimes. There's something I'd never expected about that. About being among other humans. Despite our differences, Portugonian and Ranger… in the Ruin, being human counts for something. Counts for everything, even with our differences. Because humans aren't the apex predator anymore. We ain't the dominant species. It seems there's a lot more of everyone else than there is us anymore. There are other races now, races that have lost their humanity. And are even alien to it now.

Like the orcs.

I knew the plan the wizard had made with Captain Knife Hand. Sail east and try not to attract *La Desprezada*. If we made it past the Rift, then on to our mission in the Land of the Black Sleep.

But would the Portugonians take us all the way? That had always been the big question. They'd been paid in dragon hoard. Paid well in fact. But it wasn't an easy journey by anyone's standards. There were other problems with the Great Inner Sea. The Pirates of the Lost Coast. Strange and mysterious islands of no return. Lost races, if the myths were to be believed, that lived in the shallow depths along the great northern coast of what we had once called north Africa. And then of course the Land of Black Sleep itself where the Saur slept in great tombs, temples, and pyramids, dreaming dreams of coming conquest once again.

Land of the Lich Pharaohs. Realm of the Saur.

This was our shot to take Sût the Undying himself out of the game and change the course of the coming war.

Yeah, we were getting involved now because, as Vandahar had said, "There is no other option for you Rangers here in the Ruin. Not after Toth-Azom. And the Green Dragon of Tarragon. The Nether Sorcerer will send his servants now and all the forces he can muster against you until he breaches these walls and makes certain you are dead. Until he knows you are no longer a threat to him and his plans. And… many serve that dark master, Captain of Rangers. They number like the sands of a great and very angry desert that wants to wash across the Ruin and consume it forever. Even you lot, with your impressive mastery of violence and skillful murder, would be hard-pressed to survive a wave of such proportions. For even the Cities of Men will finally fall in this last of all battles for this age."

"Why?" Captain Knife Hand had asked in the silence that followed before we left the FOB. "We are not aligned with anyone, Vandahar. We just showed up here. How does… this person you call the Nether Sorcerer… know we are a direct threat to him?"

"Your actions, Captain. Make no mistake. It's not your fantastic machine he wants. Though that would be nice, of course. He sees the advantage of it, no doubt. But it is something more. You have destabilized the West in just your brief time here. Bested his champion Triton. Defeated the termagant Ssruth the Cruel who had long been, if not always an ally, then at least a check to the Kingdom of Mourne and her wars against the Crow's March. But now those two foes are dead, and the Dark Lord must assume you are in league with the king of Mourne."

"But we aren't."

"Nor will you be," huffed Vandahar. "The elves of Mourne have their own problems and they will not come to your aid. That was where I went during your battle with Toth-Azom—to make pleadings with their king that there might be some alliance between you and them. Some friendship. But King Seron, despite his name, is no friend to anyone. And he would have none of my speech on the matter. He only covets a dark debt that must be repaid to the Black Prince himself. But that is…"

The wizard sighed.

"… that is another matter altogether that does not bear repeating here."

We all have those other stories, I guess. The ones not for now. The warts and all.

I promise I'll tell. Unless I drown, and then you'll have to forgive me. If that's even possible.

So, the plan had been made to go by boat to Sûstagul and aid the wizard's strange plan to defeat the right flank of the Nether Sorcerer's allies. If you didn't count our journey over the Ogre Wall, or the Pyrenees as they were once known if you prefer, and then down into the sunlight and orange groves of Further Navarre, then yeah, early this morning, under red skies with Portugonian sailors muttering concerns for ill omens like the morning traffic reports used to beat, the Rangers began the pump to go into the east and kill an undead pharaoh. Or die trying.

Operation Wingman.

That's how we ended up here out to sea with the harpies tearing into the sheets and canvas above our heads. Ripping it to shreds with axes and claws. Even as they died by violent gunfire from the Rangers holding their fighting positions on the deck. Even as *Dancer* lost steerage off our bow and began to get dragged south with the winds and currents of the mysterious Atlantean Rift. Even as Kurtz swore and murdered them off his boat. As Brumm held his brother's six and gunned down the vicious bird-women coming at all of us from every direction.

Ten minutes of the most insane fighting I'd even seen and been a part of, and it was over. We had wounded. But no one was out of the fight. The swarm had been so thick we'd dropped the two-forty and gone to primaries just to keep them back.

Strange spells had been cast at some of the Rangers and they were either asleep or blind. Others had resisted these effects.

The deck was littered with dead harridans. Their mutant bodies and strange leather armor lying ruined everywhere. Their broken weapons as shattered as our torn canvas fluttering overhead. Flapping madly in the wind.

The Portugonians were running for the anchor as we were dragged off course, the ship losing control. The storm seeming to inhale everything and growing all around us as we were dragged out of the Med and into the Rift. What remained of the canvas whipped and flew at the wind's behest.

Rangers were reloading. Flinging dead enemies off the deck and into the rough shark-infested waters. Grotesque harpy bodies getting dragged in the swirling current. Floating like flotsam among the waves as triangular fins raced in fast and tore at their lifeless bodies.

Tanner approached me.

Sometimes he's Tanner. Sometimes he's that other, darker thing. The thing with a mission he tells no one but me. A dark purpose that has him scanning the crossroads and watching the east. Looking for signs only dead people can see. Only he can see.

We were being dragged into the Atlantean Rift now. There was no avoiding that.

"We in it now, Talk. We in it fo' sho," said Tanner as he tapped out some dip.

I pulled out my canteen and took a big gulp of cold brew. I was burned from brass and cut from something I never should have done. Without attracting attention, I felt the wound through my fatigues. The bandage was wet. The wound had opened up.

But I wasn't totally sure about that. So I left it alone. Hoping for the best as I had more important things going on at this moment in my life, however much longer that was going to continue.

I'd just fought for my life against mutant bird-women that seemed like they'd be just as happy in hell as any other place in this savage world called the Ruin. I'd shot my share of them once we'd gone to primaries. But that wasn't the only killing I'd done in the last twenty-four hours.

Tanner must have read the look on my face. I didn't say anything. I've changed too. I know that. Maybe Talker's gone. Maybe he died back there somewhere after Tarragon. Died somewhere in the long lonely nights since.

But the look on my face said everything now. I knew that. I'd seen it in the others' faces too. Since Area 51. Since Ranger Alamo. Since all the battles... since.

That faraway look of last-man-standing survival that is the Ranger. They call it a lot of things. In it to win it. Ranger gonna Ranger. The Ranger Standard. Or... *This might as well happen today.*

But I was gonna do it too.

Ranger gonna Ranger. Whether I had the tab or not. Kurtz had failed me out of Ranger School twice.

I'd made up my mind I wasn't done yet.

"I know, Talk. I feel ya, brother," continued Tanner as we got ready for whatever came next. Barrel change. New mags. Salt water where we'd been cut and slashed. "Gonna get weird now, Talk. But hey... Ranger gonna Ranger. Am I right, man?"

I nodded.

Ranger gonna Ranger. Pity the fantasy that got up this morning and thought it was gonna win against us.

It hadn't factored Rangers.

And we'd make 'em pay for that.

The wind and the rain howled as the canvas flapped madly above our helmets. The sands of Africa scoured the deck and our exposed skin.

The smaj had authorized rolled sleeves because it was still hot.

Tanner bummed a hit of coffee and told me that dip would be part of the new me as well someday. The final piece of my transformation. "Just the natural way of things while bearing a scroll, Talk, or maybe the Ruin's baby steps workin' on ya, brother—but whatever, coffee and Copenhagen go together like, well, like a tab and scroll."

I didn't care.

I had coffee and targets.

CHAPTER THREE

"THIS is Sea Horse Three Four Heavy… we're going in! I say again…"

The netcall came in emphatically. But still in Ranger matter-of-fact. The tone was direct and serious, and the direness of the situation was definitely conveyed in that emergency short broadcast. It was Sims acting as RTO with Chief Rapp aboard commanding that element. Sea Horse Three Four Heavy, *Dançarina das Estrelas*. Sea Horse Two Four Heavy was the *Sofia*. The ship we were on. And Sea Horse One Four was the command lead ship *Sea Wolf* captained by the pirate and carrying the scouts along with the sergeant major.

Now two of those ships entered the turbulent waters of the Atlantean Rift, Two Four and Three Four Heavy, sails torn to shreds and flapping madly in the breeze. We at least had steering via oars and the massive rudder aboard *Sofia*. Three Four Heavy had lost her steering and the oars had been shredded by the sudden attack of a strange sub-surface eel-like leviathan surfacing out of the churn between a massive bay that spread away along the dull brown coasts of North Africa and the deep blue of the Great Inner Sea. Or what we'd once called the Med. A six-pack of grenades dropped into the water around the thing and drove it off, but not before the damage to Three Four had been done.

The strange and massive sea serpent was now off somewhere licking its wounds, but so were we.

In other words… Sea Horse Three Four was out of control, spinning and being sucked into the violent whirlpools of the Rift we'd been trying to avoid.

Our situation aboard Sea Horse Two Four Heavy wasn't much better. What can only be described as *Creatures from the Black Lagoon* were popping up out of the waves and hurling short iron spears tipped with jagged coral onto the decks of both ships. The Rangers were firing from cover along the low foam-washed decks of the galleys down into the raging waters, creating sudden small volcanic explosions of sea foam as they tried to dust the goonies attempting to swamp both ships.

Rangers, in their continual quest to demean anything that dare opposed them, in their own dark laconic way had begun to immediately call these new amphibious and ugly humanoid sea monster things "goonies."

"Like you know, from the old eighties movies?" asked Tanner as he popped up from behind the barrel of pitch he was fighting from, *Sofia* dipping heavily to port into the trough of a huge wave and the Portugonian sailors groaning in their angry and emphatic way that we were going over on our side. Regardless of the pitch and fall of the galley, or whether anyone heard his question, Tanner fired a quick succession of shots at a goonie in the water we were now almost looking directly down into. Landing a shot at the last second as thankfully *Sofia* began to heel back to starboard. The round blew off the top of the finned skull of the thing lurking in the water. Its jaw groaned open as brains painted the wave it was sinking under. Its inky blood carried away in the sudden swirl of the choppy waves.

"Never heard of her!" I shouted back, grabbing onto some netting and trying not to go overboard as the galley pitched back to starboard once more. I had my sidearm out because it was easier to hold on to the rigging and shoot with one hand. Not to seem too heroic, but I said this standard hardboy reply as I began to blaze away at one of the Creatures from the Black Lagoon who'd come over the side of the ship when it had dipped deep into the water, the creature swimming aboard and gaining the deck even as that side rose into the air suddenly. I ignored horizon and inertia, clenched my teeth as I repeated the constant soldier's joke of *Never heard of her*, and shot the thing in the chest and arms at least four more times. Its legs and life ran out of it and the ugly thing just flopped across the deck as the ship heeled back the other way in the violence of the churn between deep and coastal waters. Its green body rag-dolled past my head and it went off over the other side and down into deep swirling water. Limp and lifeless as our passage and the current carried it away.

Let me just pause to note something here: the smell. It was incredible. Like all the dead things of the sea. But fermented with parmesan cheese gone bad. Real bad.

The goonies smelled almost worse than Bag of Death Island.

As our ship entered the current of the bay, I caught sight of the distant sails of Sea Horse One Four Heavy far out to sea. She was heading east, pulling away from the drag of the Rift as the suddenly violent storm began to abate.

Perhaps two ships were enough for whoever had set this trap for us. Perhaps they thought they had their prizes. My guess is they probably wouldn't consider two ships full of murder hornets with Ranger scrolls, hopped up on dip, caffeine, and hatred, much of a prize. But time would teach them. They would learn.

From the helm of the ship on the slightly higher aft deck of the galley, I heard Santago, who manned the great wheel of the ship alone, call out for the Portugonian sailors below to give him hard strokes on the oars of one portion of the ship.

"Estibordo, seus bastardos!" he bellowed raggedly above the chaos of battle and sea.

He'd spotted a channel within the seafoam-and-gray chaos through which we might steer a course into the Rift and then not be smashed into the looming lone rocks and barely sunken wreckage that littered the bay we were being sucked and driven into.

Porgo, one of the comically shorter and fatter Portugonians, ran across the deck light as a ballerina, and as the ship wallowed and floundered between the waves, shouted something down into the hold belowdecks. The huge oars that spat away from the sides of the galley on the starboard side rose and heaved themselves forward, slamming down into the water and dragging the ship hard over into the current as the old man at the helm made a face like he was passing a stone to hold the wheel on the course he hoped and prayed might be our salvation from the chaos of the tempest.

Chaos of the Tempest. Ha! Look at me writing like a real writer now, Mom.

Meanwhile, on deck and in the waves all around us, the Rangers were killing everything in every direction and probably, like me, hoping another of those leviathans didn't surface and shear away our oars like that one had on Three

Four Heavy, which was now spinning faster and gaining speed in some dangerous current within the bay as it headed into the various water hazards of rock and wreckage.

It careened through a not-much-submerged old wreck, making an awful groaning sound as it snapped skeletal dead-man's-hand masts that still stuck out of the water and crawled over an old barely exposed hull. It was moving so fast and spinning so wildly that the rotten timbers of the wreck just disintegrated as *Dancer* slammed into them. The Rangers on deck hung on and kept shooting at everything.

More goonies surfaced from the waves and lobbed irregular waves of sharpened coral-studded spears at our ship. The strikes impacted, some landing in the oak with solid *thunks* all around. Rangers got hit, but plate carriers absorbed the blows as coral shattered and cut exposed skin.

There is a battle within every military unit for sleeves rolled up or sleeves rolled down, the latter of which offers the most protection. The battle is waged between everyone and the smaj.

I felt the smaj smiling with the satisfaction of being right about more protection.

I'd been hit and was bleeding, but the cuts were superficial. The salt water made them sting real bad, but I counted that as them getting cleaned out. There wasn't time for anything else so you go with what you got.

New mag in on the sidearm, I fired at a Creature from the Black Lagoon that had managed to surface nearby as the oars were heaving us into the channel leading into the fantastic bay we were getting glimpses of now. I missed, and the thing I'd been shooting at quickly ducked beneath the waves as Brumm, seeing my failure to connect kinetically, dumped a burst from the MK48 super-SAW, sending huge plumes out of the water. If it was still there, it was hit and leaking.

We were now, at last, headed into the bay and out of the rough troughs that had bridged the waters between the two areas of the ocean. Three Four Heavy was ahead of us and being carried away swiftly into the mists and miasma, the Rangers aboard her still fighting for their lives as goonies swamped the galley and crawled aboard. What looked like a sea of green and fishbelly-white locusts were swarming the sides of the stricken vessel as it spun madly within the violent current, carried forward by more of a rushing rapid within the water than a channel within this strange, cracked and ruined place that had once been a coast long ago.

Santago had told me the bay was incredibly violent and that few ships, in fact none he'd ever heard of, managed to survive entrance. It was a regular graveyard of ships apparently.

"No one would ever want to go there, Talk-ir. It is a place of no return. Ever."

Claymores went off on the deck of Sea Horse Three Four, sending goonies flying off and out into the water, away from the sides of the savaged galley. Or at least parts of them. I could see the Rangers hacking with tomahawks, knives, and newly acquired weapons of the Ruin. Swords of all kinds. The occasional axe or mace. There was some gunfire, but the ship was so overwhelmed it was clear that any shooting was likely to hit friendlies. It was coming down to who was meaner, and who could do the work at bad-breath distance.

Suddenly there was a loud thunderclap, an almost visible shock wave emitting from somewhere along *Dancer*'s deck, and Creatures from the Black Lagoon were flung away in every direction as though struck by a nuclear blast. Other goonies ran and threw themselves into the waters, leaping off the ship even as the Rangers shot at them.

"Kennedy went sonic!" shouted Kurtz.

You could almost hear some kind of pride or even admiration in the NCO's voice at the new trick Vandahar had taught Kennedy to do in the months since we'd slain the dragon. This new spell that had been unlocked.

Kennedy had failed out of Kurtz's Ranger School too.

As had Soprano.

Everyone had except two.

But make no mistake. The NCO was never going to let Kennedy hear that admiration. He still rode our ditchdigger fledgling hedge wizard harder than a cheap mule. But it was there, and I heard it in the middle of the fight so clear it could not be denied. I caught it as goonies swam into the clear depths of the bay, fleeing the spinning-out-of-control lead galley.

Kurtz was a hard NCO who took pride in the soldiers under his watch and their ability to dispense copious amounts of extreme violence. That, too, could not be denied.

I could see the bay ahead. The Rift. The no-go zone we were headed into whether we liked it or not, being dragged by the dangerous currents more than the sudden storm had ever had the power to do. I looked out to sea and could only catch bare glimpses of Sea Horse One Four. I had no idea if we had communication with them.

Tanner caught me scanning and said, "Don't worry, Talk. Smaj is gonna get that under control."

Smaj is shorthand for *Sergeant Major*. And no, you'd never use it in his presence. I had no doubt that Sergeant Major Stone, even with one hand, was going to sort that pirate out. I had a brief vision of that one remaining hand clamped firmly around the pirate's neck, throttling him until *Sea Wolf* was headed back into the bay to get us out of here.

The bay ahead was dotted with dangerous small rocky islands that rose sharply out of the waters. Like the sides of canyons that had been fractured and half sunken long ago. There were some wrecks. The skeletal remains of ghostly half-remembered ships clawing their way to a salvation that would never come, frozen in their destruction as the waters sucked at them, or smashed into them over and over again, breaking them down over the long years.

This was the Rift.

What had once been the coast of North Africa. In the Before, as the tale-tellers of the Ruin say, when the stars fell and ruined the Earth that was. The world we'd known. This and other places where the great changes in the ten thousand years since had come. Almost alien in its difference from what we had once known. Its *otherness* to anything we had ever known.

Ahead of the *Sofia*, the out-of-control Three Four Heavy began to "auto-rotate in." Like she was a helicopter that had taken a tail boom hit from an RPG and was now spinning out of control into enemy-controlled hostile territory. Going down. It had that feeling. I'd seen movies where the plot was such. The Rangers around me, some of them, had seen it in real-time.

And all around us on the shores of the strange bay that was the entrance to the Rift, lay the ancient ruin of a lost and mysterious civilization that had once been the rival of the Dragon Elves. A strange mystery from our collective past.

The Ruin called this area Atlantea.

Little was known of it, other than its inhabitants were once known as *The People at the End of the World*. There were old towers and mighty temples here.

Above all this rose the fractured remains of the citadel.

Stronghold of the medusa.

CHAPTER FOUR

MY guess is Operation Wingman planning began in secret as the sergeant major recovered from the loss of his hand. What we were getting into definitely seemed to come from him, our senior-most NCO. In short, it became the smaj's obsession. I can say that now because I see it. It was the smart plan. It was clear we needed to do something. But I think it went a little further than just that for the sergeant major. He took it personally. Not because of his hand, but because he had decided this was the right thing to do. He made his case to Captain Knife Hand, and I'm sure the captain saw it too for the sense in it. But like I said… there seemed more to it than just that. Tanner sometimes wondered if it was that injury that caused the sergeant major to send us on what sometimes felt, at least in the intel development and planning phase in the weeks leading up to Wingman, like a suicide mission for the Rangers.

But then again, they're all suicide missions really. Coming to the Ruin was a one-way trip, so besides the exotic location, time, weapons, and enemies we might face, this was not unknown territory for us.

We were leaving the FOB, the Forge, and everything, for what amounted to an assassination deep inside enemy territory. And not just any enemy territory. A strange desert land of pyramids, tombs, and powerful magic that—if you listened to any of the histories of the Shadow Elves, or Vandahar's tales, or even the dwarves' songs—seemed to be the source of corruption for the world that now called itself the Ruin.

But it was Tanner, some PFC who probably had a twenty-three-percent-interest loan on a Camaro back at Joint Base McChord and definitely had two stripper ex-wives, who called it like he saw it.

"I can see the wound that scumbag SEAL gave him, Talker. See it with my... *death vision*. He don't show it, but it's tormenting him real bad. My guess is that torment has the smaj in mind for a little epic smackdown on the bad guys, because some things can't just be let to pass. Know what I mean, brother? Some things you just don't abide. I got mine. And it's coming. I'm looking for her. But the smaj wants to smoke these guys. Real bad. I can see it as sure as I see the hand that got hacked off by that scumbag SEAL, man. I can see it straight up. Clear as life."

Death vision.

That's what we'd begun to call it once Tanner began to talk about it openly. Or at least to me. What is it? It's what Tanner can see of that otherworld of the dead and the undead. Death vision. Probably like the vision I got during the battle against the Army of the Dead when I was carrying the crow thing's *Book of the Dead* and using the ring at the same time. Those two working in combination gave me a look into that netherworld. It's a place I hope I never to see again.

It was hopelessly brutal to even get a glimpse of.

Sometimes Tanner sees ghosts. Sometimes he sees old memories. He can spot the undead and even sense them before we get close. For instance, one time when Tanner was part of the Kurtz Ranger School cadre running a night patrol and land nav exercise that was pass/fail, one of the Ranger candidates wanted to take us through an old boggy area to arrive at the objective before dawn. Generally, the cadre for Kurtz's Ranger School would just let you make your mistakes as you ran patrol, security, and kept accountability during the patrol. Then reduce you to shreds as they ripped everything you'd done to pieces during the AAR.

You're supposed to learn that way. Or get recycled.

It's a hybrid of learning and razor's-edge success or you're out. It boggles my mind but apparently it works in producing Ranger-qualified soldiers.

But that night Tanner stopped the patrol as we approached the bog, whispered something to Kurtz, and disappeared off into the forest ahead of us for a few minutes. The patrol did a security halt and conducted SLLS—Stop, Look, Listen, and Smell—for five minutes. During that time there is no movement, no fidgeting, no breathing too loudly, no smacking that bug that is crawling on your face. Sounds easy, but in reality, it's the part of all patrol halts that everyone dreads. If you ever think five minutes is not a lot of time, put a ruck on, take a knee, and try to be a statue for it. Tanner came back, and Kurtz told the Ranger who was running the patrol to alter his course. Avoid the bog. Which was unusual. Like I said, they usually let us make our mistakes and then light us up when we're dead on our feet.

I guess that makes us more receptive to the criticism. Less likely to defend our stupidity and just learn.

Later I asked Tanner what was up with the detour.

"Whole place was filled with dread wraiths, Talk," he said, spitting some dip out of the side of his mouth as we cleaned bog mud out of our weapons and gear. "I could hear 'em plain as day up here in my head. They were all down in there, lookin' like old-school Bronze Age warriors from a Conan flick, but they ain't men at all. Demons. Before the bog was a bog it was a pit, and the pit was their temple way back during what they called the Age of Darkness. They worshipped some kind of vampire shape-changer that lived down there long ago, but they all got killed and now their... spirits I guess... wait down there... for something. Wasn't clear, and I wasn't interested in finding out, if you know what I mean. If the patrol would have gone through there, we woulda had big problems. Bigger even than Kurtz recycling dudes."

He laughed dryly like that dead thing he sometimes was, going quiet and staring somewhere other at the end.

I don't mind. He's still Tanner. Still my buddy.

"Big bigga problems," I prompted, if just to get him back to our current reality. Imitations of Jabba always did the trick. Soprano had lately taken to shifting between his Mario the Plumber voice to sometimes talking scratch-voice Jabba-ese. That killed everyone—and pissed Kurtz off royally.

So it was funny.

Tanner came back to the conversation muttering, "Yeah, Talk. Big bigga problems. Those things are... *wicked*."

Wicked isn't a word I'd ever expect to be used by the guy who made disobedience an art form and who had managed to seduce two strippers into matrimony with all the goods and prizes that PFC BAQ pay might provide. But hey... words. They surface in the oddest places and always for a reason. Any linguist will tell you that's half the fascination with them and their usage.

"How do you know that?" I asked him after a moment, as I worked to clean the mud off my carbine's Vickers Sling.

"I could hear 'em talk."

Hey now, linguist me thought to myself. *This could be real interesting…*

"Could you understand them, Tan?"

"Oh yeah. Haven't I mentioned that? Yeah, all of these dead… I understand their languages when I hear 'em whispering or chanting. But not like the American I can understand in my head. I mean English. Ha! That's funny. No, I can understand their languages… *in* the language they're speaking. It's crazy, man. Crazy when your mind steps back and sees the big picture."

Literally I'm jealous. On top of which, I suddenly feel that my place in the Rangers is threatened, even though many of the Rangers can do multiple languages. It's just no one can do as many as me. I'm a value-add. A combat multiplier. Never mind that I'm still a private. I did that to me. But forces are in motion to get my mosquito wings back. So I got that goin' for me.

I know…

I'm a shallow and sick individual.

Kurtz is right. There is weakness in me in need of purging.

"What does it sound like?" I asked, because I cannot help myself when it comes to languages and coffee.

"Damnation," muttered my permanent Ranger PFC battle buddy who'd become some kind of undead warrior.

"It sounds like… *damnation*?"

"Nah, that's what it's called, Talk. Though I don't think any of 'em have ever said that. It's just… something I know. The language is Damnation. Language of a place none of them want to go to but know they're going all the same. A place called Hell."

Well, that's sounds… terrible. And fascinating. Hell's got a language. Who knew? Never mind all the eternal suffering and torment, Talker, *they have a language you can learn, you sick bastard.*

But back to why we're on this pump to the southern Deserts of Sleep to ice some mighty undead pharaoh who seems to have been a real pain in the butt for the Ruin for several thousand years since we've been gone and before we showed up.

Ice. Good word. While we're talking about languages and all. Other word choices common in Ranger vernacular for killing a target: slot, smoke, whack, bag, take down, bury, dust crush. And some other more crass ones I won't waste your time with.

But as every Ranger here says now… *Time travel's a helluva drug.* At least once a day here you think of something that's gone forever. And then you hope you can find something like it in the here and now. I feel bad for the guys who want an Xbox or a PlayStation. But I got coffee so… *winner winner chicken dinner.*

Anyway, Tanner could see the ghost hand of the sergeant major even though it had been hacked off by McCluskey the vampire SEAL warlord. And if you'll remember, that scumbag SEAL carried *Coldfire*, the sword I'm currently carrying now. *Scumbag SEAL* is how every Ranger refers to the recently deceased-again McCluskey. Sometimes worse, but I won't waste precious ink on the volume of interesting and obscene curses and descriptions the Rangers have for that particular dead scumbag SEAL. To be fair, I'm pretty sure they were already carrying those around for the SEALs in general long before McCluskey pulled his Ren faire man-in-black traitor act and tried to stab us all in the back with an orc horde.

That sword, *Coldfire*, was supposed to leave wounds that would never heal. And also burn, with a fiery cold that's probably worse than IcyHot and capsicum together. Ever get pepper juice in your eye? It's a real treat, and I'm guessing the sword's cut was supposed to be orders of magnitude worse than that.

But here's the thing. And I really will try to stay on topic this time and not get distracted by every little thought that pops into my head. Perhaps I'd be better able to concentrate if I had some coffee...

Focus, Talker.

According to Tanner the ghostly hand of the sergeant major was still there in Death Vision. And the wound should be causing him intense pain. But you wouldn't know that from the sergeant major. He went on with Ranger business just like the hand was no big loss. He rifle PT'd everyone to death one afternoon with one hand just to prove he could do it. And he did. But sometimes early on you'd see him try to reach for something with the missing hand and then remember it was gone now. The look that crossed his face was the coldest brew of icy murder I'd ever seen. But that didn't last too long. Even stranger than that though, the sergeant major never touched the wound like you would if you'd gotten it. Never rubbed the area around it or complained of phantom limb pain. I discussed that too with Tanner.

"Rumor around the NCOs is the sergeant major was Delta before coming back to the batts, Talk. Those guys are a whole 'nother level of Special Operator Operating. They ain't human even by Special Ops standards. So... maybe he just did some voodoo operator trick and turned the pain off in his mind so he could get back on mission. Who knows... those are levels of mystery operator voodoo beyond my current duty assignment, man. I just work here. *Sua sponte*, know what I mean."

Once we got back to the FOB at Castle Hawthorn, I still got the occasional coffee with the sergeant major and we still talked some, but I'd be lying if I didn't say there was a change in the weather and he seemed to be brooding about something that wasn't for public consumption just yet. Sometimes I'd come in and see him staring out the great window of the tiny tower kitchen where the old blue percolator was always waiting on the hearth with hot fresh Portugonian coffee ready to reward me with another day of servile yet wonderful addiction. Except he wouldn't be watching the hawks on the summer thermals like we sometimes did when we'd enjoy a cup or three.

He was just staring east. Looking far beyond the horizon and seeing all the chess pieces of the Ruin's geopolitics in his mind. I can tell you now, that's what he was doing. He was putting it all together. The reality of our situation and what needed to be done about it.

I could tell he was thinking about something then, and my guess now is he was thinking about Wingman before it all got started. Whatever it was, he was thinking about something hard. Real hard.

And if I was that something... I'd be worried.

The silence between him and everyone was like a wall. Which is saying something for Rangers. Seriously.

About that time, the sergeant major and Vandahar began having long conversations late into the night. Just the two of them. And no, I wasn't privy. No one was. They'd stop if you dropped in, and it was clear from the sergeant major's graveyard stare you weren't welcome just then at that moment. I had a feeling the old wizard was explaining the Ruin, the geopolitical factions of the Ruin specifically, to the sergeant major in greater detail than had been done before. The old man was downloading everything he knew into the senior NCO's mental hard drive where some incredible murder and violence processor was solving for a target to lay some serious hate on.

But then I got sent to Kurtz's Ranger School the first time. And then I got recycled two weeks later for no-going a patrol in the platoon sergeant position when Kurtz made sure everyone got two extra MREs and a good rest and I couldn't get them motivated to get moving to complete the mission. Normally during Ranger School, you operate calorie-deficient, which is great because it keeps you more alert. So the two extra MREs were like a calorie IED I didn't spot, and it killed my whole platoon while I was acting in a leadership position.

Leadership is a weak point for me.

Most of my life has been lone wolf. It was enough for me to learn to be a good follower and meet the standards of the Army and the Rangers. But now, to be Ranger qualified, and to maintain my position in the Rangers, I needed to learn to lead. Because every Ranger is a leader. This is one of the features that makes them different from other military units.

So I would keep going to Kurtz's little Ranger School until they wouldn't let me. I'd learn to lead, if just to spite Kurtz.

Don't underestimate spite. You can get a lot done just on spite alone. Trust me. It's how I learned Tagalog.

When I got back from that, I was immediately summoned to Captain Knife Hand's command post for what I thought was going to be an epic chewing-out and probably getting thrown out of the Rangers if that's even possible here in the Ruin. If it is... I'm sure I'll be the first. They'll probably make me go hang with the Air Force crew chiefs. Who are pretty cool guys. One even went through Kurtz's Ranger School. He got nailed for falling asleep. But he did pretty good up until the point he started "seeing the wizard" and treating trees like vending machines that had failed to dispense his snack. Three days of nonstop patrolling will do that to you.

Ironically, "seeing the wizard" is, and always has been, Ranger vernacular for the point when one is approaching near-total mind and body shutdown via exhaustion. The point at which the brain starts playing tricks. *Seeing the wizard* has just always been the phrase that describes that. Don't know why. But here in the Ruin we see an actual wizard near every day, plus stuff a lot more horrific and unbelievable, so maybe it's time we come up with a new phrase to apply since seeing a wizard is frankly not that big of a deal anymore.

Instead of the epic chewing-out for not meeting Ranger standards I had expected to get, it was instead the captain's warning order to the NCOs and platoon leaders for what we would learn was going to be called Operation Wingman.

Phew. Saved by the need to go and whack a bad guy.

All the sergeant major's brooding had led us to the moment when the operation to whack Sût became real *real* for reals.

The sergeant major came over before the meeting began and said to me, "Needed you here, Private Talker, because we're developing you to be our battlefield intelligence collection asset when I'm not around. We're gonna start teaching you about collection and dissemination more than John gave ya back in the Vegas that was, son. Sucks about Kurtz's little school, but you'll make it eventually… or you won't."

At that point I wasn't even sure I was going to get another shot at getting tabbed. Kurtz had just dismissed me in the morning fog with more silent contempt than I thought one human being could possibly muster, before moving on to running the next patrol in swamp phase for those that got to complete the qualification course. Then I had a three-day walk back to the FOB in silence with two other Rangers he'd recycled that morning.

"Kurtz is a hardass, Talker," whispered the sergeant major as the meeting began. "But he's *our* hardass."

So anyway, there was coffee at this meeting, and as the meme goes… I started blasting. Kurtz had known coffee was my dark master, and he'd made sure I never got any for the two weeks I lasted in Ranger School.

Ask me to describe hell for you sometime.

Coffee in hand, the captain clicked on the portable briefing projector the Forge had cranked out and began the meeting. We were looking at a map, antique and old like something made by some fifteenth-century cartographer of how the world used to look long ago in the old days.

"Rangers," began Captain Knife Hand. "We are getting involved. Our position here at FOB Hawthorn is secure as of this moment, but we anticipate, with the intel we've developed on the geopolitical situation of the world we now find ourselves in, that we cannot count on that to remain the case in the near or long-term future."

The captain didn't waste time getting down to the particulars of paragraph one: situation of the OPORD. Having just been through the Ruin's new Ranger School I was a lot more familiar now with the format and flow of a true-to-standard operations order and why it was formatted like it was. He moved to the next slide, which really was just a closeup of the big most-of-the-known-world map onto a region called Umnoth. I was pretty good at geography. You need that for languages. Umnoth was north of Turkey where-it-should-have-been and it took me a few minutes to realize the Black Sea was missing. Now, in its place, was a giant desert ringed by some pretty vicious mountain ranges that looked volcanic.

That's fairly impossible to conceive, considering where we came from. Impossible in that, during my entire life, and pretty much recorded history, there were no such geological changes of that order… like ever. But we were ten thousand years in the future and, as they say… stuff happens.

"Due to vetted information from local sources," continued the captain from the darkness beyond the projection. "We have come to understand that the primary threat to our continued survival here in the Ruin comes from this region. Umnoth. We have identified this region's warlord, gentlemen, as a major player in current geopolitical affairs. We don't have much direct intel on this individual other than that he is known locally—and to say locally, I mean here in this world—as... the Nether Sorcerer."

Captain Knife Hand paused. I could see the look of permanent indigestion on his face and hear it in his voice. Even though he could turn into a were-tiger, he had not embraced the fantasy, as I liked to tell myself. Or maybe he had, but he was still struggling with the fantasy elements. Words like *orc*, *monster*, *sorcerer*, and *spells*, along with other concepts and creatures and things that surfaced more often than not in this strange and uncertain future, bothered the very grounded and fatally realistic Rangers. But it didn't stop them. It was more of a *Well, this might as well happen today* pause each time.

But here was a funny thing I'd noticed. It was the senior-most and more hardcore Rangers who were bothered the most. The younger ones were more like, *Game on, hobgoblin. Let's do this!*

Still, Knife Hand, and the other hardcore Ranger sergeants, had embraced as best and as quickly as they could. Because they were pure survivors. Pure predators. They'd take every advantage they could find and acquire to win each and every time. Why? Because as Sergeant Chris says, *Rangers are in it to win it or they ain't Rangers anymore.*

My evidence for that?

Kennedy, a private first class now, was here in this very important meeting. Remember, when all this began, they had been trying to either kill Private Kennedy, or make him wish he was dead enough via slit trench digging to flee the Rangers. They'd even been doing that on-mission in the Ruin.

Rangers don't care where you are or how much incoming you have coming in—orcs, trolls, or boulder-throwing giants—they're constantly self-assessing and purging weakness. They need everyone to not care as Carl Gustaf don't, when it comes to murder-thirty and expending kinetic death delivered calm, cold, and preferably high dosage. If they sense you can't accomplish that… they're gonna weed you. Or as Sergeant Chris puts it… "Cut sling load, or cut that towed jumper free." Ain't personal. It's just the mission is everything. It's like a bodily function for them. That, and finding the next insanely dangerous thing they can do just to prove they can do it.

Again, as Sergeant Chris likes to say, "Rangers can do anything."

The captain continued. "This individual seems to perceive us as a threat to his existence and operations. Unfortunately for him…"

The captain paused and stepped into the light of the projector. He looked older and more tired now since the last time I'd seen him. His hair more iron-gray than it had been. But his eyes were still those burning blue murder eyes of the tiger he could become in moments of extreme crisis and stress. He stared at all of us in the dark of the briefing.

"… we weren't even concerned with him before now. But now, Rangers, we're going to be *very* concerned with this individual. We're going to make him our special project. We're going to attack his support elements asymmetrically and take the battle to him from a direction he's not anticipating. And once we've got him reacting to the problems we've created in his organization, he will stick his head out of whatever hole he's in, and at that time we will find him, fix him in place, and then we will finish him in order to ensure our continued survival in this… place and time."

It looked like it took a lot of him to get that last part out. "We're going to kill him where he lives."

None of the Ranger NCOs and officers said anything.

This was just Tuesday for them.

CHAPTER FIVE

WHAT followed in that warning order briefing for what would become Operation Wingman was a sketch of the plan all the Rangers would be developing together in order to take out the primary threat to the regiment's existence: the Nether Sorcerer.

But first we were going after Sût the Undying.

The Wingman.

Three were at least three major wars going on between the Nether Sorcerer of Umnoth and other various factions of the Ruin between us and our big bad primary target. The Stone Kings, or the dwarves, a loose confederation of lords who had rejected the leadership of the dwarf king in exile, Wulfhard Ravensclaw, were fighting a desperate battle against the orc hordes coming out of Umnoth on the eastern slopes of the Swiss alps. Or as they are known here… the Giants' March. Apparently there were giants there once but the dwarves killed them all in the wars of Malfric the Dark. Another history for another time. The orcs were coming through the Drakenwald, Eastern Europe, basically unchecked and doing a real number on the dwarven armies. According to intelligence months old, the Stone Kings had lost several fortresses along the eastern slopes of the Giants' March. If the orcs broke through, all was lost for the upper valleys and the great halls of the Stone Kings.

According to Wulfhard, the great dwarven families would turtle and get picked off one by one by the great orcish khan Sumnog.

When one of the Ranger platoon leaders asked if we could develop the dwarves as allies, it was Vandahar who spoke, though the dwarven king and Max, the dwarven champion known as the Hammer, were in the back of the room, standing against the wall silently. Fully armored and carrying their many weapons and vast array of knives. As though if the captain, or the sergeant major more likely, suddenly decided to leave at that very moment and attack Umnoth alone and immediately, they were ready to join in the slaughter.

It occurred to me that this was their posture at all times, and yet I had only noticed at this very moment. Perhaps the Wheel of Pain and the Tree of Woe that was Kurtz's School for Wayward Rangers Who Wanted a Tab had clarified my vision and allowed me to see things from an almost detached perspective while still being present.

That felt like some key to being a Ranger for me. But I wasn't sure.

Or, it was the first coffee I'd had in two weeks. And I was cruising. Cruising, I tells ya.

Me likey likey coffee mucho.

It was Vandahar who spoke from the opposite wall of Captain Knife Hand's small stone hut CP in the middle of FOB Hawthorn beneath the regardless glare of the Black Tower of the *Barad Nulla*. The old wizard was sitting on the stool provided for him, merely chewing on his unlit long-stemmed pipe and listening to "the palaver of the Rangers," as I knew he'd term it.

His presence comforted me. The old wizard had seen many wars, and what was being said sounded like we were getting into one. That counted for something with me.

"A valid question when one considers the situation," began the wizard in his subtly stentorian and naturally grand way. "Would the dwarvish lords consider your lot as allies in their defensive wars against the orcs? The answer, I fear, sadly… is no. I have encouraged the heads of the great families of the standoffish lot to see the merits of fighting alongside the Cities of Men and the elf king of Mourne, and even many others who have common cause against the dark lord himself, the Nether Sorcerer, but the dwarves see everyone not their own… as an enemy. It has always been their way. And to be frank, it has served them well until now. As you can tell by the state of exile of the most noble two of their kind in this company… sometimes they even see their own as enemies. It is, as I said, their way. They learned to tunnel deep long ago and have found dread things that would make men and elves shudder down there in the quiet deeps of stone and chasm beneath the Ruin. Ancient things. Things far darker than what we face now. Their isolation has been their strongest weapon at times, and to fear outsiders, for the world was dangerous then, was sometimes the only path. But it is dangerous now in this moment, and if we fail…"

The wizard did not finish the thought, but it was clear he saw no good coming from that path. He lit his pipe with a spark from one of his long and crooked fingers, puffed it to light, and began to speak once more.

"So… I understand their reasons, but not the longevity of their choices. There will come a day when we—and many in this room will not live to see it if we embark on this path—when we and everyone we can call *friend*… must confront the Nether Sorcerer at the very steps to *Barad Umbar* itself."

Barad Umbar.

The Tower of Doom, I translated quickly. It hurt even as my mind ran the translation. Since the dragon, I hadn't had much chance to use Tolkien Elvish. That was Autumn's job. To teach me. Now she was the queen of the Shadow Elves, consort to the king. No longer Autumn.

And that was then…

… and this is now.

The silence that usually followed anything the strange wizard said among the Rangers was interrupted by Wulf-hard from the shadows along the wall.

"It's true, Rangers. We are an… a… stubborn people." He had mastered English quickly. The fact that the dwarves spoke a lot of Germanic helped, I'm sure. "There is much I… ah… we… could have learned in having… alliances with others. But it is… hard. We have been betrayed… many times. We mistrust modern ways. And perhaps… that was wrong. If I were still king… I would listen now. The fact that I did not, the state of my people… is my fault… and it is… my fault alone."

The sergeant major cleared his throat. "We ain't doing defensive actions anymore," he rumbled. "We're gonna be all over their rear and flanks ravaging and destroying every-thing and everyone that is important to this Sût character. That's what Rangers do, boys. And that's what we're gonna do this time. No more defense. We are pure offense now, and may their gods have mercy on them when we come for them in the night. Because I sure as hell won't."

There were two other wars conducted by two city-states separately against the Nether Sorcerer. Skeletos and Accadios. Both part of the Cities of Men. Skeletos was basically conquered, but fighting a guerrilla war with mercenaries and pirates. Accadios had many legions but weak leadership, and was mostly concerned with keeping the orc hordes of Umnoth out of their cities within what we would have once called Italy.

"These three armies are all operating independently," continued Captain Knife Hand, taking control of the meeting once again, "and are effectively, through no coordinated effort, keeping the forces of Umnoth busy along a broad front that extends from Eastern Europe down into the Middle East. I'm using our geographical terms for the purpose of clarity within this briefing, but I encourage all of us to start using local terms and begin to study the maps, so we can get our minds wrapped around the current situation. It's where we're at. Might as well be there, Rangers."

I studied the map and tried to see the world, the Ruin, as it is now. Letting go of places I'd once been to or seen on maps when the world was called Earth and I thought it was mine. Those places were now ten thousand years dead. And yeah, up until now, or up until some undefined time between then and now, it had felt like we were just tourists here. Just passing through for a visit.

Sometimes you've got to forget what's gone.

And have to remember that that was then… and this is now.

I thought of Autumn again.

So… there's that too. I'll get over it someday. Right?

"This warlord…" began the captain as new slides were presented, "the Nether Sorcerer, who we will tag as

Gumby… has two allies that we can identify at the moment and one local nation-state that seems favorable toward his efforts. Caspia."

I had to ask the sergeant major later what's a *gumby*.

"When I was a kid, Talker, it was this Claymation cartoon bendy thing that was kinda green and weird-lookin'. I picked that call sign for this jackwad because from what Ol' Vandahar told me… Gumby might not be human. Might be an alien of some sort or kind. Not what they say, but… more like what I think might be. From somewhere… else, I guess. So, that's what I always thought of the Gumby cartoon thing as. Thought he was kinda like an alien. Plus, we gotta make sure his tag is humiliating enough so we can demean him and all. Makes the Rangers a whole lot happier about killing people they dislike intensely. Not that they need a reason, but a little salt makes a baked potato and a steak a whole lot tastier if you catch my drift, Talker."

Alien.

Man, can the Ruin get weirder?

"You mean like… from outer space, Sergeant Major?"

The sergeant major *harrumphed* and poured me coffee. "Maybe not, Private Talker. Maybe more like… some other dimension or such. He showed up in their histories when some huge comet hit the Earth, and that was a long time ago. So maybe he's something else if he's stuck around that long. He seems to have some pretty incredible powers. Who knows? We're gonna smoke him either way."

Some other dimension?

So yes. The Ruin can get weirder, Talker. Question answered.

Back in the meeting, the captain continued. "Gumby has two primary enablers." In Ranger-speak, people, or monsters in this case, just below the big boss are termed "primary enablers" and the guys that work from them are just "enablers" and the people that work for *them*, "facilitators." It's kinda a rank structure for bad guys so we can type-classify them according to their worth to the *numero uno* HVI at the head of the table.

"... Sût the Undying and a local warlord to the north tagged as the Black Prince by the residents. Those are Jackpots *Mummy* and *Dracula,* respectively. Mummy is basically a pharaoh down in Egypt. Now known as the Kingdom of Sût the Undying. Mummy. As we understand it, Mummy is one of those lizard creatures we faced who were supporting Lizard King when we conducted operations around Tarragon. Except he's apparently... undead. So we've done those, and had pretty good success in killing them.

"Dracula basically runs what we called Germany and Austria. That's now, as you can see from the map, the Crow's March. We've killed a vampire, so we can do him too when we get around to it. He's currently got some beef with the elves to our northwest in the Kingdom of Mourne that absorbs his attention.

"The three of these jokers have vast armies. Large forces complemented by other races and what look to be magical... unit types. Like some of the peoples we've faced so far. These are numbers we can't confront at this time in extended operations away from the resupply of the Forge. And our worst-case scenario is, these three start getting the upper hand in their respective conflicts and then get together to do something about us."

The projected presentation updated and showed the map, but now with geopolitical areas marked in colors. Black for Dracula swelling to our northeast. Green for the

Saur Mummy to the southeast. And directly east was red, and smack dab in the middle of Umnoth someone had written in marker, *Jackpot Gumby*.

It was clear Umnoth was some kind of awful, barren, and inhospitable region. Kennedy had called it Mordor. He was probably right about that. And there, in the middle of it all, was a lone dark tower.

The Tower of Doom.

Barad Umbar.

"Both Dracula and Gumby are fielding large forces against other armies," said Knife Hand, using a laser pointer to draw our attention to places on the projected map. "Both of those nations seem to be involved in direct operations. While these three elements—Gumby, Dracula, and Mummy—may not necessarily all be equal partners, it's clear from Vandahar that Gumby is the primary power source. So… we're going to take out Mummy first. Why? Because Mummy isn't directly engaged in any fighting. Knocking out Mummy grants the other players within the Ruin, who might be our future allies, the ability to come south, then come up through the Middle East, or what is now called the Eastern Waystes, and attack Umnoth directly. Whether they do that or not, if Gumby senses his flank is weak, we anticipate he'll pull troops out of conflicts to protect southern Umnoth. This again will give our future allies a chance to put more pressure on the main front and keep his attention off the kill shot we're going to execute once the situation has developed and we have a window of relative superiority to exploit."

The captain stepped out of the light and brought up a new projection that showed our route to the hit on this Sût the Undying.

Jackpot Mummy.

We were going south to Portugon where we'd get on ships and head down the length of the Med, or the Great Inner Sea, until we reached the port of Sûstagul, where I guessed Alexandria, Egypt, might have once been. Then the Rangers were going into the southern deserts to find Mummy and kill him wherever he was hiding.

That much was clear from the slide.

"This is what Rangers do. It's what we did back in our time. We break into bad guys' houses, and either kill or capture. In this case it's a pyramid, and a rather big one from what I'm told. But the good part, Rangers, is we're there to kill. And *that* we can do better than anyone. We turn Mummy back to dust forever, and destabilize the south for Gumby. Maybe Dracula flips or squirts on the alliance. At that point our Nether Sorcerer will have to make some choices and possibly do something real dumb. We'll make him pay for it if he does. With his life, or existence, whichever. We're gonna break stuff and slaughter the enemy elements wherever we find them once we get to Sûstagul and commence operations against Mummy. We leave in six weeks. Get your Rangers ready for this pump. It's going to be extremely difficult."

The captain clicked off the projector and it was dark. Outside, the morning light was soft and cool. It was almost fall now. The birds were beginning to go south and by the time we left, I was guessing the hawks who soared on the thermals out beneath the fortress would be gone.

I wondered if I would ever see them again.

"I won't lie to you. It'll be tough, and a lot of the operations on the ground to get this phase done and ice Mummy will be developed on the fly once we arrive in Sûstagul and out of initiative. Every Ranger knows the mission. Kill Mummy, then go for Gumby. I expect each and every one of them to complete the mission even if I and the rest of the command team are dead. This is a no-fail mission, Rangers."

Ranger Creed, Sixth Stanza.

Though I be the lone survivor.

Sergeant Chris would often remind the younger Rangers that the mission will complete no matter how many NCOs and officers get killed in doing so.

Readily will I display the intestinal fortitude required to fight on to the Ranger objective and complete the mission though I be the lone survivor.

Then the sergeant major cleared his throat and all I could see was the glowing ember of Vandahar's pipe as the morning sun rose out there in the courtyard of the home we had made here in the Ruin. The home we had fought for.

Outside I heard the smallest Shadow Elven children beginning to call to one another as they made games of their morning chores. I heard the soft songs of the women, the ones who had come here after finding nothing of what they had once had out there in the world.

Some had come to know the Rangers since.

I heard the ring of the dwarven forge. Knowing they had been up for hours. Dwarves were early risers and nearly sleepless when you really thought about it long enough. They kept the forge quiet until the Shadow Elves came out. Then they resumed their work of endlessly forging and sharpening. Constantly preparing new weapons for more conflicts. Warily watching the skies and shadows.

The captain had never said why we were going. But I heard it out there in the courtyard. I heard all the reasons why we were getting involved now. And I knew, somewhere in the *Tumna Haudh*, Last of Autumn was waking.

With someone else.

But she was.

Sometimes you love someone, even when they... can't... love you anymore.

I knew why we were going. I knew why I was going. And I was fine with that.

Standing in the darkness, the sergeant major cleared his throat again and spoke.

"*Sua sponte* this undead tyrant, Rangers. *Sua sponte* him good and hard."

Yeah. It felt like a one-way mission.

But hey... Rangers gonna Ranger.

Or, as Tanner would say after one of Kurtz's tirades raining down on all of us like incoming artillery fire when we weren't meeting Ranger Standard in his mind, It was Tanner who'd always remind you in the quiet after, "That scroll is the heaviest piece of gear you wear when you wear it right, Talk."

CHAPTER SIX

SEA Horse Three Four hit some ancient pillar that was still jutting up above the frenetic turbulent surface of the waters of the Rift. An ancient and carved thing, some relic from that lost civilization that had once made its home here. A marker for a memory of some war or triumph we would never know. Possibly even a religious object. Nothing now but a water hazard in this dangerous bay.

Sea Horse Three Four struck it dead on.

The current had dragged both of our ships into the maelstrom of the bay that was the great Atlantean Rift and sent us right into the sunken wreckages and ruins that littered the area. Below us, down in cool, almost clear waters despite the turbulence, we caught glimpses of structures among the drifting white sands and skeletal kelp. Old, crushed, seaweed-covered ruins of a civilization that had disappeared in a sudden cataclysm when the stars fell from the sky. A vast city beneath the waves that seemed to get closer to the surface by the second as our two ships were sucked into the embrace of the forbidden bay and sent to the rocky shore at its end. Wrecked ships were down there too. Others remained on the surface, caught on jagged rocks or the tall fortresses, the tops of which barely poked out of the storm wash of currents here.

There was no hope of navigating this section of the bay safely. It was a graveyard, and every marker told you so.

I was pretty sure we weren't gonna survive the entrance to the bay, much less the next few seconds. The entire place seemed to be a giant man-made reef of dangerous wreckage and enigmatic ruins where the bones of ships and men were slowly stripped clean in crystalline white sands.

Sea Horse Three Four Heavy, with no rudder or power from sails or oars, was in full spin within the surging current when she collided with that ancient pillar leaning at an odd angle out of the surge of the extremely violent waters. The strike on the old stone shard was horrific, and a section of the ship's starboard side was sheared clean off in one long, terrible moment. Splintered wood and rigging exploding across the waters from the sudden impact. Rangers and sailors flung into the water immediately.

But a moment later, the bulk of the badly injured ship spun away from the carved column and picked up speed, heading toward the rocks and cliffs at the bay's end. It was clear even to me that she had no possible chance of making the tiny harbor off to our right that Santago had the oarsmen of *Sofia* pulling hard for. The Rangers who had trained extensively in small boat operations seemed to see no hope for Three Four either. Their situation was bad and getting worse.

Meanwhile on board the *Sofia*, our ship, some of the Portugonian sailors were trying to get an emergency mainstay up in hopes of dragging our ship out of the current and into the safer waters of the old harbor approach from which dark and enigmatic structures rose up beneath the looming mass of the citadel we'd heard about.

Kurtz and Brumm, along with other Rangers, tried to get ropes to the men in the water as we streaked past the flotsam and wreckage of Sea Horse Three Four. *Dancer*. But the survivors in the water were being carried along as fast as we were, traveling in other currents, eddies, and whirlpools. A few managed to get aboard *Sofia*, but others were sucked along with the crumbling remains of Sea Horse Three Four, which seemed to be thunderballing into the rocks now even as she broke apart by the second. Her mainmast suddenly snapped, crashing down into the water with a titanic groan as the bow collided with something unseen, exploding terrifically after a huge, wood-screeching *snap*.

"They in trouble, Talk!" shouted Tanner above the chaos on the deck of *Sofia*. "And we ain't doin' much better, man. Here they come!"

Kennedy would tell us, later, that they were called Saw-haw-gin. I never asked him for the spelling so this was the pronunciation, and it seemed a very oddly familiar name that one of my languages should have given me a clue about.

Saw-haw-gin.

Fish people. More like the Saur in that they were monsters with humanoid shapes. But fish-like instead of lizard. Different than the goonies farther out in the bay. Fish faces. Mouths with razor-sharp tiny teeth that opened and closed as they breathed. The gills on the sides of their heads working like small bellows as they screamed through the waves and surged to catch Sea Horse Two Four. *Sofia*.

To me, they were strangely beautiful… and for a moment I was captivated by the almost balletic nature of their movement through the waves even as a huge force of them came directly at us, riding undulating inky-black eels like cavalry horses.

Yeah. Even I can't believe I just wrote that sentence, and if you've read this account so far, you've seen that I've written a lot of strange and weird stuff down. Man. If I'd thought all this up ten thousand years ago and just written it down it'd probably be a movie by now.

But then the plague would have come along, and I wouldn't have gone with the Rangers ten thousand years into the future. What would have happened to me?

What wouldn't have happened to me?

And who wouldn't I have met?

I know... tangent. But in my defense, I'd just taken the time, smack-dab in the middle of a wild battle at sea while being sucked into a rift full of sea wrecks and sunken cities, to hit a big slug of my cold brew just to get the salt water that was constantly coming across the decks at us, out of my mouth.

Priorities.

Yeah. That's the reason, I told myself. Addict gonna addict. Amirite? Can I get an amen?

Woohooo coffee for the win, man. I could face anything now. Yeah, even beautifully tiger-striped fish-men riding real evil-looking eels that slipped and slithered through the waves effortlessly, bounding like horses over jumps on some strange fox hunt. The fish-men weren't orange-and-white tiger-striped like Captain Knife Hand's other self. They were gray and a soft blue, almost like a tiger shark. They carried spears and tridents at the ready as they rode their giant eels into battle against us. When they went through the waves you could see them almost even more clearly than out of the water, the clarity magnifying them suddenly. Like they'd slipped into some other, more beautiful marine world that was calm and peaceful, relaxing despite the wind, waves, and wreckage.

Then you remembered they were probably here to murder you, and things came into focus.

Battle is weird. Things get clear. Real clear. Like this is the most you're ever gonna be alive, and you know it right there in the middle of it. I felt all that, even as my hands did the work of working my carbine. Raise, sight, pull the trigger. Stack floating corpses if you can. Slow motion all around me as the Rangers swear and open fire on fish-men riding eels coming straight at our near-out-of-control ship.

I heard Santago bellowing at the crew in his ragged old voice. Not cursing them. But shouting at them to put their backs into the oars.

It was *now or never*, he shouted in Portuguese. Or Portugonian.

"Agora ou nunca!"

I heard it in the distance as I fired at the eels. Watching my rounds smoke-trail away and then streak into the rising waves. Watching the tiny plumes five-five-six makes in the ocean. Watching the vapor bubble trail of the round through the waves.

And suddenly seeing an image of Sidra Paredes in the water in that other life not this one. A pool at a luxury resort her money had given us access to. A day that could have been the shape of all the days to come for us. Fruit and smoke on the breeze. Music until dawn. Love. Or at least the imitation thereof. At the time we probably thought it was. I know I did. She said the same, once.

A fight is a strange thing.

I know nothing. The more I know… the more I know nothing, Sensei Kurtz. I have no idea why that image of Sidra Paredes suddenly popped up as I shot one of the fishmen, the saw-haw-gin, and watched its inky blood and fish guts trail through the water behind it, the eel's mouth going wide as my next round struck it. Then it just curled and slithered away into the deeper depths, leaving the chasing of our ship by its kind and masters to others. My tracking losing both targets as the wave broke.

Since Autumn…

Since Autumn…

I'd pushed a lot of thoughts aside that tried to come at me in the strange battle on the waters of the Rift. Maybe I just remembered Sidra because… well because that was easier than remembering Autumn. You know. Or maybe you don't. Your mileage may vary.

Brumm's hot brass flew frantically across the deck, raking the advancing fish cavalry. Some of the strange creatures died. Some were wounded and hurled their tridents at the deck before breaking off. A bunch more swarmed us almost all at once as the giant eels practically coiled and threw themselves out of the water and onto the lower deck of the galley, suddenly everywhere as the fish-men dismounted smoothly and closed for CQB with the Rangers.

There was no line of battle now. They were inside the wire as it were. No enemy forward of our position. Nowhere to direct fire or concentrate for a push. The enemy was everywhere, and gunfire was ill-advised at close quarters. I can stop right here and say that in my limited military experience I could see how a lot of other military units would have been in big trouble at this very moment.

We were modern soldiers from ten thousand years ago.

Stop at that and consider what I'm about to tell you.

That's a weird sentence. But it's the truth. Soldiers where we came from worked with firearms. Ranged projectile weapons that generally did war at range. Sometimes short, sometimes long. Many engagements were at extreme ranges. Mastering the art of ranged warfare was a science, and then... an art in and of itself. Hand-to-hand combat, or what the modern military called combatives, were still taught because *hey, sometimes things just get up close and personal dontcha know*. Knives were standard for almost every soldier. And practically a religion for the Rangers who usually carried multiples. There were also tomahawks for the purists who went full Ranger. Some Rangers criticized the weapon as being unwieldy and not much good in a fight. Other Rangers disagreed and had left a trail of dead hajis and dead orcs they believed proved them right.

Since our arrival, experience had made clear to us that the Ruin was a Bronze Age, Iron Age, Whatever Age society. Weapons like swords and axes were the norm here. Yes, Rangers had a bunch of *boom sticks* of all sizes and varieties. But those *boom sticks* required kill sticks full of things called rounds. Bullets. And a Ranger, who can carry a lot and move very fast doing so, can still only carry so much. About seven thirty-round magazines for the primary. Three or four mags for the secondary. A few frag grenades and maybe a LAW rocket and that was about it or else risk being just too heavy to fight optimally.

We were less than a hundred and fifty Rangers now, and we'd faced some pretty overwhelming odds. Sometimes numbering in the thousands. The gift of the Rangers was speed, surprise, and aggression. Violence of action. Being able to hit asymmetrically and go for a kill shot on the leader types despite overwhelming odds either through stealth or airborne deployment. Rangers could also channel mass segments of the enemy into traps, usually involving explosives.

But that was just fun for them.

Assassination was their real game.

But since being here in the Bronze Age Ruin of sword and hammer, it had been made clear there would probably come a moment when we would have to fight hand-to-hand in some sort of situation that probably looked a lot like the Spartans at the Hot Gates. Using the weapons of the age, or *pickups*, as the military calls them. The circumstances could be that dire—as in being *Winchester on ammo. Black on kill sticks.* Or, if you prefer, *Sarge, I got no mags left.* That was a Tannerism he'd use doing some goofy hillbilly voice he called Gomer Pyle.

Also, no Ranger ever called an NCO "Sarge." That was a stoning offense. But the imitation was allowed.

No clue who it was of by the way. But it was funny.

I was too busy doing languages for most of my life. Wanna know about conjugating Greek? I can tell you that. TV characters not so much. I know, my life has been much less lived. But how many people will ever know the thrill of a good Hellenic conjugation?

It was the sergeant major who had decided it was imperative for the Rangers to "git gud" at swords and axes. Bronze Age Spartan-style warfare. Since the sack of the dragon's hoard at Tarragon, the Rangers had been training to fight like Viking warriors. Or other forms of warriors who hacked each other to death. It must be noted here… you didn't have to ask them twice to do this. It was like me being told, *Hey you're gonna need to drink up all this coffee before the diner closes.* You didn't ask questions, you just were amazed that the universe had decided to smile on you for once and got down to pounding the dark stuff. You've probably got your equivalent. But it turns out some of the Rangers had studied hand weapons combat in their free time or civilian life already. A couple of fencers. Some kendo swordsmen. One guy who dressed up in armor and whacked other dudes with fake axes, swords, and maces all through college while getting his degree in physics and a minor in medieval farming techniques.

But it was the dwarves who'd taught us to really fight with real axes. And I don't mean the tomahawks. I'm talking actual battle-axes the Rangers had picked up as battlefield prizes.

Some were even magical, according to Vandahar. And Kennedy, who'd recently learned to detect such phenomena.

The sergeant major had every Ranger rotating through four schools of primitive weapon combat. Swords with Autumn's... husband, the Shadow Elf king. That was a fun one for me. Not much really. She doesn't even see me anymore. Not even when she would come to watch him, leaning on a cane, teaching us how to fight with the elven longsword which is more of a katana according to Brumm.

"It's a Japanese longsword with one edge. Not a great weapon, Talker, but well made. More hype than much else," rumbled Brumm when we were in training together.

Then you did bows with the Lost Boys. The sergeant major watched that one with Sergeant Thor, and anyone who showed aptitude got made a permanent archer sniper.

Then spears with Sergeant Joe because he had some kind of Chinese martial arts background. Mainly we used spears just like we did rifle PT. Basically, just to fight defensively as a unit if we ever found ourselves outnumbered on open ground.

"Romans were bad mother truckers with spears, Talk," whispered Brumm as Sergeant Joe lectured us about the many ways you could kill an opponent with a spear easily and quickly.

I asked Brumm why he seemed to have strong opinions on every weapon, which wasn't usual for him as he normally didn't say much to anyone.

"Used to watch a lot of videos. War's always been me and my brother's thing. What we had in common when we got to hang out once a summer."

"War summer camp with Kurtz sounds... not fun," I quipped.

Brumm laughed.

But he didn't say anything. Because it *was* fun, for him. He silently hero-worshipped his brother. Like I've said. He was a mini Kurtz-in-training. But what did you expect? They actually were brothers.

Finally, we did axes with the dwarves. And they were masters of the brutal weapon. It was Max, or the Hammer as even the Rangers now called him, who taught us as Wulfhard's champion. The king merely stood and observed, occasionally allowing himself to be used as combat dummy to demonstrate the Hammer's savage tactics with the axe.

"You vill cut viz ze axe, Rangers. Putting everything you have to both cut and crush at ze same time. But know ze energy from zis cut must make the next strike. Ze axe ist always moving," he said softly in his thick Germanic accent. "De warrior follows ze axe as she does her dance...

shall we call it zhat, Rangers? A dance? You are ze partner for ze axe. She will lead, you vill follow. And lead also. And together, you do ze dance of death."

I'd trained in all the weapons. We all had. But like I said, we had our battlefield pickups. And as the fish-men, the saw-haw-gin, swarmed the decks around us, webbed feet slapping against salt-crusted, foam-washed decks running with our blood, and the blood of our killing so far, I drew my singular pickup.

Coldfire.

The dead SEAL's weapon. Supposedly it was something legendary once and long ago. The sword of the king of the Dragon Elves. There had been some intense discussion between the elves about it. How rightfully it belonged to the Shadow Elves. And not to me.

But the Shadow Elves had their own weapons of renown. Autumn's sword. Its powers expended to destroy Toth-Azom at the burial hill. To break through the necromancer's impenetrable shield at the last impossible moment. I thought she'd died that day. Sacrificed herself to give the Rangers a shot at the jackpot.

There were nights after that, when we were still... whatever we were, she and I... nights I shuddered when I remembered seeing her lying there amid the stone and ruin after the great explosion when she'd driven her blade into the bubble barrier that prevented us from harming the mage who commanded an army of dead warriors. Bad dreams in which I turned her lifeless form over... and she was gone. Gone forever.

Not how it had actually happened. She'd begun to breathe and her eyes had fluttered as though she was just in some dream. Some bad dream. Like the dreams where she traded her one chance at slaying a dragon for certain death. For us.

For me.

I thought I had lost her then. I never wanted to come that close again to losing her. Those days and nights after… they were the best. The best.

For us.

The last time she ever looked at me, it was late in the night, after her brother and the new king, her husband, had exchanged angry words over the fate of the sword. *Coldfire*.

I'd heard what they were saying. It wasn't good. It was full of commentary they had for us. A lot of things I'd never repeat to the other Rangers.

Then she stopped them both cold. Proving she was indeed the true queen of the Shadow Elves despite their traditions of succession.

Mistress of the Midnight Throne.

It was she who led them through the chaos and dark times, to come out the other side. She who had found the Rangers. She who had believed when no one else did, or could anymore.

That was what made her a true queen. Not a title. She truly was something better than any of us.

A noble thing.

And it was foolish of me to think she could ever be anything other than. That was just some… some dream we'd once had.

"He slew the bearer of the fabled blade," she declared in Shadow Elf Korean. "It is his now by right of the law of all elves. He is the hero. The Silmerána Imperator. The *Book of Dark Songs* says it must be so, and so it must be so. Even as far back as when the Storm of the North Winds was king of our peoples, so has it been done. The blade falls to the Ranger Talker."

Silmerána.

Silver Moon.

I had no idea what that meant. And she would never again be able to explain it to me.

I felt lost for a reason. Because I was.

Warts and all. I promise I'll confess. Just give it a moment.

Most of what she'd said, she'd spoken as though in a strange trance. Reciting ancient texts and laws she'd been required to know for the administration of her people. Both sovereign and law-giver. But then, at the last, her eyes landed on me when she spoke the word *Ranger*.

Telling me who I was now.

And who I was not to her anymore.

Hell, even I didn't believe I was a Ranger. I'm just the guy next to the guy.

But she is the queen. And no one disagrees with her. Because she is, in actuality, a real, live queen.

There's something *other* about that. Real other.

So there's that too, I thought as I drew *Coldfire* for the first time in battle there on the deck of the storm-tossed *Sofia*. This was it. Real live toe-to-toe no-holds-barred combat with the enemy. Hand-to-hand.

Silmerána Imperator.

The Silver Moon Champion.

The deck pitched as I let my primary dangle and went to the sword I'd strapped to the back of my plate carrier. Heard the hiss of its draw. Felt its feathery firmness as I made my first downstroke and cut right into the big-eyed face of the hulking fish-man who came at me with a spear raised a little too high to be any good to defend the cut.

I caught it in the top of its finned head, and the blade sank in far enough to reach its brain as I watched my opponent's horrid bulging eyes roll. The thing gasped, its gills flexing as it died in the next second, and I pulled the blade free and just went forward, slashing fast at the next one to come for me. *Coldfire* practically whistled as it sliced through the air and right through the next fish-man's scaly side. The thing screamed horribly with bubbles and all. Its mouth opening and closing as it pivoted fast and rammed its spear at where I should have been.

The dwarves had taught me how to dance. The slash had carried my weapon through the enemy's side, and I'd followed it around in a perfect circle. Watching the blade pass Kurtz a few feet away, slamming his tomahawks, both of them, into the gaping needle-sharp mouth of a screaming giant eel. Watching my blade pass Santago at the wheel of the ship, leaning with all his might, red-faced like he was going to have a stroke, to get the galley out of the roller-coaster current. And then watching the blade come right back at the saw-haw-gin I'd just cut. This time coming right at his head. His huge milky eyes flicked from the spear tip he'd tried to ram into me and picked up *Coldfire* just before it cut smoothly through his fish skull in one clean stroke of pure momentum and cold fury.

A moment later Tanner pushed a fish-man away from him and drove a wicked short sword he'd picked up and taken to calling *Desiree* right into the thing's bulbous throat. Black blood jetted out, and with his other hand Tanner dragged a razor-sharp sword he'd found inside the torture cell deep within the dragon's dungeon, down along the whitish belly of the fish-man. Gutting the stunned thing right there on the deck.

He laughed and said, "Just like my uncle's fish market back in the city, Talk. Get some, brother."

I was breathing heavy. That's a thing with hand weapons combat. No matter how good your cardio is, you start breathing heavy real fast like you're not going to get enough oxygen.

"Zhat is a survival technique," the Hammer had lectured us. "Your body knows it needs a lot of power to do what it's going to do. So it's helping you by making sure you have ze air and ze blood. Ignore it," ordered the smiling dwarven weapons master. "Keep killing until zhere is no one left to fight. Then you can die. Zhat is how the dwarves of our land fight. And I am guessing you Rangers know of vhat I speak."

I just do what I'm told to do.

Mostly. I'm still a private thanks to the last time I didn't do what I was told to do. But there has been talk of me getting my mosquito wings and making Private E2. So there's that also.

I struck the next fish-man with just a plain old meat-and-potatoes savage hack. No finesse now. My game plan had consisted mainly of running my first two attacks of downstroke cuts. Then cut and decapitate. I also had parry-and-strike back in my repertoire, but so far in my first fight with *Coldfire* I hadn't had the need to parry. Still I was keen to try.

My next victim was just a savage chop. The fish-man ran off screaming with a bleeding stump where his arm had been. *Coldfire* had carried on through effortlessly and easily.

Or I'm just swole. Truth be told, Kurtz's Ranger School had jacked me a little. The patrol where I carried the two-forty had given me shoulders. Strapped and carrying a ruck was pure beast mode.

But it was probably the sword that did most of the work.

For some reason I punched the next fish-man with my fist gripped around the sword. As I write this, I have no idea why I did that. I just remember that as the deck pitched and rolled and the ship groaned and heaved over into the channel leading into the bay, the sail snapping above our heads and catching some much-needed breeze to pull us out of the chaos of the torrents and chop, I was gasping for air and my arms felt as heavy as lead after just a few cuts. So I rammed my fist right into the fish-man's face. It backed away, not exactly stunned, and then thrust its spear right at my plate carrier. Without even thinking I chopped down with *Coldfire*, and the dark blade sheared right through the spear's haft. The fish-man saw that, turned, and leapt back into the waves.

I spun around, locating my next target, only to find that the chaos on the deck was winding down. Dead fish-men were everywhere. Rangers were hacking the still-living to death with their battle-axes and other new weapons. The dead eels that had stayed lay along the length of the deck, oozing dark ink blood into the wash of the sea waves.

The place was a slaughterhouse. Dead bodies, all monsters, littered the deck. High above, the harpies were back, circling in great flocks, but it didn't look like they were going to make another attack. Not just yet.

All around us the seas were now calm. We were in the bay of the citadel. But behind us, in the rough chop of the torrent that led into the bay, Sea Horse Three Four Heavy, or what remained of it, was going into the cliffs hard and fast.

That was bad.

"Ahoy, Talk-ir!" Talk-ir was how Santago pronounced my name. He was waving with one hand as he steered the galley into the waters of the bay.

"Sar'nt, I think Santago wants to tell us something," I told Kurtz.

He scowled at me as he wiped dark blood from his blades and gave me the okay to find out what was going on.

I climbed to the aft deck and made the helm. There were dead fish-men and dead Portugonian sailors here. The dead captain of *Sofia* too. Santago was bleeding across his sun-browned bony arms where the thick ropy muscles of the old sailor clung. His bloody knife was stuck in the salt-worn wood around the helm. His voice was ragged and hoarse. But that was how he spoke at all times.

"The Head of Thezuz lies ahead, Talk-ir!" shouted the old man. The harpies above were crying out insanely in the distance. Their voices echoing like a psychotic chorus of old witch-women intent on gossiping something, or someone, to death with their demonic henpeckery.

The old sailor took his hand off the wheel and pointed toward the bow of Sea Horse Two Four. Through the rigging and sail I could see a giant head directly in front of us in the water, moss-covered and cracked, erupting from the waves.

I'll admit here that the first thing I thought as I saw it sticking out of the waves there in the center of the bay, or what I would later discover was the entrance to the inner bay, was that there was some giant coming out of the waters to eat us alive. Some peaceful sleeping Buddha giant that was probably going to murder us to death. The eyes vaguely Asian and alien as the waves washed up against its stony and immobile face beneath the gaze of the looming citadel in the distance.

This might as well happen, I thought. *Brumm, get the Carl G if they haven't gone overboard. Let's see if he don't care on this one.*

But I had my doubts this time.

"Tell your captain…" hissed the old sailor desperately above the wind and the groaning of the battered galley. "The bay is cursed. No one survives the old city. It is haunted. We can anchor against the old sacred head that protects this place. The fishwives of the Obrego say true, Talk-ir."

All this was in rapid-fire Spanish. Or mostly Spanish. Which to me is like a second language. So I followed quickly and understood what he was saying. The shores of the bay and the dark port city beneath the citadel were certain death to us. The giant head poking out of the water was some ancient monument that guarded the bay, or whatever had once been here. Anchoring against it might protect us and allow us, tactically, to remain cohesive. For the moment.

I'd learned enough in Kurtz's Ranger School to know that was important. Especially right now as the entire mission had gone to hell.

Consolidate, reorganize, and figure out a new plan immediately. No plan is certain failure. A plan, even a bad one, gives you a chance at success.

And mission success is the only thing that matters to a Ranger.

At just that moment our other ship, Sea Horse Three Four, was sucked into the end of the bay and slammed against the cliffs there. I could see Rangers in the water. They'd gone in before the ship hit hard. Rangers are excellent at water survival. They had a chance. But the currents of the bay would never let them reach us. And if we entered, it appeared, judging by the number of shipwrecks in there, some along the rocks and others submerged and half-sunken, that we would never get out.

"Do it!" I told Santago, and I ran back to tell Kurtz the plan.

Our mission had gone to hell. It was survival now. Escape and evasion for those on shore. We had Sea Horse One Four, the sergeant major's ship, out there somewhere. They wouldn't give up on us.

The Portugonians began to give back oars as our ship was sucked straight toward the giant head sticking out of the waters. Santago shouted and other sailors barked angrily in reply as a chaos of short, squat, mustachioed Portugonian sailors erupted everywhere into action to anchor the ship against the giant head. The sailors danced over the bodies of dead monsters to race for the anchor and the ropes.

The head loomed and Kurtz barked, "What the hell is he doing, Talker?"

I informed my NCO and watched as suddenly the old sailor spun the wheel and braced himself against it. The ship heaved over and slammed into the statue roughly. Wood groaned but didn't snap. The anchor went out at the same moment as the current started to drag us around the statue and on into the bay beyond.

Three of the harpies swooped down, and Sergeant Thor, covered in blood and still carrying the two-handed sword he'd started using since the dragon's lair, dropped the huge chunk of steel and unslung *Mjölnir*. He fired once at a swooping harpy who'd caught what remained of our emergency mainstay, and the half-woman half-vulture exploded everywhere at once. The other two cawed and croaked, hurling curses as their foul wings flapped and dragged them back up into the sky, away from Sergeant Thor's fury.

A moment later the anchor caught, and the ship held against the giant head at the entrance to the bay, rocking gently in the swell.

It was quiet and we all stared at each other, hearing the boards and rope creak as the soft white noise of distant breakers rolled along the beaches of this deserted and forsaken stretch of lonely desert coast.

I can't speak for everyone else, but at that moment I felt small and insignificant. The black mass of the citadel looming above. Africa, what we'd once called this continent, stretching away to the south, occupying every direction that wasn't the sea. Strange riddles rippling beneath the waves like we were floating above some vast sunken cemetery of a city that was more dream than reality. Devil women in the air with the wings of scavengers singing songs that were curses of the damaged and dying. Lost Rangers along the rocks and in the water. And some strange sense of loose and wild power in the air all around us.

The power that had been there in the storm wasn't gone. It was waiting. It was here in the stillness, waiting. You could feel it coursing through the dry salty air and the silence of this lost coast. Looking for advantage.

You could almost hear it laughing at us.
Almost.
If you didn't listen too close, you could almost hear it.

CHAPTER SEVEN

"WHAT the hell are we doing?" shouted Captain Knife Hand in a rage I'd never heard from him before. It was unusual to hear that angry tone coming from the normally calm yet constantly quietly irritated ground force commander for the Ranger detachment here in the Ruin. Then I turned to look at our commander after conferring with Sergeant Kurtz on Santago's intentions to anchor the galley alongside the Head of Thezuz, whoever that was, and found our commander in full were-tiger mode.

He'd changed.

The FAST helmet obviously gone. His wide triangular tiger head couldn't be contained by it, and it had either been destroyed, doubtful, or pulled off as he got sick and the metamorphosis of lycanthropic transformation began. His clothing and plate carrier had survived the transformation though, and he was mostly dressed and looking as high-speed as a were-tiger could get. The boots had been ripped to shreds and though his tiger's growl was evident in almost every syllable of his voice, it was still Captain Knife Hand inside that killer. Just maybe sounding… innately angry… due to the tiger's growl.

I hoped he wasn't about to go on that killing spree we'd all been afraid of since his other self had been revealed by the Ruin.

His true self, whispered some voice that sounded like Autumn's in the back of my mind. But I didn't know about that. True self? What did that say about me, and what I could do?

And... what *could* I do? I still wasn't sure beyond a few tricks I could perform fifty percent of the time, and a few that came and went dependent on circumstances.

Undependable, whispered another voice that wasn't Autumn and didn't seem to like me much. Maybe that was just me. Maybe it was my mother when she felt the need to be cruel to manage me where she felt I needed to be. Maybe it was even Kurtz.

Who understands the mysteries of inner monologues?

But there on the slaughterhouse drenched in sea water that was the *Sofia,* the captain was on the main deck, crossing from the starboard side where some of the heaviest fighting had gone down when the fish-men and their eel rides had tried to swamp us. Now he was walking swiftly at me and Kurtz. And the effect of a half man, half killer big cat was not lost on anyone.

Intimidating is putting it mildly. Very mildly. Even among Rangers. Trust me, if you've never had a man-tiger walking at you, growling and angry, then you just haven't experienced what it's like for your heart to stop for a good few seconds.

"What the hell is going on, Sergeant Kurtz? We need to take this ship into that bay immediately and rescue those Rangers in the water," Captain Knife Hand demanded.

Even the stoic Kurtz—who had two settings, pure contempt and raging anger—seemed taken aback by the captain's appearance in were-form. The weapons team sergeant's mouth simply opened and closed once.

Like he was gonna say something, update maybe, give a sitrep, then remembered he was talking to a real live killer were-tiger everyone had seen in action in the middle of violent combat and who worked in excessive bloody ultra-violence like it was an art form or a bodily function.

There are killers.

And then there are killer animals.

There's a difference, and I can't tell you which one is more scary. But both are very. Very scary when in close live proximity.

Even though the captain had transformed twice in front of everyone at high-tension moments, and none of the Rangers had gotten hurt, there were still fears that Knife Hand would suddenly go berserk and start killing everyone in those moments, unable to distinguish between friend and foe. His animal side having taken over. I think even the captain had that same fear, as he'd always gone straight for the enemy line and away from his men as fast as he could once he'd changed. I'd had glimpses into his mind during those moments. I could tell he was cognizant and aware that he needed to protect his men above all else.

And because no entry in this log of the Rangers lost in the Ruin is complete without focusing on me…

Yeah, I'm aware of that. Kennedy has read a few entries to correct some of the monster knowledge, and he dryly commented in his usual way, "You sure talk about yourself a lot, Talker. Rangers don't do that. Hell, even I don't do that. Maybe that's what Kurtz dislikes so much about you?"

Point taken. But it's my log. So…

I had been made aware that leadership was my weak point, and I understood a little better that it wasn't cool to be able to turn into a half man, half tiger killing machine like Captain Knife hand could. That wasn't acceptable if you were a real leader.

Now, many of the Rangers would have sold their mothers into slavery for that power. I'm not making that up. About fifty percent of the conversations on the subject of the captain's lycanthropic nature included that very comment or some sentiment expressing same.

"Man, Talker, I'd sell my mom back on the block to be able to go all Wolverine like that! That'd be lit as it all gets legit!"

Then they'd usually act out some Wolverine slashing moves.

To be fair, some of them expressed selling their sisters or even very expensive bikes or coveted trucks to have this "superpower."

One guy said he'd even sell his tomahawk collection. And one said he'd sell his last can of dip for the power of animal transformation of the coolest and deadliest kind.

Your mileage may vary, but I noted a pattern.

But for me, trying to educate myself on how to become a Ranger, I had come to understand that as a leader, a combat leader, with the burden of everyone's life in your decision-making tree at all times and in all situations, and knowing most likely someone was going to get killed even if you made the right call, it must have burned for the captain to realize he could be a danger to his men if he couldn't control this killer side of himself that the Ruin had somehow revealed.

His true self.

You could say a lot of things about the captain.

But the one thing you couldn't say was he didn't put his men first. He did everything to make sure they had the best position and best chances for every fight we'd ever been in.

No matter how long he needed to work, dig, bury explosives, and climb sheer cliffs, to get them that opportunity to kill better and walk away from every fight with as many fingers, toes, and friends as possible. That was clear, and it was unquestionable.

Fact.

So being forced to change and get clear of your men because you might kill them, instead of leading them, was... it was unmistakable to me now... that was a real problem for a real leader like the captain.

Kurtz was right. I didn't have that in my hard drive. I'd needed to see that example at this very moment to have, or begin to have, some understanding of that concept of the burden of true leadership.

The were-tiger killer was standing right in front of us using nothing but self-control, powered by sheer will to not *go all Wolverine*, as the Rangers put it, and start killing us in lieu of enemies.

I must've inadvertently nodded as I arrived at this conclusion because suddenly the burning glare of the tiger's sapphire eyes were resting directly on me. Like ten thousand pounds all at once boring into me, and it was hard to decide whether I should speak up and try to save my life, or if I was about to be a meal no matter what I did.

Kurtz tried to speak, but you have to understand, and I know I am making this point again, but you really need to understand, as many freaky things as we'd seen in the Ruin, orcs and trolls and dragons, undead even, the captain standing there as a man-tiger in plate carrier holding an MK18, burning eyes and fangs protruding, orange and white stripes, whiskers... it was just terrifying. Even for a Ranger like Kurtz who showed zero fear in every moment, even in this moment, there was a simple stalling hesitancy surfacing about how to proceed with the lycanthropic killer that was currently our ground force commander.

"Sir," I croaked. "Santago said we should anchor here to avoid the bay. It's too dangerous to go in with the galley. We've lost our oars on the port side and the sails are damaged beyond repair. We can't steer, and power seems iffy at best. According to him, safe navigation further in would be almost certainly fatal… according to Santago."

I remembered another thing about being a leader. One thing Kurtz and the cadre had tried to impress on me during those brutal eviscerating AARs that made you just want to recycle yourself out of pure shame for failure to meet Ranger standard once again. I remembered that one of the first things a leader has to do is take responsibility. Hey, I probably wasn't the best at running a patrol, but I could take responsibility. I could do that. I had told Santago to execute the docking here at the strange peaceful head sticking out of the waves of the emerald bay.

"I made the call, sir."

Then I said nothing. 'Cause explanations are useless.

The tiger who was our captain growled and swiped a brutal animal's tongue across his chops.

My heart might have either skipped or stopped dead still at that point. I felt a cold sweat break out across my sun-blistered and salt-stung skin. I'd seen that thing sink its fangs into monsters and just bite their throats out.

No. Not bite. *Tear*. Tear throats out. I, and everyone else, had seen that.

So that was possible.

Kurtz stuck an assault-gloved hand on my chest and just pushed me back out of the conversation. Whether to protect me or tell me to shut it, I had no idea.

Turning to the captain-tiger thing, Sergeant Kurtz calmly said to the ground force commander, regardless of his lycanthropic status, "Sir. What do you need us to do right now?"

It was probably one of the bravest things I've ever seen anyone do. Seriously.

"We need to get into that bay and rescue those Rangers," growled Knife Hand. "Consolidate on shore and wait for the sergeant major to come in with Sea Horse One Four Heavy for extraction. Holding position here isn't an option, Sergeant."

As if on cue one of the Rangers on the starboard side called out, "Black sails incoming!"

Kurtz turned and grabbed his 'nocs, scanning the horizon. The captain merely turned and squinted his tiger's eyes at the horizon and the waves. I was guessing he had some kind of super-enhanced vision. And then his whiskers twitched, and those wide nostrils inhaled the salt breeze. You know, like a big giant killer cat would if it were out hunting. Yeah, he definitely had heightened senses.

All I could wonder was how much of him was Knife Hand, and how much of him was pure killer. Like no other predator ever seen before. Were-beast with Ranger skills beyond question by any Ranger. He was acknowledged by all, despite being an officer, as a Ranger's Ranger. And from what the sergeant major had let slip in our quiet coffee talks, the Knife Hand he knew back in Delta could give the killer tiger a run on body counts.

Then Kurtz told the captain what I was sure he already knew from his enhanced senses.

"We got orcs coming in, sir. Not sure of the type of ship, but I would call it some kind of longboat. Counting eight now and rowing hard under sail straight for us. Eyes on tons of archers and what I would probably term... marine-type orcs," he finished awkwardly. Kurtz did his best to never embrace the fantasy... but sometimes it just snuck up on him and there was nothing he could do. As Tanner later observed, "Sometimes you're the bug, sometimes you're the windshield."

Kurtz had been a marine before becoming a Ranger.

Sergeant Thor came aft from the low forecastle at the bow, carrying *Mjölnir* over his broad shoulders. His vision was probably as close to the tiger captain's as was humanly possible. I could see him watching the dark sails beginning to appear and grow on the horizon to our north.

I was wondering if the newcomers had engaged Sea Horse One Four and sunk her out there in the deep water and that was the reason we were getting no comm from the sergeant major, or call sign Cowboy for this op.

"Those are Viking longboats, sir," rumbled Thor with one massive hand shielding his eyes. "By the size of them... I'm guessing each one is carrying about sixty bad guys. They get in range, we can light them up with the two-forties and try to sink them. Snipers can engage the sailors, and that might leave them dead in the water. But if we leave this channel into the bay, they can bottle up that inner harbor. And that might make it difficult for Sea Horse One Four to get in and extract—if they're still combat-effective."

Fascinated, I watched the captain studying the situation and listening to the assessments and reports from two of his

NCOs. Half man, half tiger, in complete control of himself despite the utter derailment of plans and current situation. This was just the hop to get to the mission and not even six hours into what was supposed to be a six-day sail into the eastern end of the Med, and we were in big trouble already. One ship destroyed, one missing, surrounded by orcish pirates and dead in the water. I had no idea if there was some tiger form of that look of permanent indigestion, but there were certainly enough problems for there to be.

Maybe the stress had brought about the change in our commander, but the discipline of being a Ranger combat leader kept things under control.

I pounded the last of my self-control cold brew and admired the Ranger captain. I was sure I'd never be that much of a stud. The coffee whispered that I didn't need to be. *I just need coffee, and everything can just fade away, right, baby?*

Great, I was either cracking up or now my cold brew was starting to talk to me. Then again, I had put some of the magic Kungaloorian sugar in there. So... I had no idea what that did other than make me feel what I'd been told cocaine felt like.

We had no comm with either of the other elements. But it was clear from what the captain was saying that a rescue operation needed to get underway immediately. Rangers were excellent in the water, but I wasn't about to think most of the Rangers on *Dancer* managed to get their gear water-ready in time to abandon ship before it went hard into the rocks. And those waters were both shark, and monster, infested. Add in our half-ruined galley that could only make right turns if my understanding was correct as to how bad the damage was to *Sofia*, and it was clear we had ourselves a real situation.

Yes. I was glad I wasn't in charge. Because then a lot of people would get killed and absolutely nothing would get accomplished except maybe I'd get a chance to talk to the fish people if they captured us.

Then I watched a real leader do what a real leader does. Make a plan.

"Sergeant Kurtz. You will lead both gun teams in holding this position aboard this vessel to keep the bay clear of bad guys. Do not let those orcs past this point in the water. Have the indig sailors repair the ship as best they can if just to make it to the beach when the time comes. Try and regain contact with Sea Horse One Four and Cowboy. Apprise them that I'm going ashore to consolidate and rescue. Sergeant Kurtz, leave half your snipers here to assist in the defense of this position, and you and yours are going in with me and the assaulters."

Then the tiger captain turned to me, knife claw out. "Private Talker, tell those sailors we need both boats ready to launch in ten. I want their best helmsmen to take us in."

Then he turned to address the Rangers and NCOs standing nearby to receive their orders on the fly.

"Rangers, here's the situation, mission, and execution. We've got Rangers in the water from a downed transport. We need to go in there, rescue them, and consolidate at a patrol base on shore. Some Rangers will still be in the water. Most likely a lot of them have made it onto the rocks and gone up the cliff to start linking up and fighting with the local hajis holding there. Boat One with Sergeant Thor is going to secure that small tower located at the eastern end of the settlement…"

He pointed into the bay along the shore toward a squat, broken tower that looked more like a guard barracks than a lighthouse at the extreme eastern edge of the small city surrounding the towering citadel. It lay next to the cliffs where Sea Horse Three Four had gone in.

"Sergeant Thor, establish a secure perimeter there and defend that as our primary LZ for extraction. That will be our rally once Cowboy comes in with One Four to extract. Boat Two will be half our assaulters going with me to extract anyone in the water. Once we've swept the water and checked the cliffs, we'll make for the tower as a QRF and link up to relieve any counterattack on the LZ. Sergeant Thor is the GFC until we link up. Sergeant Kurtz, update your status on the half hour. I want the gun teams holding this position full on seven-six-two before we depart. NCOs, divvy up your ammo and leave as much for them as possible. They'll need to hold to keep all forces in connection until we can consolidate. The mission is still in effect, and I expect it to be completed once we clear this disaster. We leave in ten."

The Rangers set about to quickly getting their troops into fighting positions to hold the anchored *Sofia* here at the enigmatic Head of Thezuz, whoever that was, and ammo distributed accordingly. Suddenly Jabba was getting draped and piled with belts of seven-six-two and cans stacked nearby. With each deposit, the little gob murmured a forlorn, "Bigga bigga trouble coming now. Big bigga big. Smelly demon orc coming now. Bigga bad." The medics started splashing around wound disinfectant and quickly taping and wrapping up the more serious gashes, slashes, and scratches the two recent engagements had rewarded the various Rangers with.

The captain turned to me amid the hustle. It had been silently acknowledged that when he was in were-tiger form I was to stay close and be ready to use psionics, something I truly had no idea how to use other than a few tricks I'd learned to pull that left me with nasty headaches, to calm him down out of this apex predator form if need be.

That didn't seem necessary now. He was clearly in complete control of himself.

"Private, you're with Sergeant Thor's team. Need you on the ground to figure out who we're facing and try to assess how large their force is at the LZ. Get me intel about who we're up against."

CHAPTER EIGHT

WE were just climbing into the two boats *Sofia* carried, one stowed forward and one that trailed the ship via line, when the black sails of the orc longboats were within range to start their massed arrow fire.

Kurtz held fire on the two-forties to make sure they were well within range so they didn't run. He wanted his gunners to have ample opportunity to murder them for making the mistake of getting close to Ranger weapons teams.

"Heads down!" bellowed Sergeant Thor as the missiles began to whistle in. You could hear the bow twangs over the water singing out on deep bass notes. If you'd told me that day I first walked into the recruiting office to get a brochure on what I'd been daydreaming about lately at the time, before I joined up, if you'd told me then that one day I'd be engaging in Bronze Age naval warfare… I won't lie to you, I'd probably have joined up right there on the spot.

But then again, so would all of the Rangers. It was battle, and we'd done battle here in the Ruin. Defense against mass wave charges of orcs, ogres, and battle trolls built like tanks. Hand-to-hand against weird and even at times magical monsters. Raids on cemeteries full of the living dead to do a jackpot sorcerer. Even smoked a dragon with all the Carl Gs we could hit it with. Many of the Rangers had done modern combat at various hellholes around the world we'd come from. Explosives and automatic weapons on full cackle, enemies everywhere. Both sides fighting for their lives.

But this was something new. And that was like pure crack off a gas station bathroom sink for Rangers. Bronze Age war at sea. *Well why not this? What's the high score? I need something to try for*, you could almost see them saying to themselves. They welcomed this fight. But then again they welcomed any fight like most people look for extra M&Ms at the bottom of the bag. I could see Kurtz's weapons teams laying out their Middle Ages pickups just hoping the orc marines were dumb enough to try and get real close. Try and board even.

Oh boy that would be awful for them.

Hell, the Rangers would be disappointed if they didn't try.

I had to repeat all this for the six Portugonians and Santago, who had volunteered to steer us in on Thor's boat. As the linguist, my job was to make sure the indigs had a clear picture of what the Rangers were up to, so they didn't get in the way.

Thor called out, "Incoming!" and then a moment later the sky to our north was filled with its own sea of black whistling arrows arching up against the gray boiling clouds. The projectiles screamed as they fell and slammed into the water all around us. Some finding the galley and slamming home with solid wooden *thunks*.

Instantly Kurtz ordered Gun Number One to reply. A short series of *thuds* as the gunner, Soprano, found his range and then opened fire on the water line of the first galley.

"Let's go, now!" shouted Kurtz.

The captain's boat had already pushed off and was heading into the chop and currents, all the Rangers pulling hard at the oars with no Portugonians aboard, in order to have enough room for any survivors, or as many survivors as possible. The captain cut a strange figure as a were-tiger there at the tiller, scanning the waters near and far from the rocks for his Rangers who were still in the water.

I could see the remains of Three Four Heavy driven up onto the rocks, her bow snapped off, smashed by the violence of the surf raging there, and I saw that there were Rangers there also, still on board the wreckage. Others were free-climbing the cliffs above. And I heard the *crack* and *pop* of distant gunfire echoing out and competing against the replies of the two-forties behind us, having a conversation about the incoming orcish pirates who had mistakenly sailed into an envelope of talking guns they would not easily disengage from.

Eight versus one. Eight pirate vessels versus the crippled *Sofia*. Even with two-forties it was going to be a real fight for Kurtz and the weapons teams. But who else would you want directing hellfire right there in the middle of the ocean? The guy with the perfect intersection of competence and rage. He'd probably detonate one of the one-five-five shells we carried in the cargo hold rather than surrender and be taken alive.

Then I remembered Autumn's horse. He was down there in the hold. Along with some others the Rangers had brought for the scouts.

It's been said that sometimes you pray even when you don't believe. So I did, in my own ignorant way. Like it was a thought as we began to row into the open swells, heading for the beach and the LZ we needed to secure. I prayed for Kurtz to hold.

I'd lost her. Last of Autumn.

I couldn't lose the horse.

Why? I'm not self-actualized enough to know the answer. I've never been to therapy. I just deal with stuff the way we all do. Sometimes well. Sometimes pretty badly. That's true of everyone. Trust me. But I bet it had something to do with not being ready to let go.

So I sent one whatever up to the big whomever and hoped they liked horses enough to make Kurtz a killer like nothing the orcs had ever seen before in their miserable twisted lives. And also that maybe I was owed something for some good I couldn't remember ever having done at this moment when I needed a favor from the universe real bad.

I was sure there was something. I just couldn't remember when the incoming started hitting the water all around us.

Tanner waved down at me as we cast off and the Portugonians began to pull us out into the swells. He put one assault-gloved thumb up and mouthed, *I got ya, Talk.*

"Mission's canked for now," he'd said just before I climbed down the netting to join Sergeant Thor and the snipers in their assault on our identified LZ. "Be careful in there, Talk. Dead in the water say it's worse on shore than down there in their watery graves."

"How worse?"

Tanner smiled that slow dead thing's smile of his as his eyes unfocused and went somewhere… *other.*

"They say it's hell over there, Talk. Hell, man."

So, we got that going for us.

Twenty minutes later the Rangers were going ashore. Sergeant Thor had a plan developed as we crossed the rolling waters between us and the objective, *LZ Tower* we were calling it. Mainly it consisted of half the snipers on board setting up to fire at any defenders we encountered as we made the insertion, and the other half going into the water as we neared shore to make sure the boat got beached and to move forward immediately in two combat teams to seize an identified position between us and the tower, a low sea wall we could use as cover in case we encountered significant resistance. Then we'd assess and react with extreme violence.

I was going with the assaulters, and paired with Daredevil.

I'll tell you now what happened. We barely made it on shore and to the sea wall. Barely.

As we approached through the rolling waves, watching the silent city that spread away from the looming citadel, rising above the cracked and fissured bay, it was clear this place had been hit by some giant earthquake long ago. It was like looking at a city an hour after the dust has cleared from the catastrophic worst earthquake ever, buildings toppled and crumbled forever because you know no one is coming to rescue or clean this place up.

It was mostly lifeless. There was some movement in shadows and along winding streets. But it was quick and clearly moving with a purpose. No one thought we were surprising anyone.

"Expect resistance," Thor said from the tiller. "No idea how much though, boys. Just make sure it's good and dead and then keep moving on the tower."

I saw broken palaces and crumbling temples over there where we were going. City streets filled with fallen rubble like some forever frozen waterfall of stone and debris. Areas where sections of the ornate structures had slid right down into the sea and now lay half-sunken in the crystal-clear coastal waters we were pulling through.

I thought, seeing the lack of activity, that the Rangers would get the boat onto the small beach there, secure the LZ, and then move on the tower without too much resistance.

Instead, half a mile offshore, a signal fire suddenly sprang to life atop the squat watchtower we were aiming to secure. Flames like a brushfire jumped to life, shimmering in the heat of the day as the dry wood there crackled. Within seconds, black smoke was on the breeze and drifting toward the rest of the ruined city.

"Signal fire. They've figured out we're going for the LZ. Probably gonna get hot, boys. Alpha, secure that wall ASAP."

Alpha was us. Five minutes later we were slipping over the side of the boat. In the distance I could hear the two-forties still rattling out exchanges of death against the black sails circling and firing massed volleys on *Sofia*.

There were seven black sails now. Kurtz had his first naval kill.

We had no comm, for no reason we could ascertain. Magical interference was the most common guess. But who knew?

It was at that moment, as I slipped into the water in full plate carrier, keeping my rifle up on the boat and out of the water, hanging on to the craft, boots dangling and finding no soft white sand underneath, that I began to think of all those sharks and goonies, and yeah even the fish-men who'd come up from the depths farther out in the bay.

They were still down here, in the sea with us.

The water here was aquamarine and practically crystal clear. If you were up in the boat, you could see that we were clear of those enemies right now as we crossed over immense sunken statues of strangely armored warriors that had collapsed down into the sands beneath the waves as we approached the insertion point on the beach. But in the water, you had the feeling that the sharks and goonies you couldn't see were right there and coming for you. Ready to take your legs off with one bite. I had no idea how Daredevil had been able to swim through the monster-infested dark waters in the swamps of Tarragon and not lose his mind.

I sure would have.

Thor was on the tiller next to Santago, scanning the depths to make sure we were clear. Then one of the snipers, laying out and using his ruck as a stabilized shooting platform on the boat, fired.

"Got one. Orc, big one," he said just before shooting. "He's watching us from behind a column in the shadows of a collapsed building just right of the tower. Looks like a spotter or leader type. Lots o' danglies." He called all this out in the moment before firing.

Danglies meant war trophies like teeth and other bizarre totems they wore about their thick bull necks in large loops. Sometimes punctured gold coins and ears from other monsters. Our monster classes and after-action reviews had identified this as a way of spotting leader types. The bigger the dangly, the bigger the leader.

"Take the shot," ordered Thor instantly as he continued to watch for fast-moving triangular fins in the water with us. He'd ordered the Portugonians to stop singing on the way into the LZ. But I could see their mouths were still moving as they pulled at the oars to get us to shore as quickly as possible.

Specialist Edmunds, the sniper, took the shot immediately. All I heard was the terrific sonic boom of the weapon he was using. At the same time, I could feel the sandy bottom of the rising shore at the tips of my boots.

"Get ready," whispered Daredevil nearby in the water alongside the boat with me. Then, "Water's clear, Sar'nt."

"Got him," called out Edmunds matter-of-factly.

"Here we go," said Daredevil as we got our feet onto the sand. "Get ready to push, Rangers!"

We were "running" along the bottom of the sand, trying to push the boat through the waves and get it on shore when most of the snipers started calling out multiple targets in the structures around the tower.

"Open fire," grunted Thor as he worked his way forward, knelt, and started firing *Mjölnir*. The snipers were calling out their targets with little emotion just to make sure no one was picking up someone else's soon-to-be dead guy.

I'd love to give you a real movie's-eye view of what was happening. Sometimes I can, if I talk to a few other people who were involved and they can kinda tell me what happened from their point of view. But in this instance, I was with Alpha Team for LZ security and events moved so fast that I was never fully able to get the big picture of what happened around me. Alpha went left and Bravo went right. We were using bounding overwatch, under cover of the snipers, to secure the sea wall in front of the tower while the snipers shot down any targets of opportunity that were trying to react to our assault.

Now that I'd been through some of Ranger School, twice, I had some ideas about what was going on, tactically. I'd envisioned a more stealthy approach like something out of a military recruiting commercial, where we came out of the water all in a wedge and advanced, shooting down any surprised bad guys, suppressed. Those had been my thoughts while crossing the shark-infested waters from the now-besieged-by-orc-pirate-Vikings *Sofia*.

Expectations meet reality and die a hard death in the burning sunlight of a strange and weird place at the end of the known world.

It was a straight-up brawl from the moment we rushed the sand. I went left leaving the boat, as the first black arrows began to fall on the beach, following Alpha Team leader, which was Daredevil. The black arrows came out of nowhere, streaking like shadowy rockets trailing oily smoke, blurring the distances they covered. Daredevil took one through the throat. He was on his knees when two more hit him above the plate carrier. I was scrambling for cover, and I turned around and saw him get hit again. He could tell I was gonna do something real dumb, like try to get him and drag him to cover. He waved me away, his mouth working as he drowned in his own blood.

Then he just fell over. Dead.

I knew it right then.

Like you do.

CHAPTER NINE

THE incoming was everywhere all at once. The snipers were pinned down at the boat and using it for cover, firing from behind the bulk of the vessel that had brought us on shore. They were behind me and to my right as I made a large rock that might have once been a carved head just shy of the sea wall.

As the only surviving member of Alpha Team, I had to maintain security on the left. I knew that was my job. I remembered what I had to do when Bravo Team called out, five seconds later, that they were moving up. I popped up behind the slime-covered rock and laid down suppressive fire to give Bravo a chance to get closer to the wall.

I had no one to shoot at. The black smoking arrows were coming from recessed shadowy hides. So I just fired at the gaping, dark, arched entrance to the tower because I saw two streak out of there almost at once.

Bravo moved fast and Sergeant Herrera raced forward, pulled a grenade, and lobbed it up and into the tower entrance I'd just fired into after yelling, "Frag out!"

I covered and turned back to the water, seeing Daredevil lying there as the slow surf washed up against his lifeless body. His eyes were far away, seeing nothing here anymore. One thick black arrow still sticking out of his throat. Evil wisps of necrotic smoke drifting from its length.

Yeah. He was dead.

Sergeant Thor signaled me from the boat, telling me to suppress as he moved forward to assist. I popped and mag-dumped on the arch once more to give him cover. I heard his huge pounding steps come up through the wet surf as he grabbed Daredevil's lifeless corpse and dragged him to the rock. All around him more arrows slammed into the sand and whistled off into the surf. Someone was shooting at us from murder holes within the tower.

For a moment I turned away, trying to spot someone, anyone, to kill. I could hear Thor muttering as he knelt over his protégé's body. "C'mon kid…" he said, over and over. But Specialist Daredevil was gone. Finally I heard Thor rumble an "okay" to himself, and then he was up next to me, glaring like a predator sensing the kill at the squat tower he'd determined to take.

There was no anger or wrath. Just cold professionalism. At the time I didn't realize that. But now, as I think back and get it all down, it occurs to me, details like that. And so I put them down and you can make of them what you want. Whoever you are.

"We're breaching the tower. Need you to go around this rock, get up on the sea wall, and get your banger ready. I'll cover and then come up. You deploy the banger, then we go in. Go left after I go right. Slice the pie, Talker."

Not ten seconds later I was doing just that. I had cover from the sea wall and then I was pulling myself up onto it. It was old stone. Carved and frescoed with scenes of fish and sea monsters and gods that had great nets full of strange and almost comically bizarre fish. Details. I saw all this as I ran, head down, for the position I'd been ordered to against the wall of the tower, near the arch where black arrows continued to scream out, trailing evil black smoke as they came. I could see the snipers on the beach shooting into the murder holes as best they could.

Spoiler: that was easy for Rangers.

I let my carbine go and grabbed my flashbang grenade. Thor came up a moment later, literally following the front sight of his massive rifle trained on the entrance as he raised his left gloved hand for me to deploy the flashbang. I pulled the pin and at the same moment he suddenly fired. I looked up to see a not large orc, but a pretty brutal one, carrying a jagged sword and shield, standing in the doorway. He had danglies, but not a lot.

Mjölnir went off like a thundercrack at close range and disintegrated the thing's head, sending blood spatter and brain spray into the darkness the thing had come from. Even with EarPro the explosion of the Barrett was terrific and I felt my breath sucked away from me, or pushed out, forgetting not for a second that I was holding a live flashbang.

I think Thor said something but there was no way I was gonna hear it, so I tossed the banger into the darkness and stepped back, getting control of my slung carbine and ready to follow the breach.

Thor went in a second after the flashbang exploded. He went in shooting fast and hard with the huge distance rifle like he was working a slender carbine built for CQB.

There were at least eight shots in rapid succession. Thundering tremendously in that small cavern of a room. The huge Ranger sniper went in like a relentless and terrible predator that couldn't be bargained or reasoned with.

I followed using the corner of the entry door, pieing the room on angles and picking up targets as I advanced and pivoted within the portal entry. Making sure none of them were Sergeant Thor as I began to fire.

That one fragmentary grenade that had already been detonated inside, thanks to Sergeant Herrera, was a big help once we saw what was waiting for us inside the unremarkable tower we'd selected for our LZ. Or rather caught glimpses of. There were *tons* of orcs in here. It was dark and shadowy and when I thumbed my illuminator to life—unconsciously because it was so dark—I saw them twisted and sneering in the darkness there, clearly staging to counterattack.

My mind screamed, *Back out!* There were too many. Way too many. And there was something different about these. They were like animals. Malevolent and glaring in the darkness, their eyes a burning cat's-eye yellow in the gloom. Rows of needle fangs in their wide and horrific mouths. Tribal paint wild and weird, twisting and insane on their bodies in shades of blood-red and dark grease.

My first instinct was to recoil in horror. But I'd been trained to stay on mission. So I didn't, even though my mind wanted me to, or rather screamed in terror for me to. Thor had gone in and was firing at these nightmares at point-blank with the massive anti-materiel rifle he called *Mjölnir*. Some of those tremendous fifty-caliber rounds must have gone straight through multiples of the orc demons, they were packed so close.

The blinding light at the front of my rifle caught the bloody remains of those who had been ruined by Sergeant Herrera's grenade. It also caught the multitude of orcs coming off the walls they'd been pressed against, holding dirty butcher knives, toothy spears, and baring yellowed fangs as they advanced on me all at once.

They were like feral animals more than the warriors we'd faced back when we'd first gotten here.

We'd fought orcs. Fought them at Bag of Death Island. They were like dark hulking versions of us. But these... these were more demonic, more animal, the glittering madness of insanity singing in their eyes and twitching their thin lips. More feral.

If I had one word to describe them, I would choose *vicious*. Utterly so.

They lunged at once, and I started pulling the trigger.

I had to have killed some. In truth, I had to have killed a lot. It was impossible not to. But chaos reigned in the explosions and speed, and not enough died, or at least not enough as fast as I needed them to. One slender bugger with wild springy hair and a narrow chin like a pick, yellow cat eyes glittering with laughing malice, grabbed my carbine because the quarters were so close, and tried to pull it from me in one ferocious jerk. My mag was already empty and so the weapon was useless for the moment.

But my sling wouldn't let him have it.

In RASP, the Terminator had taught us all a trick for when building-clearing CQB got this intimate.

"Let 'em have the weapon, Rangers. They ain't goin' nowhere with it if it's on your sling. Now they just got their hands busy for you to do something else that's fun and interesting. And that they ain't expectin'."

I pulled my knife off my carrier in one savage swipe and jabbed it into the thing's throat. It crowed like a stuck pig and backed away while another one came out of the darkness and tried to grab me from the right. An area I'd already cleared so I had no idea where he'd come from all of a sudden. I slashed the bloody blade across my front, going left to right, and drove it into that one. This one was even uglier than the other if that was possible. I may have sliced yet another orc on the way. I honestly have no idea because this was a month's worth of chaos in about two seconds.

And Thor's rifle had stopped booming.

In some distant part of my mind, I knew that was bad. Real bad. Probably. At the same time, the orc I had just stabbed fell away with my knife jammed into a bone, dragging it out of my gloved grip.

I yanked my sling away from something else that had ahold of it, fell against the wall, never mind the sharp crack to my skull despite the FAST helmet as my legs went out from under me, and concentrated on pulling a mag from my carrier and getting it into the carbine.

The bolt slammed forward, and I fired at a nightmare coming out of the darkness.

This one was large. Easily one of the largest orcs I'd ever seen. More like an ogre, really. Also, it had four arms. Around its neck was a necklace of giant shark teeth. Huge fangs opened as it threw itself out of the darkness, swinging a huge mace that was carved like the head of a squinting demon. The mace was in one hand and aimed right at my head.

I ducked, felt my thumb flip the selector to full auto because that seemed like the right thing to do right about now, and emptied what I hoped were about thirty rounds in just seconds. I squeezed and held on.

It wasn't dead but it was on its knees, its huge eyes incredulous at what had just happened to it. A blur of walking gunfire running up its torso and leaving wounds of a kind it had probably never experienced before. I pushed myself up the wall, ejecting and grabbing a new kill stick.

Once I had it in, I shot the giant orc again, but this time just once in the head. And two more times where I thought its black heart should be.

Sergeant Thor came out of the darkness. His face covered in blood. Something had slashed him good across the brow.

"They're all dead down here, Talker. Tell Herrera to secure the perimeter around the tower. I'm going up to clear the roof."

CHAPTER TEN

THE next two hours were about consolidation on the objective. With Sergeant Thor acting as the ground force commander for the only Ranger-held position on land at the moment, things got brutal fast.

The Rangers immediately went into make-'em-pay mode by setting up hasty ambushes on the elements massing against them and placing explosives to channel the enemy where they wanted them to go. All of this under massed arrow fire that the Rangers began to measure for intervals before moving quickly to next positions for cover to conduct their mayhem. The body count started to click over fast. The enemy body count, that is.

We laid Daredevil out on the sand in a cove protected by the tower and the rocks. It was a peaceful place despite the chorus of arrow attacks and the sudden bursts of brutal gunfire. And the occasional explosion that deafened the soundscape and reminded you that a bunch of the orcs had just died on their way in to do the same to you that you just did to them.

If we buried him there at the cove, I would not have minded that for myself. But I knew the Rangers wouldn't leave Daredevil behind. Not here. Not now. Not ever.

The enemy never relented from probes or arrow sniper fire targeting the Rangers. They laid mayhem and hate like they'd just gone to a bulk supply warehouse store and picked up a couple of family packs of extra violence for the tribe. But the enemy paid heavily for these actions. The Ranger snipers holding the perimeter of the squat tower, four of them including Thor, shot every orc archer stupid enough to approach down the main road leading to the ever-more-fortified position we were holding. MPIMs and C4 were going out to be used for maximum kill blast radius along the approaches. And the Portugonians were sharpening every piece of wood they had into stakes and spears to choke off any accesses where Thor thought the tower could be rushed.

The road that quickly became the main axis of the enemy thrust came from the west, winding through the town, or city, call it what you will, packed around the only structure we had intel on. The citadel. A giant curved cylindrical structure that looked as ancient as anything I could see. It rose high into the sky, dwarfing other buildings and reminding me of the old nuclear reactor stacks from our age. Black smoke even whispered out of the top, and to me—and maybe this was the psionics talking and the impressions of memories lingering in the psychic ether about me—it looked like a place, or rather *felt* like a place, where sacrifice had once been a thing.

Human sacrifice.

And maybe it still was.

Call it an impression, call it a feeling, call it what you want—that's what it felt like in the voodoo I don't understand that the Ruin had revealed about me. And it was not a good feeling. No. Not at all.

I shuddered and turned to the work that had been given to me. Getting the stakes in place with the Portugonians to cut off any attack along the beach against the tower.

Back on the docks of Portugon, in the tavern the Rangers had chosen for their CP, Vandahar and the Portugonians had put together a tapestry of myths and accounts that allowed us enough of a picture to know what, or rather who, we were dealing with if we ended up trapped in the Atlantean Rift. The updated operation order for the hop had been to bypass the Rift, but in the unlikely event we were taken into its clutches, or ended up here in some other way due to circumstances, then the command team had given their instructions for what they wanted done.

Ice the medusa in the citadel and exfil to the east through some pretty rough terrain to link up with other Rangers in the bare ruins of a haunted dead city along the coast the map marked only as *Ruins*.

The Portugonians said Ruins was an old trading port no one could much remember the people of, that had turned into their, the Portugonian sailors', version of a ghost town. Tradition said that if you went into the port by day, you could find water, but you needed to be out of there by nightfall. Otherwise, bad things started to happen. Ghosts. They had indicated there was a high cliff west of the city and the Rangers had identified that as their emergency rally point if everything went pear-shaped. This location allowed them to use the city and the coast as a navigational marker and not enter the city if there were indeed problems, as indicated by the whispered rumors.

"But you must slay the medusa!" Vandahar had erupted indignantly when Captain Knife Hand had given the order to exfil to the city to the east in the event of ending up in the Rift.

The captain had merely looked up from his presentation and nodded that he understood the wizard and was getting to that point.

Then he continued. "In the event, Rangers, we do end up in the Rift…" He paused to accept, or rather embrace, the fantasy he knew he had to get into for purposes of the order. "In the event we do become engaged in the Rift, apparently the only way out is to terminate *Hoochie Mama*."

A few Rangers snickered. Not unheard of. They loved a good joke or pun. And tagging the medusa of the citadel, Sultria, as *Hoochie Mama* was pretty darn funny. That felt like the sergeant major's hand, pardon the pun, in the planning phase for the hop to the pump.

"At this stage in the events, she becomes a jackpot," continued the captain. "Intel indicates this is necessary to accomplish because… apparently… she won't let us leave."

Sergeant Kang asked what was meant by *won't let us leave.*

The sergeant major spoke up. Of the two senior-most members of the command team, it was the sergeant major who had most embraced the fantasy. Not that he was ever comfortable with it. But he was a hard man, and he was willing to deal with something on its own terms if just so he could kill it better.

Whether that attitude was the Texas in him, the Rangers, Delta, or some combination of all three, I don't know. More than likely all three. But one thing I did know, what we all knew, though I probably knew it better than most…

You don't mess with the smaj.

And when you did… well, you brought whatever happened next on yourself. Like I've indicated, he was the kind of Ranger you didn't want up late at night thinking about you personally. If he did… your days were numbered.

"This medusa is the head of all the medusas, or medusae, whatever you wanna call 'em, boys. She's definitely in league with the opposition, and she's got some real nasty tricks. One of her little tricks, according to Vandahar here, is she made some powerful djinn a personal slave."

"Uh—what's a djinn?" one of the team sergeants asked. "Sergeant Major. Just for clarification."

The sergeant major favored that NCO with a look of tired murder. He'd gotten crankier since his hand got lopped off, but I'm not sure that had anything to do with it.

"A djinn is a genie. A being with magical powers. Like from *Aladdin* and all. This being can do some pretty amazing stuff that will make exfilling the region fairly impossible, and before anyone asks me just what that stuff is, I'll say it's rumors and fairy tales mostly. But obviously the Ruin has taught us to consider those things when developing intel. Those fairy tales have a way of being pretty lethal. So take that for what it's worth. You've all been along on this little camping trip for the full ride. Some of this hippy-dippy stuff'll plain kill you dead, son.

"So. What we've been able to put together is something along the order of… the djinn can cause sandstorms that'll flat-out bury you alive if that's what it wants to do. Walls of fire and firestorms like something out of the big fires that consumed the West Coast back where we came from. They can maybe also suck you into other dimensions, according to PFC Kennedy. But based on myth and traditions, and

Kennedy's little game, taking out the master frees us of the guard dog. So—the key to getting clear is putting the hit on Jackpot Hoochie Mama, which should release the djinn from service, and in turn allow us to continue on mission and effect linkup at the emergency rally. The jackpot's location is most certainly the citadel, but we must assume she's heavily guarded. We get close enough, we'll go runway denial on this citadel and see if we can bring it down on top of her. Otherwise we'll breach and clear, hunt her down, and put two in her skull just for GP."

The sergeant major paused.

"But whatever that thing is… I'm talking about the djinn here… it's dangerous, Rangers. I won't lie to you about that. If, once it's been freed, it wants to go on its merry way… I say live and let live. But if Robin Williams don't wanna play nice, then smoke 'em, Rangers. Use whatever you got, but make sure you put that thing down good and dead. Kill it, and then kill it again."

If that sounds like a lot of intel on what we were facing here in the Rift we never expected to get stranded in… it isn't. We had one emergency rally, one location, one Big Bad Jackpot, and a guard dog that sounded pretty nasty. Rangers often developed intel for months when going after an HVI. This felt a little thin, and it was, and command didn't try to hide it. The Rift was one big no-go zone here in the world of the Ruin.

And yet here we were. *In it*, as Tanner likes to say.

As the orc archers crept through the dusty dilapidated sandpile ruins that clung to the road coming from the west leading off toward that pile of carved rock that was the citadel, the intel we had wasn't enough for what we were now involved in. Not by a long shot. But as one of the Rangers put it, "My wife got catcalled one time by a random guy passing by in a truck on a county road. Two hours later that guy was getting his jaw wired shut for six months. We got this, Talker. We'll adapt, improvise, and overcome once we get a good look at the situation."

Now black smoking arrows whistled out from behind corners or from within collapsed structures that surrounded the sand-washed streets near the tower. The Rangers replied with very accurate single-shot fire. The demonic orcs died just the same as the orcs we'd faced before. Pop up and show their ugly snouts and there was a pretty good chance a Ranger sniper was gonna put a high-caliber bullet right in it.

Sergeant Thor was using the MPIMs on our flanks and leaving the road open as the Rangers all had sectors covering the road within their sights. Once the high-ex was in place, he returned to commanding the defense from the top of the tower. I was with the Portugonians, our stakes made and in position, now sheltering behind the tower with Santiago sewing up a few wounds as best the old sailor could. I got the impression the old man had done this more than a few times and I wondered how many naval battles he'd fought in, limbs he'd amputated, and ships he'd watched go down into the water in flames. They'd moved Daredevil's body and were waiting for something more to do, but the Rangers were too busy fighting now.

It was at that moment the first stragglers from Three Four began to approach the tower from the rear, coming down through the rocks off the cliff. These Rangers had had no contact with the captain and had been some of the first into the water before the ship hit. Many had lost their gear and barely made it onto the cliffs with their lives. They were soaked, black, blue, and cut from the rocks and waves, but they were ready to fight with whatever they could get their hands on.

Daredevil's weapons and ammo were redistributed to two of these Rangers. The others had their battlefield pick-ups—knives, tomahawks, personal hand weapons, what have you. Many quickly took what they could off the dead orcs we'd killed here in the tower and in the roads nearby.

Ten minutes later, with more Rangers showing up, the demon orcs pushed hard. Real hard. They went for broke right at the get-go.

The Rangers accepted their challenge and met them, asking for no quarter. And giving none.

There was gunfire and explosives, yes, but this was the first battle where the Rangers embraced the fantasy, out of necessity, and engaged the enemy with the weapons of the age.

Everyone had been concerned about this moment of Bronze Age warfare without modern advantages. Would we hold the line? Could we master the art of hand weapons combat? Were our numbers not enough if suddenly we had to fight without technological advantages?

The Rangers met the challenge… and stacked skulls.

CHAPTER ELEVEN

THE Battle at Mermaid Tower was one of the most intense fights I've ever been in. Many of the Rangers who survived agree.

Our new watches from the Forge—the old ones had begun to break down due to the effects of the still lingering nano-plague—put the battle at just after three o'clock in the afternoon of the strange day of boiling gray clouds and red skies. Smoke and ash drifted from the citadel and the sound of the waves crashing mixed with the thunder of gunfire and the clash of steel on steel.

It was on, and this was the very definition of *on*.

We'd heard gunfire coming from the canyons and hills to our rear in the east, the desert arroyos the Rangers from Three Four must've gone into after climbing the cliffs upon escaping the wreckage of *Dancer*. We still had no comm with Captain Knife Hand, call sign Warlord, or the smaj. Chief Rapp was the leader of Three Four Heavy and it was unclear whether he was still alive after the crash.

But the SF operator was alive. I knew it. And not because of psionics. Because he was utterly capable. And also, I couldn't imagine a Ruin without his constant professional positivism. He was our holy man. He'd never preached a sermon out loud. I wasn't even sure what the religion was that he was advancing among the Rangers. But everything he did was a sermon in and of itself. He was preaching in all that he did.

Kennedy told me Rapp was a kind of cleric. According to his game. That the things Chief Rapp could do were the things clerics did in his game. Healing and turning the undead. They were powerful holy warriors.

That seemed about right to me. The SF operator was deadly. And kind. He cared for everyone. And even if you didn't believe in souls, like I don't, it made you want to. It made you want what he had.

"They're coming now," Thor called out when it got real still out to the front of our line, looking west down the road heading toward the pile of rock that was the old citadel.

Where the medusa would be when it was time to start looking for her. Did she know her hours, not days, were numbered now? That she should have just let the Rangers pass by and lived?

I remembered her sister. The medusa who loved a blind slave and just wanted to be seen by someone, anyone, for how beautiful she was. Just as all women do. There had been a dangerous moment between us.

Then the Rangers had blown her to shreds with an IED in the opening moments of the hit on Ssruth the Cruel. Jackpot Lizard King. They are hard men, the Rangers. It's best you let them pass by on their business… and live. And perhaps be seen by the one that you love.

I understand that more now than I did then.

That was then, this is now.

For your edification, Mermaid Tower, or the Tower of Mermaids, was called such because once we'd pulled the dead orcs out and burned them with some dry wood and an incendiary thermite grenade, we found the inside done up in emerald mosaics, the walls covered with beautiful frescoes of wide-eyed and very beautiful mermaids coming up to the tower out of the azure sea and rocks. The locals, strange humans with placid faces like that of the Head of Thezuz, threw treasure and gems, and even live victims, into the water.

The beautiful mermaids had vampire teeth.

The Portugonians, who'd done the heavy work of dragging the dead orcs out of the tower, our new command post, muttered darkly, and of course angrily, among themselves as they viewed these entrancing yet horrific scenes they'd preferred to have lived their lives without ever seeing.

There was language on the walls, ancient language, language that was old even at the time of our long-ago modern ten-thousand-years past. And yet also impossibly future. Warped, changed. An artifact of the Ruin. And perhaps of the ruin within which we stood. A language from both our future and our past, but from neither present.

The letters were mostly Greek but the words were closer to Latin. And "closer" is generous. Even for me… it was nuts. Hard to understand and really more of a cypher than a language. But I do those games just to keep myself sharp for the learning of new languages. I hear Hell's got one…

The best I could get off the walls was…

Feast of the Beauties.

The rest was nonsense and madness.

I was tasked with getting the Portugonians to drag and pile the bodies of the dead orcs because I could communicate with them. I knew enough about leadership by now, having observed both good and bad here in the military, to knew I needed to start doing it first. So I grabbed the ugliest orc, uglier than I thought possible. Sergeant Thor had shot this one in the guts and the smell was awful and the stringy corpse was a mess from the gunshot wound. I grabbed the toad-faced creature and dragged him toward the exit from the Tower of Mermaids while the Portugonians grumbled darkly among themselves.

Santago caught on and barked at his fellow sailors, and they bent to the work of clearing the tower of the enemy dead.

I was with them, watching the corpses begin to burn, when the big attack began.

The day had gotten hotter and I was sweating, standing there next to the ocean and watching the ugly orc corpses blacken and bubble in the fire.

Be all you can be, amirite?

Thor had tossed the incendiary, and he stood there with us watching his victims cook. I was guessing this was some sort of meditation in keeping with his Pagan religion for the purposes of an operator beard.

Then Thor commented about how ugly they were and dispelled the illusion by remarking, "These dudes couldn't score if they had a Lambo in Vegas and a suitcase full of diamonds, Talker. They're like Bill Gates ugly. Except they probably got more game."

Then the push came on our left flank first and Thor was off, all business and big strides as the killing work started. The demon orcs were coming from the portions of the ruins that clustered there in a section between the cliffs and the road.

Sergeant Herrera engaged and didn't stop, shooting the orcs as fast as he could reload from position two. I got sucked along in Thor's wake. He took the stairs inside the tower three at a time in full battle rattle and when I got up to the top, one of the other snipers was spotting targets and calling them out to the Rangers in the fighting positions below, but not firing yet.

"Two clusters of these bastards comin' at us, Sar'nt Thor," said the sniper from behind the salt-crusted battlements at the top of the small tower. "These got pickups of the usual kind and they're moving in behind these buildings. My guess is they make for that alley and they'll rush from there once the other bunch gets in place."

The other bunch even I could see. It was a large group of demon orcs wielding spears and small axes, thin on armor, heavy on the black grease and blood-red war paint. Easily two to three hundred moving in ragged bands. Shaman among them swinging censers of strange necrotic purple smoke that hazed out over their troops and smelled strangely narcotic as it wafted along the drafts and breezes toward us. They were coming up the road and hugging wall and building to move close to get ready to charge en masse.

Thor ordered fire held until they got within our intersecting fire nets. Then we could be sure of getting a few with each shot.

"We got the mines set up over there. If we don't get too many of 'em, the mines should rock that bunch hard and stop 'em cold."

Because radio communication was still nothing but a yawning static abyss filled with a barely audible high-pitched scream that made your blood run cold, Sergeant Thor leaned over the battlement and shouted to the Rangers he'd placed in their sectors below the tower. Apprising them of the situation and letting them know what signals were coming next. As many shooters as we had, we now had about as many Rangers using pickups. Those that had lost their weapons in the sea and along the rocks. But they were ready to roll with what they could find. They were paired with the shooters and were to handle perimeter security.

Two groups watched each flank of the defense. Three groups watched the main road, left, right, and center where we expected the main push. Two snipers were assigned to each flank with Thor picking up the center.

"We could use a two-forty right about now, Sar'nt," mentioned the sniper on the tower watching the left. "That'd clean things up real nice right about now."

"Ain't got one. Don't need one," replied Sergeant Thor succinctly.

Normally gregarious or at least friendly compared to most of the sullen and brooding Rangers, when the fight was on Thor was pure predator. I'd been in enough fights with him to follow what he was interested in and wait for the order to get done what he wanted done. My observations and anything I could contribute to planning weren't needed. Unless they were about languages... then I'm your man. But so far none of the demon orcs had wanted to converse.

Thor raised *Mjölnir* and muttered, "Big stud with all the danglies in the center..." He was calling his shot. Then he fired and blew the head clean off a massive war leader orc with a giant topknot and four arms. The head went red mist and the orcs all around this beast of an orc suddenly surged forward, running, and I kid you not, like Olympic-level track runners as they streaked toward the Ranger kill zones.

The other sniper swore at the sudden burst of speed from an entire battalion-sized mass of enemy combatants.

Again, in the world we'd come from, this did not happen. Shoot at hajis and they scramble for cover. In the Ruin, they come at you with knives out.

The orcs on the road took outgoing fire. Some dropped, others just kept running even though they'd been hit. That was clear from the blood spray in the last of the rays of the falling sunlight in the west, shafts of light coming through the clouds and bisected by the gloom and doom of the rising citadel. I popped over the battlement and engaged the road element. It was hard to tell if you were hitting, but some of them were going down. Thirty seconds later they hit our front line and the three positions out front went point-blank CQB and didn't give ground. The Rangers with pickups waded into the fray and started hacking at the screaming demon orcs like relentless jackhammers who were never gonna get tired of smashing skulls.

The shooters were picking up targets, shooting down orcs as they came screaming through the sand, hurling axes and waving spears. Some orcs took multiple shots to the torso, others caught it in the head and went down, brain matter catching the silver light coming through the clouds. Dark blood splashing out in the blue shadows beneath the pile of the citadel.

At the same moment a volley of black smoking arrows arched up into the air out from some distant place in the city and began to land all over our tower. Massed volley indirect fire. I couldn't tell if anyone was hit. But two volleys exploded with small acrid explosions in the air and we were choked with dark black sulfuric smoke drifting across our front.

I shot a shaman twice. He was waving one of those censers of purple necrotic smoke over his troops as they advanced, and I didn't like it. I hit him in the chest and the hip and he went down, black coals spilling out onto the sand. Tendrils of purple smoke erupting madly in every direction like snakes escaping a jar. Two orcs came to his rescue, and I kept shooting them until all three were dead and staring at the sky or twisted into the sand.

"Talker, head to position two. They need support," said Thor matter-of-factly as he selected another target and fired. The spotter was indicating a third group now forming and coming at us from left of center of the road. Moving through what looked like some old temple in which only the once-fantastic salt-worn columns were still standing. Like the ruins of Greek palaces consumed by the sun and sea I had once seen during lazier, better times, times when if you'd asked me whether I could even envision the moment I was currently in, I would have told you no. And that you were crazy for even suggesting such.

I pushed off the battlement, hit the stairs, and pushed thoughts away that I was the only QRF the Rangers had at this moment here in this battle for this nothing tower we were getting hit hard at and tasked with holding so the Rangers could consolidate and get their kill on the medusa.

For a brief moment I felt her gaze from the tower, though I couldn't see her. And that, for once, *was* the psionics talking. I could see her standing at some hidden window. A cloak wrapped about her slender yet shapely form, vipers undulating in her hair. Green eyes watching the Rangers fight. Knowing in the pit of her stomach we were coming for her.

The vision was gone as fast as it had come, and I only had the brief impression of the stark moment as I exited the jade interior dark of the Tower of Mermaids and saw the wind and waves out to sea.

The Portugonians were huddled near the shore behind the tower in the cover where we'd placed Daredevil's body and staying down behind the boat we'd come ashore in. They had their fingers plugged in their ears. I spotted Santago and shouted in Spanish, asking what that was all about.

Which was useless as I had no time to find out. I was the QRF for position two and they were getting hit hard. My NCO had ordered me to relieve, and I would or die trying.

I raced around the tower along the frescoed tiles of ancient scenes of sacrifice and made it down off the sea wall just in time to throw myself to the ground where some old stones had erupted through the dead sea grass here. Another volley of arrows came whistling in overhead and exploded against the tower, drowning it in a sudden explosion of black smoke that washed out and away from its surface. I coughed as I high-crawled forward. More arrows were being shot in direct-fire fashion from forward of where fighting position two was. The one that watched the right side of the road.

I saw Sergeant Herrera shoot down two orcs with his MK12 sniper rifle firing five-five-six, take a step back, work in a new mag, and then reach down to drag a Ranger back a few feet to cover who had two arrows sticking out of him. Another Ranger with a sword in one hand and in the other the standard Ranger tomahawk the true believers like to keep handy, was holding the position while the NCO pulled the wounded man out of danger.

I knew that guy. The guy with the sword and toma-hawk. His name was Hochner. One of the mortar guys who'd been on Three Four Heavy. Solid Ranger who'd been a team leader in the weapons teams before going over to mortars. He wasn't swole like a lot of mortar guys who carried the eighty-one. But he was tall and ripped. Or jacked. Whichever lingo you prefer to convey the guy was like a human python. That wasn't due to picking up heavy stuff at the gym and using the world-class pro-level athlete training Rangers got in their private gyms. No. Hochner was an MMA fighter. I'm pretty sure he could have been pro but he was too busy doing Ranger stuff, so his thirty days' leave was usually spent living in the world of high-stakes private MMA. When he wasn't on a pump, he trained Brazilian jiu-jitsu and competed whenever and wherever he could. He'd been warned by command, or so I'd been told, that if he ever broke anything and ended up on medical profile then he was out of the Rangers.

Period. Full stop.

Word was he'd actually broken stuff, like his foot, and still Rangered without ever telling anyone. I found that impossible to believe. I'd been on brutal road marches upwards of twelve miles in Basic. I thought that was brutal back then. It wasn't. But still, though it wasn't hard to road march, with a full load on a broken foot it would have seemed to me impossible.

Also, twelve miles wasn't anything. We regularly did twenty miles plus since we'd arrived in the Ruin. With everything including the full basic combat load, that was a lot to put on a broken foot.

But as Sergeant Chris likes to say, "Rangers can do anything."

So, according to legend, the Ranger just taped his foot, kept his boot tight, and didn't ever let any look of pain cross his face. He'd had fingers and nose broken too. But fingers could be hidden inside assault gloves and noses didn't count as far as regiment was concerned.

The first orc to try to overrun the position, once I made it up there, got sliced right in the throat by Hochner's sword. I shouted at Sergeant Herrera over the gunfire and demonic ululating of the orcs that I was there to help. The thing gagged as the nondescript battle pickup Hochner was using, probably one of the orc weapons from the tower, left a clean bloody gash that prevented it from ever breathing again. Then, almost dancing like he'd done this a thousand times before, Sergeant Hochner followed that up with a swift tomahawk blow and just split the thing's skull.

It gurgled and crumpled. It was dead in ways that five-five-six could never make it dead.

The next orc came in immediately and Hochner just reversed the downstroke on the tomahawk, savagely swiping up and to the right, and the tomahawk took off the side of that wretch's face. That didn't stop it from trying to jab the Ranger with a short spear, but Hochner's sword did. The pickup blade followed the axe and went straight through the screaming orc's chin and right into its brain pan.

Lights out.

It twitched horribly and Hochner shook it off the blade and slammed another strike from his axe into a newcomer who'd decided to die just as badly.

Like I said, all of this was like a dance routine. Seriously. Apparently Hochner had trained in other arts besides the grappling art of Brazilian jiu-jitsu. But his lethal passion made everything looked like choreographed prac-

tice as he slaughtered the mindlessly screaming orcs trying to push the Rangers off the position. His movements
were effortless, and as the orcs came in screaming raggedly, chanting dark things that disturbed my mind because
I just barely understood them, their words and thoughts
and eyes crazed and exhausted and dangerous, the Ranger
gracefully hacked their throats open, smashed their skulls,
and slashed up their vital organs. No rage or furious strikes.
It was as though he was merely pushing the weapons where
they needed to be to cause the worst possible damage and
the maximum amount of gore and utter horror. They were
fighting for their lives while Hochner was just running his
game, cutting them to shreds as they died badly. Very badly.

His gear was missing. No ruck. No carrier. No primary. He might have had a secondary. I can't remember. But
none of that mattered. He was some lost golden age of tele-
vision-commercial miracle-age cutting machine product
like the Ginsu knife or the Chopperizer that sliced, diced,
and whirled effortlessly. Too bad you were the tomato, the
potato, or the can of beer he was cutting through.

Chopping up orcs as easy as you please, ma'am. Your
life will vastly improve with the Hochnerizer. But wait,
there's more…

Herrera started firing at the next incoming wave, brass
shells flying away as he shouted at me to check on Skerrit.
Skerrit was the Ranger hit by arrow fire. He was choking
and gagging and I went to look for what I was sure would
be an entrance and/or sucking chest wound, trying to remember if I taped the HyFin chest seal on the sides and
top, or the sides and bottom, and to make sure to check for
an exit wound because it was no good if only one wound
was sealed in a sucking chest wound situation. The lungs

needed a good seal. Remember that, I told myself as I went looking for these wounds, running my hands inside his plate carrier after I pulled the arrows free. I was pretty sure I wasn't supposed to do that but the acrid black smoke from them was making it impossible for him to breathe. The shadowy tendrils were going right for his mouth and nose. And yeah, that was strange.

Except Skerrit had no wounds.

His plate carrier felt busted for sure. But it had held. He was gasping, trying to catch his breath. The arrow strikes had hit him so hard they'd broken the ESAPI plate.

Which was pretty incredible when you thought about it. Those things are built to stand up to high-caliber ammunition.

But the wind had gotten severely knocked out of him and now the smoking black arrows were gagging him. So like I said, I snapped them off and then poured water over them to extinguish the black snakes of smoke going for his mouth even as he lay in the sand.

Yes, I do keep my Camelbak filled with water. And also, *yes,* I have thought about filling it with coffee. Who hasn't?

Don't judge me.

I was still pretty stunned about arrows that could be fired like missiles so hard they'd break body armor. Then I got a glimpse of who had probably fired those arrows.

This dude was jacked, swole, ripped, and then some. Plus, he was huge.

The demon orc that came out of the miasma of black smoke was a giant if there ever was one. He had four arms, a topknot erupting from his shaved head, and grinning fangs. His dusty skin was streaked in black greasepaint snakes and red dried blood that had been smeared into patterns and designs that bothered the mind. His teeth that weren't fangs were more like the pointy shark teeth dangling around his neck. He wore high, heavy boots and a kilt made of netting and shells. Golden earrings were stuck in his nose—huge loops knotted like twisting, two-headed snakes. In his two lower arms, left and right, he kept savage curving daggers that gleamed in the silver light of the dying afternoon heat. They were made of what looked to be teeth bigger than those of any shark or monster I'd ever seen.

Dinosaur teeth?

Are there dinosaurs here? some background part of my mind asked.

I moved Skerrit upright and tried to clear some of the black smoke away to get him fresh air. That was my job despite Titanor the Swole Four-Armed Orc coming to kill us all despite having clearly already been shot twice and not being bothered by it. Skerrit coughed and spat out a big glob of dip as I got him upright. Swearing as he did so while his eyes watered like… a waterfall.

Look at me with my metaphors. I'm a linguist who just pretends to be a writer. But be grateful! If it wasn't for me, no one else in the detachment would be keeping this account. Writing all this horror and fantasy down of what we did here and who did what. The Rangers would just use the pens and paper to draw comics of superheroes, mainly superwomen with unusually large badonkadonks and chests. A few of them are really good. Like pro comic book good.

I'm serious. They would. They couldn't care less who knows the heroic stuff they've done. That's not their jam. They just dig doing it.

I watched as the huge and strange orc advanced toward Hochner, who weaved his blades out, almost hypnotically, ready to meet this jacked orc champion. Herrera was shooting down the smaller, screaming orcs pushing from the right, coming along the beach below the road. Fighting their way through the stakes and firing arrows from the water line.

I watched one, jabbering, get hit in the top of the skull and then fall over as his brains were carried away by the late afternoon breeze coming along the coast. The surf covered his body a moment later, and then withdrew as he stared sightlessly up at the clouds.

Meanwhile...

In the massive, advancing orc's two upper arms, right and left, was the biggest bow I'd ever seen. It was more like some ancient ballista than anything a single person ought to be able to fire. But the orc fitted a huge spear of an arrow and took aim at Hochner in a fluid, well-practiced motion. The movement, despite the thing's size and... swoleness... was surprisingly smooth and must be commented on here. For the record. Then the beast of an archer drew back, every muscle flexing, and just before he fired, Hochner under-hand-flicked his tomahawk in a sudden unexpected movement at the giant orc and struck the bow, causing the orc to fire wildly on release of the spear-arrow. Hochner then raced forward, boots flinging sand as he pounded toward his opponent in an explosion of speed. He batted away one dagger already flying from one of the orc's massive lower fists to intercept. Using his tomahawk to do so. Then his sword went for the other dagger, swinging wildly while the huge orc reached for another massive spear-arrow from the quiver on its back. Hochner leapt and was suddenly flying forward through the air and driving both boots into the brute's chest, defying any sort of physics I could understand.

The massive orc didn't go down, but Hochner turned into an eel in a moment as he twisted in the air, using the orc to—

As I write that, I am reminded this is the Ruin and putting down that someone turned into an eel might give the wrong impression of what actually just happened. No. Hochner didn't turn into a man-eel. A were-eel, I guess it would be called if there were such a thing. And note, I really hope there isn't. I've just seen my first giant eels and I could live without that scene for the rest of my life. I'd like to go into the ocean someday, just for fun, even if it is the Ruin. But now there are giant eels in there. So.

Anyway, I mean to say only that Hochner *moved like* an eel, using the momentum of the kick to twist and climb and loop about the huge orc all at once. He drove the pick-up sword into the thing's collarbone and then used that as a climbing spike in the same moment. Half a second was all it took. Still holding both weapons in both assault-gloved hands, Hochner had the behemoth orc in a chokehold one unbelievable second later. Wrapped around the giant monster like he was some killer monkey-python that would never let go of his victim this side of the waking dream we call this life. One leg flicked down an instant later and destabilized the left massive tree trunk leg of the orc, crashing him to the white dust and sand. Hochner cuddled close to the orc and choked it out almost immediately. Then he drove the spike of the tomahawk's haft into the thing's brain. It was dead, no questions asked.

I had envisioned a completely different outcome just five seconds earlier. The orc champion looked unbeatable.

Seriously. I mean, man, Hochner just rocked that thing's juice box like he was only half trying.

Don't mess with the Hochnerizer.

One of the demon orcs tried to rescue its war leader, but I shot it with my primary, putting three of the five I fired in rapid aggression into its upper torso. It tried to run off, the green skin beneath its normally pale dusty color suddenly turning gray and white from the impacts of my gunfire along its back.

It took three steps, then fell over and died.

Not quite as impressive as what Hochner did. Okay, not remotely as impressive. Not even in the same universe.

But a kill's a kill.

CHAPTER TWELVE

I heard Sergeant Thor bellowing through the black smoke, "Talker, on me!"

I checked in with Sergeant Herrera that Skerrit was back in the fight. Position two now had a crossfire on the new enemy advance and their ammunition was holding with Skerrit operational. Hochner was getting breathers, but he was still continuing to effortlessly cut down any demon orc that managed to get close enough to play.

I had no idea what was going on with any of the other fighting positions at that moment, but a wind was starting to come from offshore and push the black smoke back into the faces of the attacking orcs, and I counted that as a win for us.

The unseen orcs firing indirectly from farther out and behind cover replied with more arrow fire, supporting screaming suicide assaults on all positions as smaller, more wiry demon orcs came in savagely frothing at the mouth and swinging wicked cleavers for the Rangers before they got riddled with outgoing lead or hacked to pieces by Rangers.

At the same moment, the MPIMs must have detonated over on the left. A deafening explosion rocked the soundscape and made the ground shake near the tower. Bits of stone crumbled and fell onto the old mosaics and tiles.

History surrendering to violence. Letting go of stories we would never know, and that weren't important anymore.

The only thing that mattered here in the battle between the demon orcs and the Rangers… was who was meaner.

To the orcs' credit they understood that, and didn't fade or give ground. Or even relent from assaults that left every one of the last wave dead.

But neither did the Rangers.

Relent, that is.

More of the survivors of Three Four Heavy joined the fight and went into action immediately. Lobbing grenades that had stayed on their carriers as they cast off from the wreckage of the galley, their frags sailing out into the identified staging position of the demon orcs making ready to push and push again.

I made the tower entrance and found Sergeant Thor firing from there now. The targeted arrow fire had been too much for the top of the tower. I came over the sea wall and low-crouched to the entrance, slipping past the massive sniper and into the emerald gloom of the Tower of Mermaids.

He didn't wait long to tell me what he needed. He faded into the room, ejected a huge magazine from the anti-materiel rifle, and cocked his head, listening for a moment to something I was immediately aware of.

"Talker… you hearing something?"

"Uh… hearing a lot of things, Sar'nt. Gunfire. Orcs shrieking that madness they're doing like they're junkies on super meth. I'd like them to stop that. Seriously. Uh… explosion about a minute ago which I assume was the mines on the left flank. What else?"

"Negative, Private Talker. Getting something else and it's…"

He reached down and pulled a new magazine on *Mjölnir*. He pulled off his EarPro and listened as he counted his remaining mags.

We were all running low now.

That's not good.

"It's like…" began Thor and then stopped to listen again for a moment. "I don't know… but ever go to like a rave or Burning Man, and it's late, and they start playing that really trippy, hypnotic… trance stuff…?"

He went away for a moment. Just like that. Like he was trying to hear it, whatever it was, and then he got it… and then it wouldn't let go of his mind.

He dropped the big rifle. *Mjölnir*. Just dropped it right there and turned toward the sea wall with a strange, almost amused smile on his face.

"Where you goin', Sar'nt Thor?" I asked as he began to walk out the door of the Tower of Mermaids and into the crossfire hurricane of arrow fire and outgoing Ranger lead.

He didn't answer. Arrows whistled past him as he strolled out onto the sea wall, crossing the mosaicked frescoes of mermaids feasting on strange men and accepting treasure.

I followed and watched as Thor hopped down off the sea wall, his heavy bulk landing lightly in the soft wet sand, just feet from the water.

Then he started walking toward the water.

What. The. Hell.

There was another Ranger out there ahead of him. One of the survivors from Three Four Heavy who'd just come in. He was ahead of Thor on the sand and heading for the water, the waves rolling gently despite the frenetic battle forward of our position and at times seemingly all around us as the orcs were managing to gain new positions to shoot more arrows from.

Orcs have, like, unlimited arrows. Come on, guys, run out already. Then again, this was their sandbox and they probably had supply chains. Our nearest resupply was out there, anchored next to a giant head sticking up out of the waves and fighting off orcish Vikings. So of course they had unlimited—

Then I heard it.

It was like… it was *like* a flute. But it wasn't. Like some kind of mournful alternative rock song I'd heard once and long ago. And I was sure of that. Sure I had heard it long ago.

One of Sidra's songs on her playlists.

I could remember the name, but I couldn't catch the exact, or right, words. I could hear them in my mind though, translated and all, but over the din of battle I could catch that they were in another language altogether.

That language of Greek and Latin but not really either. The Madness Cypher, my mind started to call it.

Or was that the psionics *helping* with its useless games of *Figure this one out, Talker*?

Like I needed that right now.

This is what that sounded like IRL though. Really not a language… more of a code.

But in my mind, it was in English… and I could understand it. Like some cover band doing the original, but downbeat and in a minor key twenty years after the song had been an up-tempo and popular dance hit.

Maybe that was the version Sidra had played for us during those wild months when life and death were her playthings, as was everything else, including me.

But hey... that's another story for some other time when no one ten thousand years from now cares in the slightest.

They... were chanting it. The song I could now hear. In Madness Cypher that I could understand. And now that I was hearing it... I felt... caught.

I was off the sea wall, my slung carbine dangling as I walked toward the water and the ocean. Helpless to do anything else.

Not even if I wanted to. The song was a road and there was something I really needed to see. And if I followed the song then I got to see...

It's two songs, I suddenly realized in my mind, another part of it where sometimes I felt I could tell you the psionics hid out. But I was never really sure about that. It was just a guess and not a very good one at that. Still, my mind told me that one song was about driving your car into the ocean... *on a wave of mutilation.*

And the other... the other was about lips. *Lips like honey.*

Both trancey and hypnotic. Weaving in and about my mind the way Hochner had woven himself about the giant orc champion like an eel, a python, a murder monkey. We were being changed, and I could tell what I was hearing was a spell of some sort. But with words from our past. Spoken in Madness Cypher.

A car, my spell-addled mind thought drunkenly. Laughing to myself like I was having a regular good old time, stoned on pharmaceutical-grade heroin.

There are *no cars anymore*, I told other me from across the chasm of fuzzy ensorcellment. Shouted across the canyon and heard mad laughter in return.

But in the song… in the song from long ago I was hearing now as I entered the water… there *were* cars. *Well that's something*, I can remember thinking. I'd thought there'd never be cars again.

My usually coffee-turbocharged mind, figuring all the angles and trying to be infinitely upgraded and happy, was gone right now.

I was fuzzy and quiet. Susceptible. I knew that. I was seduced.

The opposite of me IRL. And it wasn't a bad thing. I had no fear at that moment, but, and this is the strange part, I knew I should. I knew I should be afraid. But…

Nah… not right now. I'm walking into the water never mind the firefight for all the marbles where the Rangers are holding a thin red line that doesn't look like it'll take much more.

I saw the first one in the water. She was absolutely beautiful. Dark hair. Full… full… inviting lips. She was naked but her curly hair with shells in it barely covered what she had. I've seen people in commercials that made millions of dollars a year because of their beauty who looked like lifeless hags compared to the girl in the water, clinging to the rock, smiling at me as her lips moved. Singing me that song about cars in the ocean, waves of mutilation, and lips like honey.

She looked *sooooooooo* happy. Like she was determined to be happy no matter what. I… liked that. A lot.

And there was a reminder in that. Something about Autumn that barely got through the intoxicating chant of the song from long ago I was hearing there in the water and the waves. The gunfire was a million years away. Not miles. Years. That's how you felt. But then the chanting about *lips like honey*, and the chorus coming from the others in the water, the other beauties, because there were more of them, about waves of mutilation, vanished the elf girl I'd known and all the thoughts I'd ever had of… *us*. My boots were wet and that was not a bad thing.

There was something in those waves of mutilation that would make all this not matter anymore. Letting this life go. Letting…

Going with her now. The beautiful girl with dark curly hair in the water clinging to the rock.

On a wave of mutilation.

I could do… that. I wanna… do that.

It wasn't Santago the old Navarrean sailor who ran into the waves who saved me. Screaming at us. Thor, the other Ranger. Me. Screaming at me from across the universe where all the pain I was leaving behind was.

"Talk-ir!" Santago shouted. "Don't listen to their witch songs!" He screamed hoarsely, beating at me with his bony old fists. Screaming in Navarrean.

Navarrean is Spanish, my cotton-candy mind thought from the other side of time and all its meaninglessness. Then let the trivia of that go like it was a nice big red balloon on an autumn day when it's still sunny and warm in the afternoon when the winds pick up.

And summer's gone.

Gone forever, Talker.

It wasn't the bravery of the old Navarrean sailor who ran into the waves to save us. Like we were his sailors. His sons. Like we were… his.

It wasn't that… that saved me.

It was the song the old fado singer sang in the Purple Abyss. That too was an old song. An old song from long ago. Some things had survived the Ruin of the pandemic that was the nano-plague.

Some things, many things, did not.

The radio. The telephone. Even Gibraltar. Those were things that might fade away, according to a song my mom would sing when she thought about my dad.

Which was *seldom* and *never* if you asked her.

But our love will never fade away.

That was the song the fado singer in the Purple Abyss, the song the old whore sang… that saved me as Santiago tried to drag me out of the waves. The dark-haired beauty in the water smiling at me. She opened her arms and… promised me it would all just go away…

That was then. This is now.

That was the song I remembered, from the bar in Portugon I never should have gone into ever again. The bar where I'd done killing. The bar where the stories were not mine.

For *revenge*. Trying to tell myself it was for *love*.

Santiago had tried to save me then, and now.

Pulled me from there, that bar, my hands covered in blood.

But had he? Had he saved me even then?

That was then, this is now.

I was crying because it reminded me of us. Of who we were when we were going to the Cities of Men in just an old boat I didn't even know how to sail.

You were in the bow.

And that was everything.

A dream. A prophecy. Call it what you want. It was the realest moment of my life. And it didn't even exist. It had just promised to.

Does the universe tell lies?

There is magic in the universe. Yes. More magic than what the Ruin thinks magic is.

I fell toward the dark beauty in the water, the waves around my stomach, taking one more step in which I knew I would stumble and she would…

One more step and that would be the last.

That was then, this is now, the old whore had sung and broke a heart I was trying desperately to save and couldn't. And couldn't.

My own. But I thought it was someone else's. I thought I was trying to save someone else, when it was me that needed saving. But isn't that how it is sometimes.

I'll explain if I live.

I just need to tell it as best I can when the time to tell it comes. And this is me, doing my best.

CHAPTER THIRTEEN

THAT was then…

I saw it all in real-time as the song, the whore's song in the Purple Abyss, cut through the haze and stupor of the sirens' song from the waters of the cove. They were beauties out there in the water. Any soldier's fantasy of a fantasy. Voluptuous redheads with eyes the color of the sea in turmoil, a dazzling blond who half stood on the surface, daring you to look at her. The dark beauty who'd first caught my eye. All of them in the water half submerged, drifting in the open sea just beyond the cove, or clinging to the foam-washed rocks as the battle raged all around us on the land that lay between the cliffs and the great pile of ancient rock that was the Atlantean citadel. I saw Thor and the other Ranger wading out to meet them as though on autopilot. The other Ranger was Specialist Commons from one of the assaulter platoons aboard Three Four Heavy.

They weren't deadly hags hiding some true form within their song-spell. They were indeed beautiful to the point of being epic and beyond anything the mortal could achieve. Perhaps that was half the charm. But they were deadly.

Very, very deadly in fact.

It was the look in their hungry eyes. Gleaming. Ravenous. A sly small smile knowing the trick they were pulling was working. The feminine knowledge of true power, whether they were a monster, a mermaid, or human, it didn't matter. They were among the most powerful creatures a man could do battle with. Better men than myself, or even Thor, and been bested if the game was on their terms. And they worked hard to make sure it was. Always. Luring as they'd always lured.

Two suddenly lunged up out of the water around Specialist Commons as I became aware. Maybe they sensed the spell was broken. Perhaps my psionics was broadcasting my immediate fear… but I don't think so.

If anything was broadcasting… it was anger.

This pissed me off. For reasons I couldn't quite put my finger on. But it was a long time coming. A long time building within me.

The two that lunged up out of the water and grabbed Commons in an instant, glistening water cascading off their perfect bodies, practically shrieked with delight as they yanked the Ranger down under the surface of the gentle swell within the cove.

I pulled my slung carbine up to the shooting position, unable to tag the dark beauty who'd had such a mind hold on me. She'd ducked and streaked through the water, disappearing just under the surface and going straight for Sergeant Thor.

Instead I landed my red dot on a red-haired stunner who'd crawled up onto a flat rock, her mermaid's tail fully out of the water and splashing. I shot her twice. The look on her face was pure horror. Then she turned, despite the two bullet holes suddenly sending blood into the water, and screeched, baring her vampire fangs as she slid from the rock helplessly, her hands reaching for me as she slipped back into the depths, mortally wounded.

Sergeant Thor just stood there, a giant in the water as the surf came in. In a daze or a trance. Not in the game was the point. The dark beauty coming for him streaked like one of those sharks we'd been so worried about. The quizzical half-stoned daze in his eyes was far away and *otherwhere*.

I was wading forward when Commons surged out of the water screaming frantically. He was awake now, that was for sure, both mermaids still hanging on to him, fighting to pull the Ranger under once more. But one had Commons's knife firmly planted in her chest now. Her mouth was open, and she was screaming at the sky while still trying to drown him. Note: that's a nightmare right there you won't soon forget. Trust me on that one. Vampire mermaid trying to drown your buddy with a bloody knife planted in her. Sign me up for less. The other, another dark beauty, pulled Commons close to her sensuous body, almost lovingly, and then sank her gleaming white small fangs right into his throat.

He tried to punch her right in the face, but the pain of being bitten in the neck, probably the jugular, was a lot to deal with in all fairness. Speaking in his defense.

Then I did something I would have never done under any other circumstances. Truth is I was never a shooter at the level I'd seen the Rangers and the SF operator shoot at. All of them were excellent. Some of them were crazy good in areas of speed and accuracy. I'd qual'd expert every time at the range, but that really doesn't mean anything when you're talking SF levels of shooting.

Still, I could hit what I needed to hit in most situations given enough time and ammunition. And had been doing that fairly regularly since arriving in the Ruin.

Still, in hindsight, I don't think I would have ever normally done what I did in that blink of an unthinking moment, waist-deep and advancing toward the transfixed Sergeant Thor in hopes of doing something to prevent him from becoming Vampire Mermaid food. Anything. It's just I wasn't sure, at that particular moment, exactly what I was going to do about Thor's dark-haired siren. No shot. She was too close already and Thor was a big target. My only hope was maybe I could do something if I got close enough.

But for the moment, the other Ranger needed help because his situation was critical and all.

The mermaid Commons tried to punch in the face, the one biting his neck, was a better shot, but not great. At least I had a sight picture as the barrel red dot landed on her throat and danced a little side to side, weaving as I tried to control my breathing despite the killer mermaids and bloody knifings going on all around me.

I can't even tell you the thought to pull the trigger was a conscious one in that instant. Because before I knew it, a single shot from my rifle smashed her face right open. Bullet climb and range turned the throat shot into a face punch at twenty-four feet per second and ruined all that loveliness in detail.

She just let go, then slithered down under the water dead as Commons thrashed free of the other.

The freaked-out Ranger ran toward me, shrieking.

I'm shouting at him as he passes me in the water that he's bleeding and to get his hand on his neck. But I think in that insane moment all I managed to do was scream at the freaking out Ranger, "*Put pressure on it!*"

He probably had no idea how bad the wound on his throat was. If it was the jugular, without Chief Rapp I was pretty sure he was gonna die of arterial blood loss in about two minutes.

Spoiler… it wasn't. And one of the medics from Three Four who'd held on to his bag during the crash came pounding into the water to assist the shrieking Commons who'd just been bitten by a mermaid.

I don't think less of Commons for shrieking insanely. He'd almost just been drowned and bitten badly by two beautiful monsters, probably only figuring that out once he began to be unable to breathe under the water and came out of the trance held down in a nightmare and choking. You do better in that situation, and we can talk. If it'd been me I probably never would've slept again. But then again maybe that would just be an excuse for me to see how much coffee I could consume just cause and not really having anything to do with ever wanting to sleep again. Junkie thinking right there, folks. Warts and all. That was probably when the dream trance of their spell broke and the mindless fear exploded inside Commons.

I get that.

My guess was they liked the fear. The mermaids, that is. Made the meal taste better maybe. Who knows? Monsters. They ain't human. Except the more I understand the Ruin, maybe they once were. Their ancestors. Maybe they were once us on that long-ago day when the nano-plague started turning people into nightmares.

And the ten thousand years since had forged them into something not human anymore. I don't know. The Ruin is a big mystery.

But despite the shrieking freak-out, Commons had straight-up Rangered. He'd stabbed one and tried to punch the other within seconds of waking up. He didn't go quietly to his drowning death, and in no way did I save Commons's life. His actions got him out of there, and he was a killer about getting it done.

He did lose his knife though, and the other Rangers did, during down times, reenact Commons's screams and fall over helpless with laughter.

"Help!" they'd whisper-shriek comically. "Stripper mermaid got me, guys!"

Or, in an imitation of Commons's voice they'd say matter-of-factly, "I got bit, man!"

For some reason they thought that was the funniest thing ever said. But I think they were just glad he was alive. It was pretty freaky, and sometimes the only way you can deal with stuff is just to laugh at it. What else are you gonna do, roll up and go fetal?

Not Rangers. That's not an option. So you make it into the worst joke ever and you hammer it until it has no power over you anymore.

Bitten by a vampire hottie while being drowned? Been there. Done that. Got the bite marks, man.

Sua sponte'd that wench. Straight up.

Commons is a stud. Fact. I give him mad props for surviving and continuing on mission.

It was pretty funny that he screamed though.

"I got bit, man!"

But that was all later. I couldn't shoot the mermaid now coming out of the water, the dark-haired beauty, climbing the tall Sergeant Thor to go for a bite. I surged forward through the waist-deep water, pushing myself forward, getting deeper, no easy task in chest rig and plate carrier, fatigues waterlogged and weighed down by all my gear. Then I reached out, grabbed her hair, and pulled hard, yanking her away, twisting my assault glove and making a larger knot as she was pulled off the giant Ranger sniper.

She shrieked and gave me a glimpse inside her mind as my psionics kicked in in a way I'd never experienced. Hard and shocking like suddenly falling into cold, deep, dark water in some abandoned quarry way out in the forest where no one goes anymore. Suddenly my mind was flying down what I could only call... *a space-time tunnel?* I have no idea what that means, but right there in the water as she screamed in anger and I used her hair to jerk her from Thor's massive frame, that's what it felt like. Flying down that tunnel at the end of *2001*, the movie.

Which I didn't understand. The movie. Or the tunnel.

But that's neither here nor there. I just work here. Let someone who knows all the secrets explain it in the lecture at the end of the film. I just write down what I saw.

Don't expect much. I'm not that good at writing. But I am probably the greatest modern writer in the Ruin. So far. *Hey-yo!*

Her name was Allandria. That's the psionics peeling away the impressions and memories released by her sudden terror. She was a priestess of the Sacred Grotto. No idea what that was at first, but then as soon as I thought about it... tumblers unlocked in her mind, and I saw it clear as looking at it IRL. It lay farther out in the water around the point below the cliffs. Then history popped in and made me understand what it meant to her. The mermaids, who had long ago been wanderers for ages after the great Ruin of the Lands Above, had come here in the After. Meaning the fall of the stars. And they'd found much of the strange city here around the citadel, beneath the waters. So had the saw-haw-gin and the other undersea races we'd fought on the way in. But the Sisters of Blood had claimed the point beneath the high cliffs, where in my mind I could see that Three Four had crashed into the rocks, as their own.

Those were *their lands* along the seabed.

The maids had a king. The only male in their society. He had once been a sailor they'd captured, then turned into a… *mer-person* let's call it… and then made their king. Merman works I guess too.

He was really their prisoner. But they went through this bizarre play of pretending he was their king while keeping him in a gilded cage of sorts. They kept him pretty happy if you know what I mean, and from the visions I was seeing he had shed his humanity and become one of them eventually. Fighting and leading them in vicious undersea wars against the goonies, the saw-haw-gin, and the shark people who were the Sisters of Blood's worst enemies.

The Shark Nomads were hated by everyone.

They, the mermaids, worshipped an ancient beast that lived in an undersea canyon called the Mouth of Madness, and all the gold and treasure the ancient Atlanteans had given the Sisters of Blood had been cast down into the shadowy depths off the sides of the great undersea cliff farther into the bay and just beneath the citadel. When I caught an image of this place, where the Sisters of Blood carried their treasure once a year and cast it in, I did not like what I saw. It reminded me of the thing in the crack, when Autumn and I had hidden in the ruined Dragon Elf temple to avoid the gotaur hunters and centaurs.

I saw the mermaids floating there in the water before the great chasm, staring out and down into the black titanic depths and seeing nothing that lived. Even the other fish avoided that place. Then they threw the great treasures of

Atlantea into that crack and prayed that the monster would not come forth. Watching gold shower into the black, shimmering as it caught the last of the sunlight at these extreme depths. Jewels that once adorned the lustrous raven hair of lost princesses becoming pinpricks of fading star light in the cold universe below. Fantastic shields of ancient Atlantean warriors, the medusa's image stamped on their large circumference, tumbling end over end and lost to the current that sucked the Great Inner Sea into the crack and off into the reaches of the Lands of the Lost.

Even the Sword of Aerax was given. The fabled blade of the greatest and most fated Atlantean Spartan to ever adventure beyond World's End was given to the dark titan of the depths that both the maids and the ancient Atlanteans worshipped.

There were a lot of images, and more to it than my badly drawn rough sketch for what was about ten thousand years of history. But in short, that's what seemed to be the situation.

I caught one image of the medusa. But then the images flipped like ancient photos and there was an impression of danger beyond the Great Bridge that connected the city of Atlantea to the citadel. A great barrier.

I had no idea what any of that meant. Psionic images like this only gave me parts of the stories, and the vaguest of impressions of the meanings of such things. Like skimming through a book and only reading chapters that catch your eye. The maid knew of people, monsters within the ruined Atlantea, who knew the secrets of the bridge, the barrier, and the medusa.

I needed that…

Suddenly I was sucked backward out of the space-time tunnel the psionics had opened up. Vandahar would explain the mechanics of this to me later. I was back in real-time, breathing heavily and trying to figure out my place in the universe. The dark-haired killer mermaid beauty was flailing, thrashing her huge tail in the water, twisting and squirming, trying to get away from us so she could swim off to her sisters and run for the deeps.

The sudden violence had scared them all for a moment.

I heard Thor rumble, "Uh... what the hell..." as he came back to reality.

Then she smacked me, no, walloped me in the face with her huge scaly tail. That wasn't as pleasant as you would think it might be.

My bell got rung for a good solid five seconds. But I held on. Because I needed that intel inside the photographs in her mind.

"Sar'nt!" I shouted at Thor, hoping he was back in real-time too as I struggled to hold on to the wild killer mermaid. I could see the other mermaids coming for us now, sensing the confusion. Seeking to take advantage. Swimming from the rocks and farther out. Not fast. But slowly, once more starting their trance-y, lyrical song. Hoping to pull the hypnotizing trick again.

That's when I realized Santago had been with me all along. Fish knife out and keeping them back and off of us as we struggled.

"*Recuar!*" he shouted raggedly in Portugonian. "*Recuar!*"

Get back!

Then switching to Navarrean Spanish as if to help me understand because I was still struggling with the feisty mermaid, "*Volver atrás, Talk-ir! Ahora! Ahora!*"

Now! Now!

Thor had figured the situation out. Either from the fact that the struggling mermaid was trying to drown me again, or the looks on the hungry mermaid faces coming for him now, vampire teeth glistening among those stunner faces. Or maybe it was Commons shrieking, "I got bit! I got bit!" from the shoreline as the medic tried to get him out of the water and help him.

"Let her go, Private!" bellowed Thor, grabbing me with one arm as he decided to leave the water immediately. "Fall back!"

"Negative, Sar'nt!" I shouted back. "Need to interrogate... She's... got a line on how we can hit... Hoochie Mama."

CHAPTER FOURTEEN

I held on to her dark curly hair as she screamed like a savage, untamed, feral animal. We dragged her through the surf and sand to get her on shore, Thor picking up her massive tail as we hauled her out of the water, dripping wet with seawater.

I'd say she fought like a feral cat. But that would be underestimating the battle.

To make matters more interesting, orc indirect incoming whistled in from high above and fell down along the wet and dry sand and into the water, the arrows making strange noises as they hit and exploded in dark smoking fizzles. It would be dark soon, and the battle didn't show any signs of letting up.

Then out of nowhere we suddenly had comm. Our radios sprang to life from other fighting positions with dire news of two new major players the enemy had thrown into the battle in the last few as both sides decided to invest all their marbles in the outcome.

We dragged the screaming, fighting mermaid up the sea wall and into the tower, still fighting hard and whimpering harder the farther she got from the water. It was a sad sound that tried to break your heart until you remembered what she was. She managed to rake Thor's biceps hard with her nails and tear through his fatigues before he roared and backhanded her with a solid smack. That took the fight out of her and we were able to get her inside the tower and down around the statue of a beautiful mermaid that had toppled in the center of the chamber. She slithered across the floor, clung to the statue, and cried out plaintively, appealing to it for help like it was some god.

Meanwhile PFC Kennedy was breaking through the comm. His position as wizard and intel specialist on all things magical allowed him to perform feats among the Rangers like suddenly overriding team leaders and platoon sergeants in the middle of a critical fight to disseminate specialized information.

"Netcall, netcall, this is Merlin…" That was Kennedy's permanent call sign. Merlin. Whether he liked it or not. He'd told me *not*. But he'd accepted it nonetheless. "We have two spellcasters in play. Indications are, they are *name level*. And—"

"Say again. Clarify *name level*, Merlin," barked one of the irritated team sergeants who sounded smack dab in the middle of *in it* and well forward of the action. The bark of automatic weapons could be heard and then someone desperately shouted, "Heads down, Rangers. Frag out!"

The net cracked and cackled wildly. Both Thor and I heard the dull boom of the explosion off to our left behind the tower walls of the deployed grenade.

Then the team sergeant was back over the net.

"Say again, Merlin. *Name level*. What's that indicate?"

Kennedy keyed the mic and cleared his throat like the pros don't. But hey, he was Merlin. And if anyone was gonna get us an airstrike of the magical order and clear the orcs off our flanks it was this guy.

"Name level indicates very powerful. Approach with extreme caution. They have a lot of spells at their disposal and some of them are heartbreakers. Merlin over."

Silence for a moment.

Someone sitrepped the position of one of the spellcasters who'd just entered the battle.

"Name-level bad guy holed up in blockhouse one hundred meters forward of our position on the left. Tangos have clear field of fire on our position. Enemy firing... spider webs at us. Effective fire is useless for some reason. Carter and Spaz down. We cut 'em out. SDM had a shot... suddenly six of name level. We can't hit the blockhouse without taking heavy fire. Bravo Two-Six out."

Kennedy came back over the radio.

"Bravo Two-Six, that's a wizard. Do not approach. I'll come forward and see what I can do to get you close for breach. Merlin out."

I heard Thor rumble "Hero" as the mermaid whimpered in the silence of the tower and the gunfire rattled out in short bursts beyond the walls. I couldn't tell if it was meant as fact, or sarcasm. But there was Kennedy going out to do his thing as a Ranger upon whom other Rangers were depending.

"Merlin... this is Charlie position on the main road. We're putting fire on... cathedral... off the main road. Two recons in force and we can't get close to push. Lotsa protection. Effective fire is useless also. Grenades won't detonate. I played D&D back in the day, Merlin, and this feels like a pretty high-level cleric in there. If we can get close, we can bring the whole cathedral down on them. But we can't. Wards all over the stone and in effect. Anytime we get close some of us get confused. Others fall asleep. I think he used a spell—called a *flame strike* if I remember—on our support position. Please advise. Charlie position over."

For a moment Kennedy said nothing, and in the pause, Thor looked at me.

"How critical is she?" he asked after a moment. "Sounds like they need me out there."

"I saw something inside her mind, Sar'nt. This place is still… I don't know… active. There're people that the Maids of Blood—her people—deal with in the city that can get us a location on Hoochie. I think. If I can get that out of her, then we can send in Reapers?"

Thor nodded.

"Get the old man to help you," he said. "I'm going to go take out that cathedral."

I yelled for Santago, then was surprised to see him already standing just inside the tower doorway. His thin form a silhouette against the coming darkness falling out to sea. It would be a long night.

The comm crackled.

"Charlie, this is Merlin. Let me assist Bravo Two-Six and I'll shift and see what I can do after. I'd hold back. High-level clerics can flat-out kill you with just a word. Advise extreme caution."

Thor cut in. "Charlie Actual, this is ground force commander. Moving forward to link up. Hold position."

"I need your help," I said to Santago as he stood there in the gloom. His fishing knife out and ready to plunge into any skulkers who'd managed to get around the Rangers.

He nodded once. Then whispered a gravelly, "*Sí*, Talkir. Let's get it done now. This night feels very evil already. And it be long too."

The comm crackled once more.

"All elements Task Force Pipe Hitter. This is Batman…"

Because the Rangers called all Green Berets *Super Friends* when they weren't calling them *Green Beanies*, they'd assigned Chief Rapp the call sign Batman.

Of course, the Rangers were also jealous of this.

"… we can get a Javelin out of Three Four Heavy. Merlin, will that do the trick if this… cleric has a heat sig?"

Even I knew the FGM-148 anti-armor, fire-and-forget Javelin would do the trick on a single target. When talking weapons and tactics against *heavies* during our monster classes back at the FOB—the term we used for some of the big monsters we'd face—Sergeant Chris had told us he'd once considered using a Stinger on a haji when he'd missed an extreme-range sniper shot.

"Wouldna missed with that bad boy. But… it's a pretty expensive kill. Government accounting woulda had a heart attack in the cost-analysis section of the report."

The Javelin would detect a heat sig off a human and that could take out this cleric. Expensive or not, that was a way to get it done. And that's what Rangers did. They figured out ways to get things done that others didn't consider. Whatever was required to ensure the mission got accomplished. Mission accomplishment drove all Ranger thinking, planning, and problem-solving.

"That would do it, Batman. Merlin out."

Two clicks came back over the net to acknowledge that this was now the plan. Later I would find out about Specialist Crouse's marathon to lay the hate with a recovered Javelin on the orc high priest stalling the attack from Charlie position.

But for now, I had a mermaid to interrogate.

CHAPTER FIFTEEN

SANTAGO understood what I needed to do once I explained it to him.

"We need to know how to reach the medusa," I told the old Navarrean sailor. "I think she knows."

"And you can talk to her, Talk-ir?"

"No. I don't think I can speak her language if it's the one on these walls. I can... kinda speak the languages that it's based on... or the ones I think it's based on... but I think the meanings have been obscured by time and it's more of a code now. It would take too long for me to figure it all out. But... there's another way. I think."

The old sailor had no idea what any of this meant. He shrugged.

"What can I do to help, Talk-ir?"

I took a deep breath. Vandahar had taught me that when I turned off my senses, made myself blind, I could do things... like see. It was a psionic meditational trick that, so far, had been the only way I could control what the Ruin had *revealed* about me. The problem was, it made me vulnerable—not only because I was blind, but because I had to turn off my body as much as possible.

And, bonus, I got a really big headache as a parting gift for trying.

But hey, the medics had lots of Motrin. Which they affectionally called *Ranger Candy*.

"I need you to hold her still, Santago. I'm going to put my head against her and start a conversation you might not be able to hear. Just hold on to her no matter what, okay?"

"*Sí*, Talk-ir. I will hold the maid. Will you be able to understand her? You say you do not speak her cursed tongue."

I didn't tell him that I was intending to basically open up my entire mind and turn it into a translating algorithm that could decipher codes and that, perhaps, if I could show her pictures of what I wanted, then maybe she'd say something that would give us a clue about how to get to Hoochie Mama.

Listen—I'll admit this was pretty thin soup. I only *hoped* this would work. But the Rangers were gonna need a hit location fast if we were gonna end this little detour and get back on mission.

So… maybe Sergeant Chris is right.

Rangers can do anything. You just gotta give yourself permission to try and be open to what *anything* really means.

Does that still apply even if you haven't passed Ranger School—twice—and went through an abbreviated RASP?

I won't lie to you. I wear the scroll and try to earn it every day because that's what they do.

But I don't feel like a Ranger.

Nope.

I'm just the guy next to the guy who did the Ranger thing.

But there was what Autumn had told her king, and her brother, Carver.

And oh yeah, Carver and the Hammer were the only ones who made it through Kurtz's first Ranger Class. Probably Kurtz did that just to spite the rest of us. But not really. I knew Kurtz the Ranger purist wouldn't let that happen. You had to be a Ranger's Ranger for him to have less contempt for you.

Carver was as bitter as Kurtz.

The Hammer was… he was unstoppable, indefatigable, and probably the happiest, most proficient killer you'd ever meet. If the Forge could crank out a 249 that would fit him… the Grim Reaper was out of work.

New sheriff in town.

But when Autumn said the sword was mine in the argument with her king consort, and her brother who would never be king now—*The blade falls to the Ranger Talker*—well…

I have found that sometimes when you can't believe in yourself—and only a sociopath or psychopath believes in themselves all the time, all of us doubt, all of us question ourselves and how much we can really do in the face of it all, don't ever doubt that, that it helps—when someone else believes in you…

Even when you don't…

… It helps.

And sometimes that's all you need. Just a little wind in your sails. Or as my dad would have said when training a rider for a horse, *Sometimes you need a leg up, and a horse that's kind. That's all. Then maybe you can cowboy a little.*

I never forgot that. I'll never forget that. I wouldn't be me if I did. I wouldn't be his son.

Yeah. That dream we had, Autumn and I, the dream of the Cities of Men. That's gone.

That was then. This is now.

But she called me a Ranger. She did. So maybe I was. And maybe, like Sergeant Chris had said, I could do anything.

So why not try and see what can be done when you embrace… *anything?*

I nodded to Santago and moved fast to get ready. He grabbed the maid and held her in a bear hug. She screamed once, the beautiful dark-haired mermaid, then began to whimper. Her vampire teeth biting her full lips as crystalline tears rolled down onto her cheeks and she began to hyperventilate.

"It's okay," I told her, whispering as I approached with both hands out. Open. Friendly. Assault gloves off. Palms up.

I closed my eyes.

I'd gotten good at this part. Turning off my senses. I could do it in about thirty seconds. There's Talker. Making a game of things and seeing if the teacher will give him a gold star for being the best, the fastest.

First my eyes.

I didn't even see the darkness behind my lids. I was in a coffeehouse. I could hear the steam from the espresso machine steaming milk. Espressing the dark roasted bean. I love that sound. Love the steam. Love its feel on your skin.

I took a job in a coffeehouse, a really craft one when I was doing graduate work. Just to be close to coffee.

I know. I have a problem.

I turned off the sound of the steam.

I was blind. And now I couldn't hear.

You'd think smell would come next in my little meditation of turning everything off to pull the psionics trick as I held my hands out just in front of her. Within my blindness she was coming into focus as a shadow. She was beautiful. A killer. But like a little girl. Not really bad. Just naughty. A vision like a shadowy angel.

Maybe that was the empathy speaking.

Vandahar told me the empathy helped with what I was about to do.

And as I was saying, you'd think smell was the next sense I turned off to reach the state I needed to be in. But it was actually taste. In that coffeehouse I used, that perfect, best-ever coffee house where I could smell the roast and feel the warmth of the heavy porcelain cup, heated just right so the coffee wasn't damaged when it was poured in and ready to consume, I took a mental sip of the coffee in my mind, inhaling as I did so.

She was coming into focus more now with the vision I was creating where we could meet. I could see her falling tears of fear like silver moonlight on the waters of the deep.

I leaned forward, putting my hands on her cheeks. Feeling the wetness of her tears. Santago struggled to hold her tight as she suddenly surged to be free. I heard his breath. And then, with just a mental flick of the switch, that too was gone from where we were going inside our minds.

It's not taste that's the most important to me about coffee. Don't get me wrong. I love the taste of coffee. But of course… you know that. You've read this far, faithful reader of this account no one will ever read.

You are special.

And so I'll tell you a secret only Talker, me, knows inside the Coffeehouse of the Mind. The place where I go to turn everything off. The quietest, most perfect place you've ever been. Trust me. The silence there is like… peace.

There is nothing that can get you there.

And all is right with the world, or it isn't. It doesn't matter there anymore.

Smell.

Smell is the most important sense. And I use it to turn off taste as I sip and inhale the coffee at the same time. In the world of high-class coffee-tasting, this is called... *cupping.*

Slurping and inhaling the roast at the same time. It's how you get the taste, flavor, and aroma profiles. Nuts. Shoe leather. Toffee. Tobacco. Hints of citrus. And so forth.

The smell is more important, your mileage may vary of course, than the taste. To the aficionado. The pro. The junkie. This is where the magic is.

And the feely-feel-good-superman-I-can-do-anything rush excitement of the stuff.

I let go of taste and concentrate on smell so it's the last thing before there is nothing, inhaling as I lean my head close to the weeping mermaid. I've taken off my FAST helmet and I have no idea what's going on out there as Sergeant Thor goes to direct the desperate battle around the LZ. Trying to affect the outcome by sheer savage competence and brutal action done extremely violently. As Kennedy runs up dark alleys to link up with Bravo Two-Six and prevent Rangers from being turned into toads or struck by fireballs and lightning...

... *very, very frightening.*

As Crouse goes down into the half-submerged wreck to get the Javelin.

I let all that, everything, go. Even the smell of coffee. The most wonderful smell in the universe.

So says I.

My head is against hers and I can smell her hair. It is perfumed and I wonder how a mermaid does that.

I wonder…

"Please don't hurt me…" she whimpers in the pool we are in. The midnight moonlit whirlpool that is the psionic mind-meld I have effected for us to have… *palaver*.

As Vandahar would say.

I won't, I whisper in my mind and hope she's seeing a picture that reassures her so.

It is just the two of us. She can't move. And I stand there in the pool that is the entire universe. Projecting calm and safety.

I'll let you go, Allandria.

She cried for a moment more, and then started sniffling. Whimpering like a mewling puppy. I just kept thinking the most non-hostile thoughts I could think. And the truth was, I felt bad for her. I could tell she was just a wild thing, a beautiful wild thing that wanted nothing more than to swim the ocean depths and be free. Finding pretty shells. Seeing strange sights none of us would ever see.

Inside her mind I could see she loved whales. Big giant wanderers of the ocean's wastes. Loved following them when she could, and when she heard their mournful songs, she considered those her best days ever.

She thought she would both live and die when she heard their calls over the great gulfs and distances of the oceans. She collected them and sang them back to herself when no one was listening.

That was my in. I didn't have a Coke for a haji. Or moon god potion for Jabba. But I did have that.

You will hear the whales sing again, little mermaid, I said calmly. In my mind. *You will. I promise.*

"I will," she said softly.

I nodded and brushed my hand through the waters of the pool between us.

I need to know about the medusa.

She looked up, concerned. Uncertain about what I had just said. There were just the two of us here. I thought hard and showed her a picture of the only medusa I had ever… "seen."

Alluria's sister.

The one the Rangers had blown to smithereens to get their hit on Lizard King, Ssruth the Cruel. Those thoughts surfaced and she tried to back away in the pool from the violence of the images on the waters she was seeing that were coming from my mind. Edging toward the circle of moonlight that was the boundary of the entire world here.

Don't, I said.

Here was an unknown. I had no idea what happened if either of us left the circle of moonlight in the pool I'd created. But I had a feeling bad things happened if you did. If minds linked and went into the darkness beyond the moonlight… because yeah, that was here and it was like a living, breathing, dangerous animal waiting, those were the terms of the deal for being able to do this… then perhaps… I don't know. Perhaps madness that way lay, and you didn't want to find out what was beyond the moonlight.

Don't, I said once more.

Then, *You're safe here.*

She didn't move. But she didn't go any farther.

The medusa… I need to reach her, Allandria.

"You know my name?"

I do.

Her eyes sparkled for a moment. A shy smile covered her vampire's teeth.

I pushed away thoughts of McCluskey. The dead murderous SEAL who'd become a vampire wouldn't help matters right now. I was amazed at the number of dark thoughts that tried to creep into the moonlit pool I'd created for communication. And honestly, I wasn't sure how much longer I could hold it. The headache that came from psionics use this heavy usually came afterwards. But right now, I could feel it creeping into the back of my skull already.

You're beautiful, I told her. And meant it. *And so is your name. Allandria.*

She blushed and swam forward, beginning to stand up out of the water, and I was pretty sure certain assets she had were going to collapse this whole thing as my concentration went... well... you know.

I sank down into the water and moved closer to her.

The medusa, Allandria. Tell me. And then I'll take you back to the water and you can swim away. Hear the songs of the whales.

"Will you come with me, Man of Land? It's possible. If I kiss you, and you live... we can live in forests of azure. I will show you things none of your kind have ever seen. Strange and beautiful things that will make your heart stop because they are so beautiful."

She was getting close.

And the kiss. Her lips were parting. The vampire fangs biting her lower lip. That was the kiss. And we'd have to tell Commons about that. The Ruin had its way of revealing, and I had a feeling we were about to get the best combat diver the Rangers had ever had.

I have to kill her. The medusa.

My headache was already bad. I had no guile. Just the truth. I was shaking. I wondered if my body back where we were was starting to have seizures.

I took a breath in the moonlit pool and let all that go.

Rangers can do anything.

The blade falls to the Ranger.

It was a fight out there and there were casualties. A genie and a medusa. The Rangers were gonna get one shot to whack Hoochie Mama.

Rangers can do anything, Sergeant Chris whispered in the moon above.

I'm sorry. But I do. I have to kill her, Allandria, so we can be free like you want to be.

Allandria began to turn over and I saw her body in full. Her whole body. Not the fish part. The tail. But the human she could become… if she wanted to. She was so beautiful I ached. Her hair flowed in the water around her full breasts.

"*Hang in there, Talk-ir,*" I heard from far away. As though the old sailor was shouting in the storm that the ship was still there.

Santago. Far away. I was losing my mind. The pool was starting to collapse now.

The medusa, little mermaid. Tell me how to find her… and you'll swim away.

She smiled and laughed. A little cute delicate laugh.

"You'll never kill the snake hair," the mermaid said in the darkness as the pool began to fade. As the moonlight disappeared. "But over the Mouth of Madness you'll need to go, Man of Land. And only Kaffir can tell you the way and where she sleeps. Kaffir along the Mouth. On the

Street of Dreams. But it is dangerous, so very dangerous, Man of Land. He is dangerous. Come with me. Come with me and swim in forests of azure. I will love you. And make the pain in your heart go away. You will see my pretty shells I have shown…"

I was drowning in the darkness. The psionic doorway had closed. The dark animal lying in the shadows was the darkness. And I was in it.

Then I heard Allandria from far away…

Just the whisper of her singsong voice over the endless depths of that ocean where the giant nomads swam.

"… *shells no one has ever seen, Man of Land. I will…*"

And then I was gasping, coughing and hacking like when you're in a dream and you can't breathe anymore. Rolling on the bloody floor of the Tower of the Mermaids. Hearing the distant gunfire. Santago letting go of our prisoner. Allandria. Rolling me over to slap me on the back.

"Talk-ir! Talk-ir!" he shouted. "Breathe!"

***

We carried her down to the water. She was unconscious. The thing I had done to the two of us had taken its toll. My head was pounding hard, but I stumbled down to the water, carrying her torso and watching her, then the water. Watching for her sisters. Santago with the tail.

Waist-deep into the cold ocean, and her eyes fluttered to life like a child coming awake in the morning of a new day.

She smiled like she was having a pleasant dream.

Then I let her go, and she slipped off into the water, disappearing and never looking back.

The battle raged behind us in the darkness along the shore and the outskirts of the citadel. The fireworks of death.

I watched the water and wondered about her out there, thinking of the forests of azure she would go to and swim among, and shells no one has ever seen. Shells she would have shown me.

She was a strange and beautiful creature. And I knew I would think about her now and then, for as long as I lived, and wonder what might have been had we kissed.

CHAPTER SIXTEEN

I was useless for a moment. Imagine the worst headache you've ever had. The Portugonians had started a small fire against the darkness to the rear of the tower. I passed the covered body of Daredevil and pushed thoughts away I couldn't take right at this moment.

I'd pay for those later, I told myself. There would be time for grief when the fighting was done. We'd do right by him. I had no doubt of that.

I got my ruck.

Fished around and got my own blue percolator out. My hands were shaking badly. Penderly'd had the Forge crank one out for me. In exchange, I'd taught him some French because he thought that would impress the cute little ponytailed Air Force drone operator co-pilot.

Word was, she had it bad for Thor.

But hey, everyone runs their game.

My hands were shaking as I opened my watertight bag and got my *fixins* ready just like any other hardcore addict. Grinder. Beans. Water.

Time. I needed time. But don't you always?

Did I tell you my hands were shaking, and I was seeing double?

I'd gone deeper than I'd ever gone before.

I found the Motrin.

Ranger Candy.

I took five.

It was that bad.

The radio traffic was heavy. Huge firefight between the Bravo element supported by Kennedy and the wizard in what the Rangers had identified as the blockhouse.

Who knew what strange purpose the ancient building within this weird and haunted city had once served? But someone had decided it was a blockhouse, and so it was a blockhouse on the Rangers' mental map of what stood in their way of smoking the enemy.

The wizard fired magic missiles at Kennedy.

Vandahar had taught Kennedy a shield spell that negated those. Kennedy was supported by a wedge of four Rangers, one of whom was carrying the MK48 super-SAW if my ears caught the sound of barking gunfire bursts right.

The coffee in the blue percolator was bubbling and the Ranger Candy was doing nothing. My head felt like it was going to split in half right there. The Portugonians murmured among themselves, and I could tell they were saying I didn't look so hot.

Good guess, boys. I don't feel so hot either. I pushed thoughts away that I'd damaged myself permanently. I checked myself for stroke by raising both arms and curling my tongue.

I could perform both actions.

I kinda wanted to throw up.

But the smell of the coffee… well, it's a magic deeper than the universe. So I held on as it finished brewing and listened to the traffic.

Kennedy fired off his prismatic color sprays and blinded a bunch of archers trying to flank the Rangers. The SAW gunner opened up on the alley and ruined that bunch in high-dosage seven-six-two.

The Rangers advanced and Kennedy used the dragon-headed staff, firing a huge fireball right into the blockhouse.

They thought the wizard inside was dead until stones started getting pulled from the pavement and flying at the Rangers.

"Tango is using telekinesis!" shouted Kennedy over the net. Then, "Firing counter spell!"

This was Kennedy's new, most powerful spell. If he employed it on a certain effect, according to what he'd told me, the opposite would happen. He had to be careful, according to Vandahar, because opposites can be hard to predict.

So, Tanner had hypothesized, "It's like, what if someone sends a blast of wind spell at me, Talker?"

"Is there such a spell?" I asked.

"I don't know. Probably. But let's say I counter-spell that. What if instead of a gust of wind, the counter is no air at all? What if I suddenly create a vacuum and the universe implodes, or everything gets sucked into a black hole that just opened up?"

"Can that happen in your game?"

"It could. But like I keep telling you guys… this might not be totally the game. Sometimes it is, sometimes it isn't. It's a great spell the old guy taught me, but even he said it was dangerous. But as he likes to say, dangerous times call for dangerous spells."

In this case, the counter spell just stopped the telekinesis, which was supernatural, and turned everything into natural. The flying rocks became just regular old rocks and dropped to the ground.

At this point the Rangers took the opportunity to rush, stack, throw bangers, breach, and straight-up murder the stunned orc wizard who looked like a real lunatic to them according to what I got told later.

"You shoulda seen the look on that cat's face…" one of them told me. "He was all, *This ain't supposed to happen.* He had one eye like them cyclops do. Then Marks just hoses him a whole bunch with the SAW. Used a whole belt. Marks gets a little freaked out. He comes from Appalachia and says he's jittery around witchy stuff. Fine by me, Talk. I was glad we saved some grenades. This ain't done yet."

By the time they stormed the blockhouse, I had a full canteen cup of coffee, and I drank a big gulp even if it burnt my tongue and the roof of my mouth.

I had to get intel into the system.

First I needed to get mobile.

First I needed to stop dying.

The Ranger Candy kicked in because I took two more and just sat there. Drinking coffee while the Rangers fought all along the line with guns, grenades, knives, axes, maces, and bows.

I had no doubt that the incredible run of Specialist Crouse was underway. Twenty minutes from the wreck to Charlie position forward to deliver the mission-critical Javelin.

The orcs were in retreat by then. They'd been fighting up on the cliffs. They'd been pushing the Mermaid Tower since we'd inserted. Their two spellcasters had halted the Rangers' mayhem as the Rangers shucked any kind of defense and started hit-and-run raids against columns of demon orcs surging through the sand-filled ruined streets to try and take the LZ.

Spellcaster one got riddled with bullets, thanks to the jittery Marks who told me later, "I don't abide black magic, Talk. Regular magic's okay now that we're here and all. But none o' that wacky voodoo around me. I was raised Pentecostal. Sure, we handle snakes. But wrong is wrong. And I'll cut a witch that fast, brother. Only way to be sure."

Spellcaster one was down and the orcs were pulling back to the Mouth of Madness. A bridge from this section of the city over to the citadel proper. Spellcaster two, on the other hand, was being much more difficult to dislodge. The Rangers could have bypassed and flanked according to doctrine, but Thor wanted this thorn removed. Problem was, no one could get a shot. No one could get close.

The cathedral only had three standing walls, and everyone had good sight pictures on him. But even *Mjölnir* could not penetrate the magical shielding surrounding the orc shaman. And any assaulter getting close got confused or fell asleep. Worse, Kennedy was identifying other runes that looked much more deadly once he was on scene five minutes later.

The orcs were beginning to rally behind the cathedral, and this was going to be a problem pretty soon. Other creatures were coming in now and we had no idea about their capabilities. Thor indicated we had to break this defensive position and then they'd run.

Second cup of coffee down, I stood. The net was wild. The Rangers were full of murder and nowhere to go unless they could punch through the cathedral. That passage allowed them access to the rest of the city this side of the

Mouth. Otherwise they'd have to fight alley to alley and house to house to reach the bridge.

"Hang on," said Chief Rapp. "We almost there!"

CHAPTER SEVENTEEN

CHIEF Rapp had fought a separate and desperate battle from well before the moment Three Four Heavy went into the rocks hard on the cliff below the point. At sea, the ship had borne the brunt of the attack by the Harpy Aircav because it was the closest southern ship in the column of the hop advancing from the west, heading deep into the eastern portion of the Great Inner Sea. When the storm hit *Dancer*, as the Rangers and her ship's captain called the heavy galley, they struggled to get the sails set for the oncoming storm in order to outrun the tempest.

The Rangers focused on the fight.

But it took time for Chief Rapp to realize the sailors of *Dancer* had a bad captain. Or at least a bewitched sailing master. A drunkard, the captain issued strange orders that the Rangers, skilled boat handlers already, knew weren't right from the start. The situation of transport on private vessels had already been a delicate matter, but it rapidly became apparent in the tension and stress of the battle at sea that it was almost as though the captain of *Dancer* was *trying* to be incompetent. Trying to lose the ship to either the storm or the enemy.

Sergeant Joe, the platoon sergeant for the assaulters on Three Four Heavy, remarked to the Special Forces operator in command of the element of Task Force Pipe Hitter,

Chief Rapp, "It's like the guy works for the government there, eh, Chief? Can't tell if he's just incompetent, or real bad on purpose-like."

The Rangers suffer neither incompetence nor betrayal lightly. Several offered to sort things quickly via the trailing sharks. Sergeant Joe had everyone in plate carriers and ordered them to be ready to go into the water if need be, using water survival protocols. Flotation items and improvised rafts were under construction when the harpies hit the ship hard and fast from the air just off the ocean's stormy surface.

A wave of the flying hags the other two ships might not have seen came in low across the water. Sergeant Chris, running the gun teams, opened up hard, devastating this first assault even as *Sea Wolf*, the third ship commanded by the pirate, cut away to the north to avoid the clutch of the Rift.

Once the harpies were hitting all three ships, the fighting heaviest against Three Four Heavy, Chief Rapp spotted the problem for his ship in the chaos. *Dancer's* captain was in a trance and merely swigging hard from a pear-shaped bottle of rum near the helm while the Portugonian sailors grumbled and expressed that things could be done better. One of them, a man named Valvao, tried to give the order to at least lower the sails in the current configuration so they weren't torn to shreds by the force of the oncoming gale blast of the witch storm out of the south.

The captain raged, angrily drew a saber, and charged the smaller sailor, screaming incoherently. The Portugonians fought off the brute of a captain to protect the capable Valvao, and the chief told Sergeant Joe to keep the

Rangers in the fight while he sorted things out with the indigs.

He'd handle things. One way or another.

This was all that was told to me by the Rangers from Three Four Heavy when I was able to put the story together before we made the final assault against the citadel. There wasn't a lot of time, but there was some during the inhaling of MREs and the brewing of coffee. And the binding of wounds.

Remember, this all went down while the harpies were storming the sails on our ship, the seas were rough and getting worse, and the goonies were just getting involved. Everyone was busy when *Dancer* suffered a command malfunction and Chief Rapp had to diagnose.

So if we thought it was bad aboard *Sofia*, apparently it was downright out of control on *Dancer*.

On our ship, *Sofia*, Santago battled as much as we did by keeping the ship moving and watertight despite the sincerest intentions of the enemy to drown us all at sea. I was grateful for the old sailor's dedication and competence then, and even more thankful when I learned of events aboard *Dancer* to the south.

I heard most of the story from Sergeant McCarty, a squad designated marksman with the assaulters. He told me he watched the chief studying the battle, taking shots with his tricked-out SCAR-L he preferred to the Ranger-issue MK18. Because Rapp was SF and here to advise the Rangers, he was allowed to have his own say in what weapons systems he worked as he often operated independently with the indigs of late. The SCAR worked for the kind of encounters he was concerned about. Alone, and needing range to engage at distance and close at hand. The SCAR was flexible enough to meet his needs. On the other side of the detachment, the sergeant major wanted the Rangers to run the weapons systems they'd trained with until there was a formal decision to switch over to new, better, advanced systems the Forge could print up for us when the time came.

This did not include the personals everyone except me carried. Backups like everything from Sergeant Kurtz's Rampage to the Taurus Raging Bull firing .454 Casull with an eight-inch barrel in matte-black that Monroe the Ranger Minotaur carried in addition to the special M60E3 with a powerful laser designator that he wielded because his bull head and massive neck made aiming through iron sights difficult. Add the foregrip and he was a regular killing machine. The Raging Bull made matters even more violent in close encounters.

Chief Rapp left the battle on the deck of *Dancer* to Sergeant Joe, who ran the defense of the stricken ship excellently despite taking the brunt of the enemy attack. Once the harpies tore open the sails and the goonies came out of the depths, it was clear the fighting was going to center on that galley as the most exposed in the wedge that had never formed. Sergeant Joe ordered the rails mined with claymores after the assaulters repelled a massive attack by the Creatures from the Black Lagoon attempting to swamp the galley out beyond the bay and drag her over onto her side in the waves. She would have sunk fast and the Rangers would have been lost that far out and surrounded by enemies who lived below the ocean. Instead, the next time the enemy tried that, they'd be blown off the sides of the galley regardless of the consequences.

"Might collapse the superstructure of the ship if we have to det," warned Sergeant Kang.

"Sometimes you're the bug, sometimes you're the windshield," shot back Joe as he redirected the gun teams to the forecastle being threatened by a new push from another direction. The harpies there were coming in with smoking pots of flaming oil and trying to land them on the ship's hull and start a fire that would have been yet one more out-of-control crisis for the overwhelmed crew and the heavily occupied Rangers fighting from every position of the ship they could cover. "We're gonna get a thousand-yard stare out of this one, Sergeant Kang," noted Sergeant Joe. "Might as well have a ton of dead to look at while we're there staring off into space."

Meanwhile, Chief Rapp had diagnosed the problem that *Dancer* was having, according to McCarty the SDM. The chief approached the SDM and ordered him to shoot a black seagull trailing the galley.

"He just comes up to me, knife hands the seagull he wants dead, and says, 'Ranger, see that bird? Show me some street magic and make it disappear!'"

McCarty shoulders his MK11 SDM rifle and sights the bird weaving in the wind, trailing off the aft deck of the galley getting hit by the storm from the south.

"Never mind it was a weird ask," McCarty told me. "The wind was tricky and there was sand coming at me. I'll be honest, I'm a good shot. But the deck of the ship, the roll and pitch of the sea, the storm and the harpies shrieking... one of the toughest shots I've ever been asked to make."

"Did you?" I asked.

The Ranger nodded.

"Then I turned to the chief and said, 'Gotta ask why, Chief?' He turns around and stares at the drunk captain on the forecastle fighting with the sailors. Then points. He says, 'I think that bird was some kind of evil sorcerer. He cast a spell on the captain. Lookit there, Sergeant.' And he's right. The captain has dropped his sword he was waving around at the crew, and he just collapses on the deck in a pile."

"Then what happened?" I asked.

"Chief takes over. Orders Valvao to take command. And that's when the ship starts to run smooth for what's left of a real rough ride. Truth be told we were already doomed. Right about then is when the big sea snake hit our oars and sheared off the starboard side. Sails were ripped to shreds, oars snapped, we were starting to spin. We were going in, man."

What happened next, we saw from the deck of *Sofia*. It went from bad to worse as more goonies and fish-men kept trying to sink the galley right there in the bay, never mind that it was out of control and spinning in.

The chief ordered the Rangers that were ready to go into the water, to go then. It was that bad and he knew the ship was lost.

He stayed on board until the ship hit the rocks because the Rangers holding the aft deck couldn't disengage from the enemy without taking fire from the archer harpies.

And for some reason, that's when the enemy, or at least those under the water, pulled back from the wrecked ship. Just before it exploded all over the rocks and snapped in half.

Once that happened, the chief gave the order to abandon ship, and the Rangers started making their way out onto the rocks where they could or climbing straight up the cliffs with as much gear as they could haul. Those that did the latter found themselves climbing right into a force of orcs waiting at the top of the cliff and looking for a fight. The Rangers went from the frying pan right into a fight for their lives.

Chief Rapp was one of those who made it to the top of the cliff, trying to get ammo cans slung on the deck below and hauled up to the defense the Rangers were already fighting up there. Once there, the Special Forces warfare doctrine specialist assessed the situation and found Sergeant Joe's defense was sound and meeting the needs of the operation as far as consolidation was concerned. The Rangers quickly expanded their perimeter, taking control of some Stonehenge-like stones on a small rise just beyond the top of the cliff. The wind came off the cliffs hard and the Rangers could smell the ripe smell of more orcs massing nearby.

They were low on grenades and Chief Rapp had shucked most of his ruck to climb with a crate of grenades and get them to the Rangers. The Rangers, busy shooting down orcs from the cover of the stones, were getting pushed hard fast.

Chief Rapp commandeered a Ranger who'd lost his weapon in the ocean, and the two of them cracked the crate and became the defense's indirect fire team, tossing grenades out into the press of orcs growing by the second on the rolling hills all around up there at the top of the cliff.

From nearby dry dusty desert canyons, heavy orc infantry was boiling out of the caves and hills. Later, the separate elements of the Rangers would come to the conclusion there were at least two different orc tribes engaged against the Rangers. The ones near the citadel were smaller and augmented by four-armed giants that definitely had lots of danglies and seemed to be war leader types. This tribe preferred the blood and black grease warpaint for identification. They seemed more fanatical, and we guessed they were more religious of some sort. The orcs coming from the desert canyons beyond the citadel and attacking the Ranger defense at "the Stones," as the Rangers called the Stonehenge-like area, were more like desert nomads. They wore dusty robes, kept their heads covered by turbans, and carried mainly scimitars and spears with curved knives as backups they kept on knotted belts.

Their method of attack, these desert orcs, was twofold. They had heavy archers who carried massive war bows that they fired by lying down on their backs, bracing the bows with their hideous legs, and then pulling back with powerful arms. They launched these arrows skyward en masse, then shifted positions to fire again. Because they were low to the ground, and because of the rolling terrain, they were hard to engage and only the few Ranger snipers with the Three Four Heavy element could get shots on the squads of orc tribal indirect. Mostly teams of eight made up an orc archery battery. One group fired while two other groups shifted position and made ready to fire again.

"It's like they understand the concept of modern artillery batteries," Chief Rapp would note from the cover of the Stones as Sergeant Joe organized intersecting fire to hold the position until more Rangers could link up.

Meanwhile, while the indirect squads shelled the Rangers, combined arms groups of heavy infantry orcs, supported by the orc version of designated marksmen with small, curved bows, made savage mad rushes on the pinned-down

Rangers at the Stones. Ululating bloodcurdling war cries as they came.

By the time Chief Rapp made the top of the cliff with the box of grenades, literally a stud feat of strength for the massive special operator, there were already piles of the slaughtered orc skirmishers combined arms teams dying in the sun and the hot winds coming off the desert up there on the cliffs above the citadel. But more orcs were coming, and more arrows were falling. The situation was far from under control.

By this time most of those who'd gone in with Three Four Heavy had consolidated on the cliff. The battle was raging between both sides, with outgoing fire intersecting waves of arrows and typhoons of turbaned orc foot. Between assaults from the orc assault elements, the Rangers rushed out into the narrow lanes of access to the Stones, created by either the geography of the arroyos or the trails that led there, and quickly mined them with what explosives they'd managed to retrieve from the wreck of the galley below. Two scouts were sent out to find a trail leading down into the citadel and off the cliffs.

Chief Rapp could see that, out to sea, Captain Knife Hand and his boat were busy pulling Rangers out of the waters, and another assault boat had gone ashore to secure a perimeter at the tower. Despite lack of comm, he had a pretty good idea of what was going on.

The two scouts returned and indicated there was a narrow canyon road leading down through a graveyard beyond the limits of the citadel, but that the orcs were using that road to come up to the fight too. Plus, there was some witchy stuff going on near the tombstones, but the scouts couldn't get close enough to say more without getting into combat. So they pulled back to report.

Daylight was fading and this was about the time we were getting ready to get involved with the mermaids.

At the same time, the two serious spellcasters had entered the battle against the Ranger elements inside the city surrounding the citadel. Kennedy, with the help of Ranger assaulters, took out one. But the powerful orc shaman holding the old cathedral and rallying the fleeing orc forces was a problem getting worse.

That was when radio traffic opened up, and the Ranger element on the cliffs finally had comm with the rest of the Rangers on land.

I had no idea if we had comm with Kurtz holding *Sofia*, or the smaj with the pirate who had disappeared.

We were now four hours into the battle. Low on ammunition, separated by two hostile forces, and facing a major enemy war leader who could not be dislodged by the Rangers. That spellcaster was threatening to lead a second attack against our most forward elements, never mind we had enemies all over our rear.

We were winning in that we'd established a toehold in two positions, but we were thin enough that our line could break if the orcs could consolidate and push through. It was clear they had the numbers.

But the Rangers had the violence.

At this point I was back on the top of the tower with Sergeant Thor, watching the battle in the ruined streets below. Listening to *Mjölnir* boom out and ruin targets of opportunity. As night came on, we were switching to night vision, those of us who still had NODs, that was. But not quite yet. It wasn't full dark.

Twenty minutes prior, Specialist Crouse had climbed back down the cliff to the wrecked galley to hopefully retrieve one of the clamshells containing the M-148 Javelin anti-armor weapon.

The plan organized by Chief Rapp was to lead a wedge of Rangers down the enemy-overrun canyon and link up with the element preparing to assault Cathedral and ice the enemy shaman holding up the retreat and threatening to collect a force of enemy large enough to counterattack through the Ranger line there. The Rangers would protect the Javelin carrier, another Ranger who'd take the weapon from Specialist Crouse once he secured it.

Then the QRF wedge would move out, fighting their way through the canyon, engaging bands of orcs, and protected from arrow fire by the sides of the canyon, due to the fact the tribal orc light artillery batteries were targeting the Stones up on the hills above the cliffs and canyons that led down to the citadel.

Chief Rapp confirmed the message with the GFC fighting forward, but Specialist Crouse was already down the cliff via a hasty rappel and crawling across the disintegrating wreckage of the ruined galley on the rocks.

Because Rangers never go alone, Private Davis went with him. At the bottom of the rope, they saw the galley beginning to break apart as the waves got more violent and the evening tide started to develop.

The Javelins had been located in the aft section of the second deck, behind the rowing benches. That was where the cargo was kept and where the Rangers had kept much of their reserve weapon stores intended for use against the forces of Sût upon arrival at the mission insertion point in Sûstagul. But now, with Rangers Crouse and Davis assessing the disintegrating wreck, it was apparent that that portion of the ship, and reserve weapon stores including the Javelin clamshell, were now submerged and sinking further into the increasing violent waves below the rocks.

Crouse called for more rope to be sent down, and since there was none, the Ranger on the cliff working belay, under fire and guarded by two other Rangers, cut the rappel rope and sent it down to them.

Crouse tied himself off to Davis who acted as a belay on the rocks, anchoring himself in the rising tide around an outcropping, while Crouse went out into the wreck.

When I talked to him later, Crouse said the whole galley was coming apart around him as the waves hit. It was pretty freaky. He could see mission-critical gear getting carried out to sea and sinking down into the whirlpools and grottos around the cliff. But a clamshell containing a Javelin was not identified in this location of the ship. He needed to get aft.

Unfortunately, just as he approached the aft section, a particularly violent wave hit, and when it receded it took that entire section with it. According to Crouse, and Davis confirmed, Crouse untied himself and leapt to the section now floundering in the waves. The entire section was sinking fast, and Crouse went belowdecks, recovered the Javelin, and came back up on deck. He signaled for Davis to hold the rope where it was dangling against the rocks and not to assist him. Then he dove into the turbulent water carrying the twenty-six-pound Javelin, timing the leap between an outgoing wave and an incoming wave.

Davis told me Crouse was sucked down into the trough instantly and he lost sight of him as the waves suddenly revealed a jagged cove of sheer rocks and dangerous currents. He was pretty sure Crouse was a goner.

Crouse told me he thought he was a goner too, but he held on to the strapped Javelin in the clamshell, and it effectively acted as a flotation device while he rode the next wave out of the violent trough and back up onto the jagged rocks.

He was cut up pretty badly, ignored it, and barely, according to Davis, managed to get hold of the rope Davis was in control of before the next huge wave hit and flung Crouse with brutal impact against the rocks. Davis was pretty sure Crouse had been knocked unconscious, so he started to haul the other Ranger in. But Crouse was, miraculously, not knocked unconscious. He just couldn't get his boots under him due to the torrents of water coming off the rocks as the last wave receded.

Eventually he found his footing and, using the rope, pulled himself up the face of the sheer rocks and to Davis. The two Rangers climbed back up the cliff—using no ropes as none were now available—and arrived at the rally to link up with Chief Rapp's QRF wedge to deliver the Javelin to the GFC for the assault on Cathedral.

The QRF wedge consisted of Chief Rapp in the lead, or point position. Sergeant Stott on the right flank. Corporal Mercer on the left. And PFC Gonzalez taking up rear security. Private Lee was supposed to take the Javelin from the exhausted and waterlogged Crouse, who'd just free-climbed a cliff after surviving a shipwreck and engaging in active close-quarters combat with the enemy for the better part of an hour. But as the QRF wedge moved out under fire from the cover of the Stones, Lee was hit by arrow fire right through the left leg. Medics dragged him from his exposed position and dealt with the wound.

Upon effecting linkup, Chief Rapp decided to carry the Javelin himself as he maintained point on the wedge. But Crouse said, "I can hang, Chief!" and the special operator agreed to let Crouse carry as far as he could, and then they would switch if he got too tired or became injured.

The QRF had to immediately fight their way off the hill under fire from archer batteries and rushes from random directions by orc jihadis. Six orcs in turbans and robes, supported by three archers, engaged the wedge as they made the twisting trail that led off the cliffs and down into the canyon. Chief Rapp shot the two lead orcs down, while Mercer and Stott set up a base of fire to eliminate the three archers coming down off the hill to intercept. The archers were neutralized, but not before the other four orcs closed to within meters of Chief Rapp, hurling spears and charging with knives and scimitars.

Chief Rapp switched the SCAR to full auto and ran a line of fire across this snarling front while taking a spear in the plate carrier. The spear shattered and, according to Crouse, it didn't affect the big SF operator in the least. Two orcs closed and swung blades at the chief. Stott shot one as the chief switched to his secondary and put one round in the other orc's head at point-blank range.

New mags in, the team moved down the trail and engaged two more groups of orcs. Both groups were neutralized, and the QRF moved on to the old cemetery.

The scouts that had identified the road down into the old city surrounding the citadel had indicated something strange going on at the graveyard. Witchy stuff. "Firesnakes and orcs" was the only intel they could give before pulling back, and that wasn't much to go on.

But the mission was critical, and so the QRF team advanced into what PFC Kennedy, our wizard and lore expert, would tell us were most likely salamanders supported by the demon orcs tribe.

Vandahar would later tell Kennedy the cemetery was an old Atlantean noble burial ground, and there were strange tombs beneath the surface where great artifacts slept.

The salamanders, or what the scouts had identified as "firesnakes," apparently servants of some powerful efreet, were robbing the graves looking for something in particular. The demon orcs were complicit, working with picks and axes to crack the doors to a massive tomb in the wall of the cliff. The triangular stones that served as the door and the lintel were carved with weird runes of the madness language.

When the QRF entered from the southwestern edge of the graveyard, the stone slab entrance had been cracked, and the salamanders were busy inside. The demon orcs were unaware at first, and the QRF, moving fast, tried to stay low and skirt the opposite edge of the place to avoid contact. But they were spotted and quickly pinned down. The orcs attacked at once, hurling spears and firing arrows. Two groups of enemies flanked the pinned-down QRF, now fighting from a series of low monuments carved in the reliefs of long-dead Atlantean nobles.

Four orcs flanked Stott. He shot them all down. The rest went through Mercer's sector and overran the Ranger. Mercer was stabbed repeatedly, but with the help of Chief Rapp, Gonzalez, and Specialist Crouse, they were able to drive off the orcs and rescue the downed Mercer.

Chief Rapp held the QRF to administer first aid, and it was Crouse who later told me, as the other Rangers lobbed their remaining grenades and laid down suppressive fire to keep the rest of the orcs back, that he actually watched as Chief Rapp... *healed* the badly wounded Mercer.

One particularly bad slash to Mercer's femoral artery would have killed him, and the only answer was a tourniquet. Chief Rapp was busy working on a head injury he thought was the worse injury—Mercer's face was bloody and the head wound was deep—when the femoral wound just started suddenly spurting blood.

Crouse said that Chief Rapp, still focused on the head wound, placed one massive hand on the spurting artery and simply said, "Not now..." before mumbling something else.

The blood stopped, and the wound was healed.

According to Crouse.

At this point, the salamanders who'd been down inside the tomb entered the battle. The word "salamander" doesn't do these things justice. Perhaps I should stick with calling them "firesnakes," which is what Crouse and the others called them. But Kennedy says they're called salamanders. According to Crouse they're tall, like snakes that stand upright, but with arms and claws carrying pitchforks. Their skin and scales are the color of the worst sunburn you've ever seen. Crouse's words.

These fiery upright snakes cautiously advancing on the QRF seemed immune to gunfire, and so the decision was made by Chief Rapp to exit the graveyard and continue on mission.

Fireman-carrying the badly wounded and unconscious Mercer, Chief Rapp led the QRF at a run out of the graveyard and made the main road leading down into the ruin of the outskirts of the citadel. Off to their right they could see the battle going on around Mermaid Tower. And even hotter forward of those positions. Chief Rapp, while under fire from the enemy archers within the city, confirmed the location of the cathedral, identified the route to effect link-up with the GFC staging at Charlie position to begin the assault, and then made sure the QRF understood they were going for broke to reach the linkup.

They had to reach the staging area for the attack at all costs.

"Anyone goes down, just keep moving," ordered Chief Rapp calmly as he stood there getting a new mag into his SCAR with one hand. "Specialist Crouse goes down, grab the Javelin off him."

"Ain't goin' down, Chief," I'm told Crouse replied.

Reports were coming in that the orcs staging behind Cathedral were getting ready to resume the attack. The Ranger line was too thin due to the hit-and-run raids they were employing and the lack of resupply and wounded, and holding against a significant attack against any point in its line seemed iffy at best right now.

The Rangers were holding on by offense. Defense was going to be a whole other problem.

Chief Rapp continued to carry Mercer and suppress one-handed with the SCAR as the QRF moved out once more.

When Crouse told me about this moment, when no one else was around and he was just making sure Talker got it in the record because everyone knows that's what I really do around here, he was brutally honest.

Brutally honest about himself. Warts and all.

Let me just stop and say, that's the thing about Rangers and maybe in the reading of this you've gotten that point already. They don't seek glory. And they don't BS. They just tell it like it is, despite how it is.

And in this moment Crouse did just that.

"Man, Talk. I was smoked. I'll be honest. I was out of gas. Even my fumes were running on fumes."

He paused and worked some dip in as we sat there in the darkness, talking about what had happened. I knew there was more to this story. And I knew I was about to hear the really important part. Not the ending. Not the success. But the honesty. So I shut up and listened.

The standard. What he was saying was about the standard Rangers don't just try to meet. They live by it. They really do.

"You know how in RASP you learn the Ranger Creed and you think it's all…" said Crouse there in the dark of the morning as we waited for the next mission.

He didn't finish the sentence, but I think I understand. I'll just leave it at that.

Then he said the rest.

"The part that goes… Energetically will I meet the enemies of my country. I shall defeat them on the field of battle for I am better trained and will fight with all my might. Surrender is not a Ranger word. I will never leave a fallen comrade to fall into the hands of the enemy and under no circumstances will I ever embarrass my country."

When he said that… I had chills. Just ran up me as we sat there in the dark and he told me hero stuff without knowing he was doing so.

"You know that part?" he asked me.

I did.

"I was so tired that when the chief told me the plan… it felt like the biggest hill ever that I needed to climb. No— scratch that. The biggest mountain. Ever. Felt like Afghanistan after your sixth valley. Felt like what those Rangers faced on Anaconda going into QRF, the hajis firing on them. All uphill, nearly vertical, through waist-deep snow. Carrying all the ammo you can do and with no other way than upward to get through it all. We all know the story that happened that day. That's hero stuff. Everyone on that mountain. I never thought it would happen to me. But there it was, monsters coming out of the dark on us. Mercer hit bad. And an SF operator telling you, 'It's time to dig down, Ranger. This is what you boys is made for.'

"I was so tired, Talk, all I could do was nod. And I knew that part of the creed. Knew the whole thing. But I was so smoked all I could say to myself was… *energetically.* The first word, Talk. That's all I had in me. And that was everything and I never knew it before that moment. Told me what I needed to do now, right then. For whatever was left. I'd do it that way. I'd do it energetically, Talker."

What followed, from what I've been able to piece together, was a running gun battle through the streets of the old ruins surrounding the citadel.

Stott held an intersection they were getting pushed hard from. The demon orcs were flat-out chasing the QRF at that point. Some shaman appeared out of the darkness and fired blue lightning at them, hitting the chief and knocking him to the ground. He shouted for the rest to go on, grabbed Mercer off the ground with one heave, and started toward a building for cover once they got separated. He lobbed his last grenade and mag-dumped on the orcs to get them back while Gonzalez and Crouse continued on alone.

Gonzalez was a shooter. He was dropping orcs on the fly as they came out of the darkness, trying to cut them off. Two streets from Charlie staging position for the attack, Gonzales was black on mags.

One left.

They ran fast, pushing hard now just to move fast enough so they didn't have to engage. Arrows came whistling out of the darkness but missed.

Crouse was gasping raggedly as he carried the Javelin. Gonzales offered to take it. But as Crouse said, "I was so out of breath I couldn't even say yes to that, so I just kept carrying it." They were close and almost got lit up by the Rangers pulling security on the staging area.

They made it, Crouse handed off the Javelin, and three minutes later, an ad hoc force of Rangers advanced on Cathedral, smoked the shaman with the anti-armor fire-and-forget Javelin missile, then swept the objective, double-tapping the wounded orcs who hadn't fled yet.

It was full dark by then and the orcs were pulling back to the Mouth of Madness.

For a moment, the Rangers had a break in the action.

And Crouse's run would go down in Ruin Ranger history. Because I was putting it in the log. Telling whoever would listen what heroes do when you're all outta gas and surrounded. When your buddies need you. When it's no fail.

He'd live forever.

I like that.

CHAPTER EIGHTEEN

NIGHT fell deep and dark across the strange battlefield, and within the hour a chill cold began to wander the body-littered streets and ruined fighting positions where the Rangers had battled for their lives after gaining a toehold on shore.

Meanwhile, out to sea, intermittent gunfire could still be heard centered around the Head of Thezuz and *Sofia* anchored there. Kurtz and the weapons teams had not been dislodged, and of all the things I doubted, the rough Ranger NCO who'd failed me out of his Ranger School twice, was not one of them. He would not relent. They'd never take that rock.

Several of the black sails were on fire. One exploded dramatically, lighting up the night sky. We had no idea if more were joining the battle, but it seemed likely.

Up on the cliffs, the tribal jihadi orcs had disappeared into a sudden dust storm that had come up with the evening, consuming them in its brown billowing front. Sergeant Joe, holding the defense there at the Stones, remarked on how eerie the silence was once the orcs had pulled back and disengaged from the Ranger slaughter.

"Eerie if you don't count the wind in the Stones," he muttered to the Ranger junior enlisted faithful who attended to his hard-earned wisdom and made efforts to know it so they could Ranger at that level. "Makes me feel about as uneasy as my ex-wife used to three days after I got back from a pump. Joke's on her though—pretty sure I ain't comin' back from this one. So I don't gotta beat that PFC Tanner and make the same mistake three times in a row."

Tanner had married two strippers. But one of them twice. Hence three.

Or as the disciples of Sergeant Joe would tell you when pinching dip and imparting the lessons to me, "Spend no energy on what ya already done... good or bad. Spend it on what's in front of you. The good or bad that came before will catch up to you soon enough. Book of Joe, Ranger. Book of Joe."

The Rangers on the cliff were able to consolidate, get an accountability of those who'd come ashore with the boat hitting the rocks, then climb to the cliff to face the assaulting orc jihadis. Amazingly, there were no KIAs. Wounded, yes. But so far, the Rangers had hung in there and told the Grim Reaper to pound sand.

And the Angel of Death *had* pounded sand. But the feeling was, he hadn't gone too far off and was looking to get a sequel together along the lines of *Empire Strikes Back* where he wins and the plucky Rangers all buy it heroically.

The Rangers were fine with the ending if that's what it would be. But they had their own ideas about how the sequel would go, including strong ideas on the body count and the plot points therein.

That was straight from Sergeant Chris, who was a movie buff. Specifically, Tarantino.

Chief Rapp appeared carrying the badly wounded yet still-alive Mercer, having hunkered down inside an old library full of rotting scrolls and ancient candles long turned brittle with age. The orcs had made two serious attempts to dislodge the special operator from his hole inside the alcoves of the old scholarly place, but in the end, once the orcs pulled back as the evening shadows began to fall over the ruined city beneath the cliffs and the looming citadel, he'd left with Mercer over his shoulder and a lot of orc dead littering the floors. They'd come looking for him and had gotten a lot more than they bargained for.

He was Winchester on ammo, and down to his secondary. And still he was incredibly deadly. After that, he had his knife, six-foot-six of raw muscle, and an endless capacity for smiting those who would oppress, especially if the oppressed were under his medical care.

He took that personally. And it was the only time I ever saw him truly, righteously, angry.

There was still no sign of Captain Knife Hand and the assaulters, or the boat they had taken to pull the survivors of the wreck of Three Four Heavy out of the water. Some of the last Rangers to make it down to the LZ, in groups, informed the GFC that the captain had taken the boat farther west, following the currents that might have carried off some of the Rangers who'd gone into the water before the ship hit the rocks.

"If they got their gear in flotation mode and they just laid on their backs, then they have a good chance of surviving and being found farther up coast," noted Sergeant Thor. "Went helicopter surfing twenty miles off the coast of San Diego one time and missed my ride one night when the fog came in out there. Ended up in San Felipe. Some fishermen rescued me fifty miles out."

"But you had a surfboard then. They don't now," noted one of the Rangers.

Thor didn't say anything and kept working maintenance on *Mjölnir* while keeping a weather eye on the quiet front out there across the darkened half of this section of the old ruined city that lay beneath the pile of the citadel.

Then he replied after cleaning something that had bothered him within his weapon system. "Negative. Those waves are hundred-foot board-breakers out there. My board was cash after a wave I thought had to be one-twenty, maybe even one-thirty-five. Transponder got wrecked. I just inflated my wetsuit and laid back to enjoy the current."

Yeah, I thought to myself, standing watch with my NODs on, that woulda freaked me out that far out, that deep underneath you. No one in forever to come get you. Drifting into Mexico to get picked up by fishermen. And believe me, the irony wasn't lost on me that here I was inside a half-ruined cathedral to some long lost and weird god that looked like an octopus with swords in its tentacles stamped on the mosaic in the body- and debris-littered floor, way downrange, plan *canked*, and watching for monsters while I got my own plan ready for Sergeant Thor to greenlight me on going out there alone to find a contact that could get us some intel on how to ice Hoochie Mama.

It wasn't lost on me that I was about to suggest my own version of Thor's little extreme surfing adventure.

Hoochie Mama was a real-life medusa who could turn you to stone. And I'd pulled my psionic meditation trick for the week already. My head still hurt a little. And the trick was only good once every few days.

So I couldn't blind myself and still *see*, as it were. And I was not eager for a face-to-face. One glimpse, and that's that. But most likely I was gonna have to end up interrogating her, or at least translating for the command team, unless—and I'm really hoping for this one—the Rangers just smoked her early on and outright. Or managed to IED her like they did her sister. Even though I had mixed feelings about that, I wasn't particularly into engaging with another medusa. Felt like juggling nitroglycerin.

Day made if they whacked her, as far as I was concerned.

Listen, I know that sounds grim. But how many times in your life has *getting turned to stone* been a real live option in your work environment? Lately it had been a real possibility regularly for me on at least two pumps now.

I was full up on that.

I could use something else. Maybe death by instant poison. Or cursed to become a werewolf. Getting turned to stone… it just seemed a little too permanent for my taste.

Sergeant Thor got *Mjölnir* back together and approached me where I was keeping watch at the far end of the shattered cathedral.

I told him it was quiet out there and I'd seen nothing. Then…

"Sar'nt. Captain tasked me with going out there to gather intel on who we gotta kiss to get out of this. Hoochie Mama is our target, and best guess is she's holed up in that big chunk of stone across the bridge over there. Word is she's got a genie."

I paused to gather myself for my big ask.

In the pause, the hulking giant of a Ranger sniper prompted me with a quiet, "I copy that, Talker."

Meaning he understood the situation as I was laying it out thus far. And he probably did, having been a problem solver among an organization full of stoic problem solvers who didn't problem-solve lightly and usually did so with much forethought and care, being that anything anyone suggested was gonna get ripped to shreds intelligently in order to find the critical weakness that might get everyone, planner and participants, killed.

It's best to rip a plan apart, rather than getting ripped apart yourself.

The Rangers are problem solvers.

"Intel from the… mermaid…" There's me hesitating, not embracing the fantasy. *Embrace it, Talker,* I told myself. Otherwise, it's gonna kill someone. Maybe even you. "The mermaid indicates there's a local indig located nearby we can gather intel from that may give us a way to cross the bridge and approach the citadel to get the hit on Hoochie Mama."

"Are those things going to be a problem? Bridge and approach to high-value target?" asked Sergeant Thor sharply.

"Yeah, according to a chick that swims in the sea and collects shells when she's not singing hapless Rangers to their death in chorus with all the other mean girls in the undersea high school cheering mermaid squad… yeah. There are barriers, magical I'm guessing, to going direct and kinetic on Hoochie Mama in that tower over there." She hadn't said this last part, not in words. But I'd seen images in her mind that led me to believe this was the case. "And we're running low on ordnance as it is. We needed an anti-armor smart missile just to do that shaman whose head Herrera just stuck on a pole. We're gonna be dealing with that at least that same level of offensive and defensive magical power here. So unless someone gets a ship ashore, or we send Crouse down into the wreck of Three Four Heavy to get more gear in the middle of the night, then as this lowly private who was once just a PFC and is really a linguist figures it… we are low on kill sticks and other things that go boom. Is that right, Sar'nt?"

Thor muttered a, "I feel ya, Talker," as he watched something moving out there in the dark. Trying to see what it was and if he should kill it now, or later.

"Apparently, Sar'nt, this source, Kaffir, is this side of the river on an access road called the Street of Dreams. If I can locate him and get something valuable, maybe we can do this smarter and not harder. Let me go out there. I got the ring and I can move fast undetected, locate the source, and see if there's something to this. I think I know where the street is."

I didn't explain that I knew where the street was because I had seen it too. An image of it. In the mermaid's mind.

Psionics. It's the new GPS.

Thor remained silent. And I thought about what I'd just said. Perhaps I'd offended him with the *smarter not harder* part.

I didn't care.

Less dead of us, more dead of them. I bet there was something in the Book of Joe about omelets and eggs getting broken.

Less… Daredevils on the sand wrapped in their ponchos.

"Negative."

I kinda felt it was gonna go that way. I said nothing and just accepted the decision of my leader. I'd made my plan, offered it for consideration. A guy like Sergeant Thor who had more real-world experience than I did had made the call. I had to defer to that. That was how things got done in the regiment.

I was about to say *Copy that, Sar'nt* and just move on, when he spoke again in the silence of the night.

"You'll go out with a four-man Reaper Team. Herrera on point. Kang as lead tactical. Monroe in support. Get ready to move in ten. You'll do the operations order so they know what's up and what you're going out there to accomplish. Kang'll lead tactical movement to the source. Then you'll take over to collect. Interface with Kang now. You got this, Talker. It's your show, Private. RAH."

Rangers acting hostile.

CHAPTER NINETEEN

TEN minutes later we were on the move.

The operations order I'd learned in Ranger School, though most candidates already had that down before they showed up to RASP. Maybe that was why I sucked so much.

I'd given up on the notion that Kurtz had it out for me.

The truth was I was weak. I could see that now that I'd had time to consider where I didn't meet standard. That wasn't necessarily my fault. Most kids, because they're kids before they're soldiers, just eighteen-year-olds who've figured out early on through some guy they know who's been there and done that, they've figured out they wanna be Rangers. And they've taken the steps to get their shot. They've enlisted with a RASP agreement. They've done the PT work and learned as much as they can to be ready for just to get a shot at the show of getting selected for a battalion. In pre-RASP they get a master class in a lot of the things I missed. Mine was abbreviated because the situation was critical, what with the end of the world and all, and they needed me for their one-way trip to the other side of that end of the world.

But a kid going through RASP and then entering the Ranger battalion is going to learn how to patrol and lead patrols. That was something I'd pretty much gotten taken care of in and during. I'd tried to learn what I could, but it wasn't expected of the linguist, due to the situation. Normally yes. And In Kurtz's Ranger School, it occurred to me how many of the NCOs had been getting me up to speed all along ever since our arrival in the Ruin. Mentioning things. Informing me of standards. Applying those standards.

But still, Kurtz's school, it wasn't like being thrown into the fire after the frying pan. It was like dousing the frying pan in napalm and throwing it into a fire, then knocking over a fifty-gallon drum of gasoline to make matters more interesting. Oh, and did I mention there was C4 under the stones of the fire that Kurtz could detonate anytime he wanted.

That's Ranger School.

And I was weak on leadership. Op orders are a big part of that. I had to admit that and be honest about the situation as I got my gear together and we rallied for the Reaper mission to gather intel from a possible source deep inside enemy-held territory tonight.

It was a long day getting longer that now turned to a long night out there on the stalk. It would be heads-up ball with no room for failure.

The chill in the air was what we told ourselves was the reason for the mysterious fog bank that came up and covered the city as we got ourselves night-mission stalk ready. Stripping down all our gear to basic minimums for fast and quiet movement. Assault packs gone for everyone except Kang, who was carrying extra explosives and extra mags. Three mags for each of us except Monroe, who was draped in two extra belts for the sixty. Suppressors and night vision on thermal because of the fog.

The operations order, in my opinion, was weak, but not as weak as it could have been. I got it down and gave it out. That's what you do, and I did it in two minutes. Your mileage may vary.

"Here's what we gotta do tonight. Situation. Uh... we need to terminate Hoochie Mama. Developed intel says there's a local who can assist with more intel on how to get that done. Name's Kaffir. Mission. Locate that guy, Kaffir. Make Kaffir talk. Execution. Go forward on a stalk through enemy lines. Locate a house on a street near the river that intersects the city proper from the citadel on the other side. Locals call this the Mouth of Madness. There's a bridge nearby. Surround the house and I'll go in using the ring to see if... to assess..."

I had no idea what I was going to do. I just needed this whoever he was, Kaffir apparently, to talk.

"... to get intel. Use comm to get the information to the GFC and then..."

This is where it got lame. Or rather I got lame.

"RTB, then... I guess. Is that right?"

No one rolled their eyes.

Sergeant Kang in his controlled, quiet manner simply stepped forward and took control from there on. "Perhaps. Sometimes the intel we develop on-site might lead us to roll on another loc. So let's keep that in mind and be ready to exploit. Good brief, Talker. All right, here's how we're gonna move. Talker pointed out the location to me before the fog rolled in and I've got a route in mind. Sorry, no time for a sand table. No time for a map recon either because there ain't one. We move silent and engage only when necessary. Copy?"

Kennedy was busy re-memorizing his more powerful spells, which was a thing he had to do. But he would be available on the net to advise should we run into anything too weird, or too magical.

A few moments later we moved out beyond the perimeter just about twenty yards and hunkered down inside a small alley, listening to the night and getting acclimatized to its breath and silence. Sergeant Herrera was on point. Kang came second and ran the reap. Then me watching my sector on the flank and working the scan with my head on a swivel. And finally, Monroe on rear security.

We crouched there in the darkness after we'd left the Ranger perimeter around the cathedral. I turned around toward the dark part of the ancient stone alley we were acclimatizing in and caught sight of Specialist Monroe, forgetting for a moment that the Ranger had been revealed into a minotaur by the workings of the Ruin. He looked like a giant horned demon there in the darker part of the alley. Then I saw his muddied plate carrier, the draped belts of 7.62, and the wicked machine gun from back in the Vietnam-era of old-school bush fighting.

Most of the Rangers were pretty jealous he got to carry that beast of a weapon. I was too. It was pretty sweet.

"Can you see?" I whispered, because he had no night vision on.

He nodded once and put his massive hairy finger to his lips. Reminding me we were being quiet for the acclimatization of the patrol.

Once we were underway, getting ready and following Herrera down the alley, he came close, leaning down—he was eight feet tall now—and said, "I can see in the dark now. It's like night vision but way sweeter. K-man calls it

Darkvision. Plus, I can smell. Blood especially. Smells real sweet. Smells good. There's lots of it out there tonight. Lotsa orcs over there. I'll be honest. Makes me wanna tangle real bad."

K-man? Kennedy I guess.

He said all this in the basso rumble of what you'd think a wild beast would sound like if it could talk to you. And I'll be honest, it made the hairs on the back of my neck stand at attention. I was glad he was on our side, and I hoped we didn't meet any enemy minotaurs.

Herrera took us down a tight alley and through the ruins of a building whose walls were still standing. The roof had collapsed long ago but it had probably been made of some other material than stone. It was gone and the orcs had fought a battle here against a Ranger ambush.

Clearly it had gone badly for them. Real badly.

Before entering the place to cross over and through a crack in the wall that would lead us toward a north-south street we hoped would link up with the Street of Dreams, Sergeant Kang whispered into his subvocal throat mic.

"Watch the dead. Some could be playing possum. Don't need that right now."

Herrera went first and Monroe took up a position with the sixty to cover the crossing. He did not activate the targeting laser. Kang went next once Herrera had secured the other side of the crossing, and then me.

I moved fast and silently, something I was not bad at to begin with, and had gotten better at thanks to working with the Rangers for the better part of six months now in the hostile environment of the Ruin. I scanned the bodies of my dead, my eyes roving across their twisted and misshapen features, their bodies that had been ruined by explosions and gunfire. They snarled and gnashed their fangs permanently, setting their anger in the rictus of death until decay made all of us skeletons laughing in horror forever.

Good. Better them and theirs than me and mine.

I pulled security while Herrera moved through the crack and then checked the street we were going to cross through. Monroe gave me the tap and we were all accounted for. We moved through three more intersections, encountering dead orcs each time who'd been ambushed by sudden explosions they hadn't anticipated, or simply shot a whole bunch by concealed Rangers. Or done at distance by the snipers located around the Tower of Mermaids and other high positions they'd been able to attain and shoot from.

The fog was thick and silent in these areas as we got farther away from where much of the day's fighting had taken place. The calming whiteness floated ethereally across the strange buildings that were like no architecture we'd encountered in the Ruin so far. There was almost a weird off-kilterness to the patterns of the buildings, as though they were oddly and not always coherently laid out. Doors were never straight. Always crooked. The stones used were all odd sizes with no uniformity. More like they'd been selected for their oddness, then pressed down and crushed into place by some sheer magical force.

There was something in that. The whole place radiated a kind of tense and uneasy power that felt not just dangerous... but strange. Giddy. A giddy kind of madness was here. You could feel that in the air tonight.

Just before we reached the Street of Dreams closer to the Mouth of Madness, which we could now hear the rush of off through the blanketing fog, we encountered a strange creature.

It looked like a human. A human man. But with red skin and dark armor. And here was the weird thing. It had bat wings. Huge red bat wings. The look on its face was a cruel sneer as it scanned the street it moved along.

Herrera spotted it coming up that street. Slowly. Cautiously. A dark iron spear out. It scented the darkness and took a few steps at a time. Feral, but intelligent in its infernal armor.

Herrera alerted us to the target. We were stacked along a wall getting ready to make the Street of Dreams when we encountered this being. Whatever it was. It was like nothing we'd faced so far. And Sergeant Kang must have had the same thought because he looked back at me and whispered, "Call it in to Merlin."

I did.

"Merlin, this is Reaper. Be advised we've spotted a bad guy…"

Then I went on to describe the creature, hoping for some background we could put to use on how to deal with it.

There was a pause, and in the silence, Herrera noted the distance to target. Seventy-five meters. That was more than perfect for effective engagement range for all of us.

"Blood smells foul, but I don't mind," rumbled Monroe in the darkness. "Let me light him up with the sixty and let's see what that does to it."

Kang held up one gloved hand as we waited for Merlin to advise.

"Reaper, this is Merlin. That sounds like a cambion. Long story short it's a fiend-class monster. Pure evil. Its intentions would not be good and it's probably a good fighter. They're like… soldiers in hell."

Soldiers in hell. Oh, okay. That's not good. I don't speak Hell yet. Or what was it…? *Damnation.*

Sergeant Kang came back. "Merlin, are you saying this thing's the devil?"

Oh crap. We just met the devil out on the street and the Rangers are gonna wanna kill it. I just know it.

"No, Reaper," replied Kennedy. "It's *like* a devil, though I'm pretty sure the details don't matter considering the situation. They're fiends. Offspring of a demon and human female. Could be the other way I guess too. Anyway, it's not the devil. But… kinda… yeah, works for that operations group, speaking organizationally."

"Advise, please. Is this devil something we can kill kinetically?"

I could almost see Kennedy lowering his head, then rubbing the bridge of his nose over his RPGs. Getting ready to deliver the *I don't know if this place is the same as the game, guys* speech for the I've-lost-count-of-how-many-times-he's-told-us-this number of times.

But he didn't. He just sighed audibly over the channel.

"Yeah, sure. Go ahead, Reaper. In the game, demons are affected by metals like silver and cold iron. So yeah, shoot it. Kill it. GFC Thor says green light to do the devil."

We all looked at each other. Or rather, the Rangers all looked at me. Kennedy had said that last part as though he was basically saying *Fine, whatever, kill it.*

Out here in the dark beyond the wire, with a thing from hell advancing, that felt a little thin on the you-can-do-it-Rangers vibe.

That was the look Sergeant Kang gave me.

Herrera just muttered, "Really?" over our comm.

Monroe on the other hand rumbled, "All right, let's get it on," and I heard the click of the sixty's safety going off.

Okay.

We're really going to do this. We're gonna kill a devil. This might as well happen.

Kang nodded to Monroe to shift to the far side of the street and set up the base of the L for our ambush. Surprisingly the huge minotaur moved lightly across the street, hefting the light machine gun and belts quietly with a minimum of gear rattle as he switched position to anchor the attack.

"Monroe, once Herrera takes the shot, open fire if this thing doesn't go down. Private Talker, watch our six. Sergeant Herrera, once I put my hand on your shoulder, shoot this thing in the head. Make it clean."

That was Sergeant Kang's simple and effective plan made on the fly as the mission was introduced to a variable.

I hadn't been able to do that when I was leading a patrol in Kurtz's Ranger School. I'd ignored the new variable and continued on mission.

We'd all gotten dead a few minutes later.

Two minutes passed, and I watched the strange being walk into view. Coming down the street, advancing cautiously through the fog, dark iron spear ready and held in both hands. Clearly ready to fight. It looked like it knew what to do when it came to that, and I was expecting it to be crazy fast. Its movements were graceful almost. But confident like it had worn armor and fought in countless battles both weird and hellish.

Its eyes glittered cruelly in the darkness and fog as it scanned the streets. Its face was handsome in that spoiled trust fund rich kid movie star way. But yeah, the skin was pure flame-red, as were the folded bat wings rising out of its back. Its armor was better than anything I'd ever seen worn by the enemies we'd fought in the Ruin so far.

I didn't see Sergeant Kang place his hand on Herrera's shoulder. Just heard the *clack* of the suppressed shot through EarPro.

I watched the top of the skull of the cambion—I have to get a class on that one, or maybe on fiends in general, from Kennedy—but I watched the top of the skull just disappear and turn to red mist as the body of the thing pitched forward and fell dead in the street.

Well, that was easy. For once.

We waited in the silence and then Kang put in a call to Kennedy.

"Merlin. Tango eliminated. Advise... do we... touch this thing?"

Good call, I thought. We'd probably get cursed. And I was pretty sure it'd be me doing the sensitive sight investigation.

"Negative, Reaper. I'd stay on mission. But your call."

Kang was a Ranger of all business. He didn't need to know the bigger questions. He'd been ordered to get this team to the source intel and collect. Random variables in the mission that didn't specifically point toward yield weren't important to him.

Then a thought occurred to me.

Oh crud. What if *this* is the source? What if this was Kaffir?

"What?" asked Sergeant Kang as I went blank for a moment. We were ready to move out down the Street of Dreams. At the end was the Mouth of Madness, and she'd said, the mermaid Allandria, that this Kaffir, whoever he was, lived near the Mouth. We were still a good quarter mile was my guess from the Mouth, as I could see the city in my head from when we'd been able to see it before the night and the fog.

I tried to use my psionics. Tried to study the corpse of the devil in the street. Tried to get some giant stay-away from this guy's signal. As in a *Do Not Poke Dead Body With Stick* image. Nothing.

But my gut told me this wasn't Kaffir. When she'd spoken the name *Kaffir*, I'd gotten another image. It was of something that wasn't what it was supposed to be. Clearly the dead thing in the street was what it was. A dead devil lying in the street that had been shot by Rangers.

Bet you didn't think that was gonna happen when you got up on the wrong side of the bed in hell this morning. But hey, life comes at ya fast, as they say.

Sometimes you're the bug. Sometimes you're the windshield. So sayeth the Book of Joe.

In the brief image I could barely remember, I'd seen a dark figure when she'd used the name Kaffir. A dark figure putting on a coat, and becoming... Tanner?

Except not. But that's how psionics had explained it to me. Make of that what you will.

"Nothing," I told Kang. "Let's get back on mission."

The Ranger sergeant studied me briefly for a quick moment, then nodded to himself. Then we were on the Street of Dreams, making our way down its length. The minotaur Ranger tapped me on the back and rumbled breathily.

"Killed the devil, didn't get the T-shirt, man."

CHAPTER TWENTY

THE house of the rakshasa named Kaffir lay near the Mouth of Madness. Because why wouldn't it? I had no idea demonic entities could also be shape-changers, it would have been nice if somebody would have told us that, but all we had was a name to go on as we made the approach to the intel source that might give us a clue on how to smoke Hoochie Mama and get back on mission. Later, Kennedy would fill us in on what a rakshasa was. Or rather, what it really wasn't.

The Mouth of Madness was the great inlet from the sea that bisected the ancient city of Atlantea. The rush of the water sounded like a great roaring monster that would never be satisfied. There was something in that sound of endless unfulfillment that bothered your soul in the night as we scouted the location and got ready to go for it. We'd identified Kaffir's residence after smoking two orc patrols in the district. The orcs were holding the river, but closer to the coast and directly lined up against the Rangers at their position centered around Mermaid Tower.

What the orcs didn't know was the Rangers were all over their flanks and probing to figure out disposition of forces. Yes, there would be a big fight in the morning, or at least sometime tomorrow, but the Rangers would definitely not be where they were expected to be when the time to exchange harsh words and gunfire began in earnest to see who the king was of this particular little hellhole.

We eliminated two patrols with suppressed weapons as we scouted the block around Kaffir's dwelling there by the river that opened up into the bay and the sea. Neither fight was fair. Which is the way it's supposed to be.

"Fair's for the movies," grunted the minotaur, swapping in a new belt and blowing on the glowing suppressor. "They can run, but they'll just die tired."

Through the fog we could see the monolithic citadel rising up into the gloom of the late night we were out and about in. It was close to midnight now. At midnight I was going into the location to see what could be seen, and to hear what could be heard.

The elimination of the orc patrols hadn't been silent. Whoever was in the house we'd identified as Kaffir's had to be aware of it. The orcs around their bonfire camps to the north, in the streets before the bridge that threw itself over the Mouth, were aware as well. They sent another patrol, their version of a quick reaction force, to find out what had happened to their buddies.

They found out.

Monroe hosed them good and long when they tried to break and run from Herrera and Kang's ambush.

Me, I swept and double-tapped.

After that, the demon orcs back at the bonfire didn't seem much interested in finding out anymore. They'd found out all day. Now they were content to turtle and watch their fires, chanting like demonic Gregorian monks.

That last bit was oddly disconcerting.

Every time you caught hints of it in the distant night, coming down the alleys and not smothered by the thickness of the foggy mist, it made you feel like you needed to be home soon. Like when you were a kid and the street-lights had come on. Why wasn't your mom calling? It was dark now. It was past time for you to be home from playing in the park that afternoon that had turned to evening so suddenly because you hadn't noticed it amid all the fun you were having. And the friends you usually played with, they had gone home, and now there were strange, older kids here you'd never played with before there in the darkness around you. You couldn't quite see them clearly, just hear their older, more dangerous voices. They had something they wanted to show you, in the dark, down by the train tracks. Why not go see it with them?

And why wasn't your mom calling you home?

I know, that bit's a little poetic and all, or, I don't know what the writer word is. But that's the feeling you got when you caught weird snatches of what the demon orcs were chanting out there in the night around their bonfires that would burn till dawn.

What you heard made you feel that way.

Kang and Herrera were reconning the block, making sure it was cool for me to go in while Monroe and I waited inside the debris of what had clearly once been a temple to some bizarre shark god.

"Musta been crazy for gods," rumbled Monroe in the shadows as we watched the street. "Half the buildings we been through here are some kinda holy place."

"Agree," I said noncommittally and unlike myself. You know, I am called Talker for a reason. I blame it on the coffee I didn't have. I'd drained my last bit of the good stuff post-mermaid, just to get the brutal aftereffects of the mind meld out of my head. And to wash down the Ranger Candy.

And because, if I was gonna die, then no sense in leaving any coffee undrunk.

Except I hadn't died.

And now I didn't have coffee.

I'd even hit my two emergency freeze-dried packets I'd been holding back after the fight at the cathedral.

Now I sat quietly in the darkness of the shark god temple not being me. Watching for something to light up and trying to figure out how I was gonna get intel out of someone, or something, called Kaffir. Sounded Arabic. If it spoke one of those dialects, then I was good there and we could do communication.

Monroe tapped his can of dip and held it out to me.

This might as well happen, I thought. Then took some.

It ain't coffee. But it's something when it's dark and the night feels dangerous.

We had no idea it was a rakshasa before we went into the source location. Kennedy would tell us that later. And even then we had no idea what a rakshasa was. But we had the location. It was the only place on the street in the weird gloomy graveyard of a city that had lights on at this time.

A place that seemed occupied, a dwelling, in the middle of a long-ago ruined city overrun by orc tribes and under the thrall of some medusa in a tower across the river.

That it was occupied and lit at this time of night like it was just some other dwelling with residents still watching TV late in the night in an ordinary town or village, was odd.

The light coming from within was almost cozy. Especially when you're sitting in the dark with a gym-bro minotaur Ranger who keeps snuffling and scenting the wind and talking about blood while cradling his death-machine M60.

And there's no coffee and you're working some dip instead.

And to me... on that other level of psionics and feeling and intuition... call it what you will... it felt like the place where a *Kaffir* would live.

I just had the feeling it was.

Kang gave me the all-clear, and for a moment, just before I went in, I could feel something out there in the darkness, watching us.

Something dangerous.

I didn't say anything. Why? Because right now everything is dangerous here in the ruins of Atlantea and the Ruin in general. How was this thing I could barely sense any different than all the other dangerous things here in the Ruin. How could I tell everyone and not sound like a freak to the Rangers?

Specialist Monroe was already creeping us out with the blood talk.

I crossed the street and just... knocked on the door. That's the plan. Good call on making me the battlefield intel collection asset, Sergeant Major. That's the kinda pro-level secret squirrel spy stuff you get from Talker when he doesn't have coffee.

Coffee would have given me a cool plan.

Instead... knock knock.

Good evening. Sorry to bother you so late. Tell me how we can kill Sultria, if you don't mind? Hope you're not on her side and all.

Yeah. We coulda breached and cleared on this guy. Monroe was all for blasting our way in, hog-tying Kaffir, and getting some answers the hard way. Truth be told, the other Rangers were too. Kang and Herrera had each proposed lesser themes on Specialist Monroe's bullish charge, pardon the pun. He's a minotaur. They're half bull. Get it?

But I suggested we do it this way.

"Why?" Kang asked after hearing my plan.

"Because this Kaffir, whoever he is, seems to do… business here despite what goes on here, before we showed up, and even now. Business with the mermaids. The orcs leave him alone. And he does have some kinda relationship with Hoochie Mama. So he's probably some kinda non-player in the events. If he was on their side, he woulda come out to fight us already. Instead, the lights are on, and I can smell…"

I smelled coffee.

And food.

But hey… *coffee.*

There's a meme going around among the Rangers where it's Leonardo DiCaprio in *Once Upon a Time in Hollywood* watching TV with a beer and a smoke, leaning forward and suddenly pointing at the TV. They use it for a bunch of things. Like one Ranger used it to make a meme on his smartphone basically saying, *When you spot the giant you did with the Carl G on the sweep.*

I could use that DiCaprio image right now based on me smelling coffee. It would be spot-on.

I spit my dip out as I crossed the street, telling myself it was because I needed to talk now and I couldn't be working a pinch of dip. But really there was coffee in there, I could smell it, and hey… you never know. Amirite?

My mom used to say every day to get me going when I was little, *Hey, maybe you'll get to ride an elephant today.*

Coffee is my elephant.

I'm a simple man.

"I'll leave my mic on. You listen in. I'll try to talk to this guy. If it does go bad, you come in then."

Kang agreed to that, and we went with the plan. Me going in to get coffee. I mean, me trying the friendly approach with the intel source.

I knocked on the door, and then Sean Connery told me to, "Come in, Talker."

You know the voice. Sounded exactly like that.

Okay, that's odd, I said to myself as I stood there staring at the door I'd just knocked on.

I cast one quick look back at the Rangers stacked on the other side of the street and ready to breach and clear to get me out of there.

Then I made the wrong decision to go in, thinking I could do my talking thing and get us something to go on. Earn my place in the Rangers by doing it my way and trying to show how extra-special I am. I'm pretty sure that's why Kurtz kept recycling me. Not 'cause I do that, but 'cause I think it. Because it's my motivation for trying so hard. And Ranger purist that he is, that's not good enough.

He's right. I know that now. The Purple Abyss taught me that.

The door opened and I didn't push on it to get it to do that. It just did.

Creepy, man.

Golden firelight washed out over me and into the dark and foggy street I was standing in. Inside I could see ornate Middle-Eastern-style cast brass bowls and eastern pottery, delicate and filled with unknown herbs. Small cages with sleeping birds hung from the ceiling. Richly woven rugs lay on the floor. Fine tapestries on the walls depicted ancient scenes of other races we had not encountered here in the Ruin.

It was like some… fantastic curiosity shop from another age when adventurers wandered the world looking for the curious and bizarre.

Like I said, Sean Connery told me to come in. That's what the rakshasa's voice sounded like. The old James Bond actor, Sean Connery. I once had a colleague at a language department who could do a dead-bang impression, despite the fact he was native-born Mandarin Chinese.

Do you see the beast, Miss Moneypenny, he'd say. And slay everyone.

"Come, come, Talker. Come in out of the cold and the night," begged the rakshasa I was staring at with my mouth pretty wide open.

Every time you think the Ruin is weird, it says *hold my beer.*

I was talking to Captain Knife Hand, but wearing silk robes and smoking a pipe. A man-tiger standing in the room, speaking like Sean Connery, had been expecting me.

Buy the ticket, take the ride, Tanner would have said.

If that main don't open wide, I got a reserve by my side. If that one should fail me too… look out world, I'm a-comin' through, the black NCOs would cadence call in jump school for the morning run.

It felt like that. Walking through that door into the den of the rakshasa.

If that one should fail me too… look out world I'm a-comin' through.

CHAPTER TWENTY-ONE

IT wasn't Captain Knife Hand.

But it was that same kind of were-tiger form. Half man. Half human. A deadly killer wearing red silk robes. And smoking an ornate brass pipe.

He stood in front of me there within the room, tiger arms open wide and beckoning me to come in and out of the cold night.

Like some grandfatherly gentleman glad you have arrived even if the hour is so late.

The switch from *Dude we almost flash-banged your house and went in shooting* to *Cheerio, my good fellow* was a little jarring. But pro that I am… I dealt.

"Come, come, come in now, Talker. You are safe here," he lied. Everything the rakshasa said was a lie. I know that now, unfortunately. Wish I'd known it then.

We'd have had a drone overhead by dawn. Now that comm was back up, the Air Force crew back at FOB Hawthorn was able to get our version of a Global Hawk up. Couple of AGMs would have done the trick on this cat. We should have just hit the place with an airstrike. But that's hindsight. And it's always twenty-twenty.

I entered because… what else?

"How…" I started off like a pro. Not.

"… do I know your name, Talker? Well, where I come from… let's just say they've begun to talk about you a lot. Don't let it go to your head, my dear boy. But… there have been conversations… regarding you. Events are shaping, one may say, if I say so myself. There's been much discussion regarding what to do about you, in particular."

Well that's just creepy.

"I suspect you met Abomnabusbus out there tonight, out there in the streets perhaps? Chap with the wings. Looks like your representations of the devil?"

I said nothing.

The tiger-man in silk robes scented the air as the door closed, as though looking for something. His cat's eyes closed for a moment and the effect was unsettling in that it conveyed he feared me not in the least.

And then his yellow eyes went wide. Just for a moment. He did not have the same *tyger tyger burning blue* eyes as the captain. His were more… *a demon's dreaming,* as Edgar Allan Poe might have written.

"I see I will no longer have the company of that particular fiend. Which is for the best as now a small debt has been dispensed with for the moment. I sent him out to… welcome you. But I see that you and your friends across the way have slain him, as your kind is wont to do rather excessively."

Kang was in my ear.

"How does this guy know English, Talker?"

Obviously, I couldn't respond.

"You seem to know a lot, Kaffir…" I prompted.

The rakshasa smiled slyly.

"Why yes, I do. And you are correct, I am Kaffir. At your service, Talker of the Rangers. I know why you are here and… I am all for it. Death to Sultria! The time has come, and I stand ready to assist you in any way I can."

"And how can you do that?" I asked.

The tiger moved over a giant brass urn, took up a delicate cup, and filled it with coffee.

Oh boy! my mind screamed.

And then psionics, or whatever, warned me that it was probably poison. Or at the least… to be careful.

The rakshasa purred as he set the cup down on a low and ornately carved teak table between us.

"Clever boy," he murmured when I didn't reach for it and instead adjusted my sling, flexing my fingers on the pistol grip of the MK18 carbine. Indicating I too could be dangerous, in that all it would take was for me to lift the barrel with my left hand as my whole body went into a shooter stance, thumb flicking the safety and landing the red dot right on his furry chest poking out from the crevice of the ornate silk robes, swirling with patterns of delicately stitched Chinese-style dragons.

I thought of the sorcerer HVT we'd first done. On my first Reaper. And the shape-changer that had been operating nearby.

Doppelgänger.

Shape-changer.

Why was my mind firing on that as the upright tiger speaking English in a deep Scottish accent offered me coffee and help?

If I was Spider-Man, then my Spidey sense would be tingling. Right?

"I'll be… *honest* with you," the tiger said. Softly. "Kaffir plays the game for himself. The medusa, Sultria, the one who controls the power Al Hallu, she plays for a team. And it isn't yours, dear boy. I, shall we say, *set up shop* here twenty years ago with one purpose in mind. Long have I schemed and bargained. I've been fair in my dealings with her, and others, to obtain what she possesses. And try as I might... I have not. Then along come you lot with all your weapons from the Before. Out of time and out of luck, falling into the hands of the first charlatan to come along and tell you grand lies about even grander struggles and oh, all the good you could do if you'd just go off a-questing with that old fool. Fine. The affairs of men and monsters don't affect me, nor do they concern... me.

"Let's just say I am a collector. Of sorts. And there's something I want. And that thing I want, want very badly to possess, and here's me being completely honest with you, Talker of the Rangers, is within reach now that you've shown up. So of course I mean you no harm—because your interests coincide with mine. And now, if you'll let me show you..."

He took a long pull on his ornate brass pipe and fragrant smoke flooded the room.

Instantly I felt... warm and fuzzy. I wanted to like this... old, comfortable... cat.

I considered biting my tongue. Literally. But that would stop me from doing my most very special trick that makes me Talker and lets me try to Ranger at the introductory level.

Speak languages.

So don't bite that to get some good old clarifying pain, I told myself.

But I could tell, immediately, that the coffee was a trick to... dominate me. Drugged, probably. And the smoke was the next trick to disarm me. Make me more suggestible.

Kennedy would later tell us the rakshasa monster in his game was really a devil from the nine hells and that they tried to dominate their victims for grand schemes. But I didn't know that at the time. I just knew someone was trying to sell me that off-post-car-lot used Camaro at twenty-three-percent interest with my enlistment bonus down.

That the stripper in the club was selling me the fantasy in exchange for the big PX in the sky.

And to be fair, despite all I'd been through in the last six months with the US military's most elite fighting force, I had not actually had those experiences. But I had heard about them extensively enough to understand the hard sell and ill intentions that came with it.

Plan number one was to bite my tongue so hard my eyes watered. But hey… Talker do languages, need tongue.

Plan number two was to pull my knife and stab my exposed arm a little. A nice cut to get some clarity. But that's… crazy.

I felt my mind slipping into a dangerous complacency I knew I couldn't control. I needed…

True story. Wanna know what helps you really concentrate as though your life depends on it, 'cause it does?

Grenades. Live ones.

I pulled my last one from my carrier, held it up in front of the rakshasa just so my blurring rose-colored-vision eyes could see it, moved my other hand through cotton candy syrup, and pulled the pin.

I was wide awake now as I told myself to do two things.

One, keep a real tight grip on the spoon because right now Mr. Grenade was not my friend and the spoon was the only thing keeping him from losing his temper in a really explosive way.

And two, hold the pin because I was gonna need that.

And hells yeah, I was wide awake. Big bigga.

Live grenades'll do that, Talk, I could almost hear Tanner telling me.

I was back in control… and holding a live grenade.

"Ya wanna get crazy… Kaffir?" I said, trying to remember his name as the fugue of his narcotic smoke cleared from my mind, driven away by the overload of adrenaline I'd just spiked my system with. "Then let's get crazy."

I said that last part low and deadly like I knew what I was doing.

If you can't make it, then fake it. Amirite?

It was stuff like this that pissed Kurtz off.

LOL.

"No," purred the tiger-man rakshasa with a hesitancy and caution that hadn't been apparent in our conversation so far. "I am not interested in… getting crazy… as you put it. I was offering…"

"You're trying to drug me. Trying to control the outcome to solve for what you want!"

Hey, I'm still holding that live grenade, and even though my mind is high-mountain-lake-ice-water-plunge clear, the rakshasa is slowly fading from view. Turning invisible like I can with the ring, which, because I'm holding a live grenade, I can't put on.

Didn't think of that.

"Oh, that," pshawed the rakshasa in silk robes. His essence now nothing but fragrant smoke, smelling of jasmine and sandalwood. "I do apologize if that means anything to you. I was just… soooooo hoping we could work together to get the things we both want."

"And what do we want, Kaffir?"

I kept holding that live grenade, turning round and round to find out where he was speaking from now that he'd turned invisible.

"Talker, we're stacking by the front door. Stand by." Kang in my ear.

Something hit the roof. Heavy, but light. Was that him? The rakshasa?

But then I heard Kaffir speak from over in a corner. Or at least that's where I thought he was as I pivoted fast with the live grenade. My hands were getting sweaty inside my assault gloves and, to be honest, starting to shake.

"Ah… a new player has entered the game," murmured the rakshasa almost to himself.

So, to sum up. Rangers stacking at the door with automatic weapons.

Invisible demonic tiger in the room.

And… something on the roof.

"Don't worry about your… friends, Talker. They'll never get through a held door."

And just like that, all the lights went. The fire. The many candles.

Darkness.

And me holding a live grenade.

My plan didn't seem great at that point.

CHAPTER TWENTY-TWO

THE room had just descended into a blue darkness when the loud blows against the outer door started. I was assuming Monroe had gone into extreme door-kicker mode. Probably Kang and Herrera stacked on opposite sides of the frame ready to move in, pie the room, and hopefully not shoot the guy holding a live grenade.

Some distant part of my mind told me I should probably warn them about that.

I had a feeling also that the rakshasa wasn't in the room anymore, but suddenly I was aware that something else was. Something... dangerous.

"Don't move, Talker," growled Captain Knife Hand. His voice low and deadly. And yeah, my heart flat stopped, or at least took a giant skip across the Grand Canyon. "He's still here. Can smell him. Don't move. Hang on to that grenade, Ranger."

Monroe continued to beat on the door. It didn't seem like it was making much difference.

And I was worse than useless. I was a threat, what with the live fragmentary explosive in my gloved hand.

Might wanna do something, I told myself, if I was ever going to see those mosquito wings.

I heard Santago's voice then. Pulling me out of the Purple Abyss. Telling me, "You're made for something better than avenging whores, Talk-ir."

Reminded me as he tried to stitch the cut I'd received. "You owe me, Talk-ir. Go make the Ruin a better place. Succeed where an old hidalgo like myself has failed."

Hidalgo.

He called himself something I never would have thought. A term usually reserved for lower nobility. Also meaning *son of someone*.

Santago was a sailor. A competently gifted, drunken wanderer of all the ports the Ruin has to offer. Not usually the profession someone associates with the word *hidalgo*.

I'd thought that was odd then. But I'd been in too much pain from the cut. And the booze.

Go make the Ruin a better place, Talk-ir.

"What is it that you want, Kaffir?" I asked the silence of the room where the rakshasa might not even be anymore.

There was a long pause, and then a slowly growling chuckle from what might have been another room. But wasn't.

"Never you mind, Ranger. Now with your beast leader in control, and isn't that funny? You really don't know half the story about him. I'll get what I've come for, Talker. But I didn't lie to you when I told you we both need the medusa dead to depart this place. And so… before your captain finds me… I'll tell you what to do."

Captain Knife Hand was moving through the room. The door was taking a hammering. Even though it was probably magically held, the door itself, Monroe's ferocious kicks were shattering the frame around it. They'd get through in a moment.

"She'll use the djinn to destroy you," said the tiger. Kaffir. "And the djinn will do precisely that. I tell you no lies. Al Hallu can wipe you from the face of the Ruin and make it so you never existed. There are things you don't trifle with, and he... he is one, Talker. Go for the citadel in the morning. Bring it down with your powerful explosions and you will crush her within. But face the djinn... and you will die. That's all I can give you. And yes, Talker... and the one you call Knife Hand... yes, I think we will meet again."

Now his voice was far away. As though fading into another reality.

"I would bet on that, Rangers. Most assuredly, I would wager everything on a reckoning betwixt you and me. Powerful forces are aligned against you. And that will be interesting to watch, after having bested me in this encounter and gotten what you wanted at no charge... pleasant for Kaffir of the nine hells. Pleasant indeed."

Then he was gone.

The door shattered.

The Rangers didn't kill me.

And slowly, very slowly, with a concentration I thought beyond possible, I threaded the pin back into the spoon.

And disarmed the grenade.

CHAPTER TWENTY-THREE

WE linked up with the captain and made our way back to the Ranger lines. It was close to oh-two-hundred in the morning at that point. The captain assumed command of the ground force and called a quick meeting between all leaders for thirty minutes later at the CP inside Mermaid Tower.

While preparations for that were underway, the captain took me aside.

"Private Talker, I heard most of what the intel source had for you. Sounded like we were being played. Is that your assessment?"

"Definitely, sir. He was holding back on us, and it was clear what he wants us to do for him. We were being manipulated. Minimum. The question that's been bugging me, sir, on the way back is… Do the source's wants coincide with our needs like he was trying to indicate? For me that's the question, and thinking about what he told us, sir, if I were planning the next op… that kinda determines things going forward for us, as in what we do next."

And I didn't add *but that's me, low-level private who got recycled from the combat leaders' course of Ranger School. Twice even, sir.* Like I wanted to.

I was learning how to Ranger by at least keeping some things to myself, occasionally.

"So what's the deal then, Talker?" asked the captain matter-of-factly.

He'd changed. He was no longer the tiger that had scared the living daylights out of me in the rakshasa's den. On the way back, following Herrera, he'd changed back into a graying, almost middle-aged combat leader who carried the weight of everything on his shoulders and was determined to accomplish the mission and walk away with as many Rangers as he could.

I don't think he ever asked himself why. Why try to save everyone. There was no home to go back to. I think keeping his men alive was just a bodily function. No... no that's not right. That sells him short. It was like a calling. That's what it was. Like... a religion for him. Keeping everyone alive. And maybe that's what I lacked as a leader.

I didn't know.

I just knew that some people are different than the rest of us. And we call those people heroes. Sometimes.

Heroes are the ones, enlisted and officer, and sometimes the two-DUI private with the two stripper ex-wives, who put everyone else first when the hammer falls.

Say what you want about officers. There are good ones. And Knife Hand... he was good. He was heroic. At almost three in the morning with death in the wind and full dark glaring you in the face and daring you to walk into it just one more time, he was doing his best to give his Rangers a killing chance.

Even if that meant wringing the stupid linguist for some vital detail that might just save us all. Even if the linguist didn't believe in himself after the Purple Abyss.

He looked tired. Knife Hand did. That look of every commander. Too much mission, too little me to spread around to make sure you get the best possible chance on the objective. And here's how desperate the situation really was: he was asking me to assess. He was hoping there was something I had, and maybe I didn't even know it, that we could all use to walk away from this one.

We needed the smaj here, that's what I was thinking. It was always murder-thirty inside the smaj's West Texas heart. Or Chief Rapp, but he was busy with the wounded. The Rangers weren't beaten. They'd had a long day, yeah, and there were wounded. And there were dead. But the Rangers in the darkness and the wet fog, ignorant of fatigue and hunger and cold, were busy like they were getting ready to go out again right now and meet the enemy... *energetically*. I was hoping for fifteen minutes to brew the old you-know-what. Even twelve, universe. I could do it in twelve. Gimme ten. Lemme just crush some beans and swallow 'em down with seawater. Please.

But the Rangers, the studs all around me, even if there wasn't a frago, they could smell one coming in the night as sure as they could smell the orcs a few streets over. The only thing they were hoping for was the order to go on the offense and run major amok with as much ammo as they could carry.

In the end, that is the unspoken paragraph of every Ranger op order. Once it goes to hell... screw it. Let's break stuff.

About that time, right as the captain and I were talking, the first of the enemy catapults across the river started firing on us. We heard the low *thooooonggggg* of the weapon's release far away, out over the city and across the Mouth of Madness.

Then the giant flaming missile came in and exploded.

Thor was in the tower immediately, alerting the captain to the incoming indirect fire and assessing what he thought was going on.

"Late in the day, sir, we saw them bringing disassembled siege engines up under the citadel. Musta got 'em ready and are firing into the fog on best-guess last-known positions. Suggest we shift the TOC to locations they aren't considering as primary targets. Let's move down to the beach, sir."

"Agreed, Sergeant Thor. We'll shift the new op order in eighteen minutes to there. Let everyone know we go at first light. Cowboy is coming in with both ships, *Sofia* under tow to support. We'll link up the other side of the bridge. I'll have the full plan in seventeen minutes."

Then we hustled out of the tower under incoming fire. The giant shots were like balls of fire coming down through the misty gloom of the fog and then splashing all over an area in sudden explosions of flames and debris. The aim was bad, and the general consensus was we were in no real danger. Still, every Ranger watched the sky as the next incoming shot sailed in, often overhead, all of us ready to run a short distance to get away from the next impact point.

Once the captain and I were on the beach he turned to me once more.

"Go," he ordered without ceremony.

I'd had enough time to figure out what I wanted to say in the shift to a new CP location, now a patch of sand not far away from Daredevil's still, poncho-wrapped body. Two other Rangers had joined him since to lie there in the sand, but I didn't know right then who.

"I asked Kennedy for a quick sketch on what he thought this monster was," I began. "One of the adjectives he used

241

stood out to me, sir. Rakshasas are liars. Deceivers. Supposedly they are spirits from hell. But your mileage may vary on that, sir, depending on your system of belief. So, we could say we got nothing of value from source. Or we could use induction to reverse-navigate what he said, and then make our decisions based on that."

The captain rubbed the bridge of his nose and sighed.

"Do the work for me and I'll follow, Private."

I nodded.

"Roger that, sir. Okay, what I got is he wants the medusa dead. So do we. Okay. He wanted to make sure we were aimed right at her. Second thing he wanted was to protect the thing he told us not to mess with once we attacked Hoochie Mama. He was real clear about that and went to great lengths to make the point. Big problems. *You'll most certainly die, Rangers.*"

"And what was that thing, Talker?"

"The djinn, sir. He said it would flat-out smoke us even though he knew we—you Rangers are real killers. He—"

"Lemme stop you right there, Private. You're a Ranger. You're a killer and expected to be to meet standard. You got that scroll. That's what you do. Proceed."

"Copy, sir. Okay... he wants us to stay away from the djinn and not engage. Go for the kill. But... source said he was here for... *something*. And I'm guessing... if I use what we all know about genies and magic lamps... well, I'm betting he wanted the lamp, or whatever the djinn comes in. That's what he's here for, and source doesn't want us to mess that up. Kaffir wants us to smoke the medusa so it can run off with the genie, sir.

"So what we do, sir, is what he doesn't want us to do. We jack up the djinn hardcore. Instead of ending up trying to go for medusa and getting surrounded, and maybe even killing our primary jackpot on this location… we take out the guard dog. According to Kennedy and Vandahar, a djinn, or efreet, whatever this thing is, has the powers to stop us. That's what she, Hoochie Mama, has been using. So we kill it, and we stop her. As I see it, sir. It makes no sense just to bypass her most valuable asset to go for her in a hardened position. Not outgunned and low on ammo and resupply as we currently are."

"So…" said the captain slowly.

I finished because I'm me and that's why guys like Kurtz hate my guts.

"So we smoke the djinn, and Hoochie Mama is powerless going forward. She's just got orcs. Those aren't going to stop us from getting out of the location and back on mission. And smoking the djinn actually opens up shipping traffic out of Portugon, so we can get a resupply from the Forge if someone takes a ship back, meets a shipment in Portugon, and links up with us farther toward the insertion point. Sergeant Major said the djinn controls the weather. It brings the storms. It causes the shipwrecks. It *is* La Desprezada. Stop it, and the medusa can't use it to keep us here. Stop it, and this place is just a wide spot on the highway no one stops at anymore."

Twenty minutes later I was in the operations order down by the surf. It was simple. This was the plan of attack. Before dark, the Rangers on land were going to be breaking into two teams. Assault and support. The assaulters would enter the water, in the ocean, near the Mouth of Madness and cross over to the other side to secure the new LZ for the incoming ships, which would need at least an hour to thread the wreckages of the bay and make the landing at the new LZ. At the same time, the support element would take the bridge, pushing through the orc forces on the ground this side of the river. Then we'd pretend to get held up this side of the bridge while the assaulters and the Rangers coming in by ship secured the LZ on the far side of the Mouth, basically now in the enemy rear in front of the citadel. On the beach and three hundred meters from the citadel, weapons teams would support the attack. The hope was that the enemy commander would freak out and deploy all forces against the flanking attack from the beach there, and with forces drawing away from the bridge, the support element on the bridge could move forward and load the bridge up with explosives to cut off any orc haji force coming down out of the hills to try and counterattack our rear.

And then it would be up to Vandahar and Kennedy to engage the djinn and banish him. Which, in conferring with the wizard aboard Cowboy's galley, was possible, though difficult. If the Rangers kept the harrying forces off the wizard, it could be done. The Rangers, if everything worked, would have all their enemies flanked from two directions, with intersecting fire set up on the base of the citadel, which was where the battle with the djinn was expected to take place, in that it would attempt to defend its jar, a giant brass bowl set out in front of the towering structure.

That was where the magic would happen. Literally.

Captain Knife Hand said we were hitting the bridge at dawn. We'd secure the bridge, the assaulters would link up with the smaj's two boats full of weapons teams and ammunition, and then we'd hit the djinn when it came out to play.

I was going with the assaulters. Assigned to Sergeant Joe's team to set the explosives to deny access to a counter-attack.

It was on.

CHAPTER TWENTY-FOUR

I was going to leave.

I was going to walk away from the Rangers and the pump we were going on. Back in Portugon. I'd found something… someone else.

Something I could lose myself in to make the pain go away. If not forever, then maybe just for a little while.

So it's confession time. I told you I'd get to it. Warts and all with one hour to go before we hit the bridge. It's still dark in the east, so dark it feels like it'll be night forever if we fail this time. The Rangers are ready. I've talked to Crouse. Heard his story. Gathered as much as I could from everyone with a spare minute to give the best possible account of what happened. Sorry if I talked too much about me, or coffee. I get it, not everyone's jam. It's just mine and it keeps me anchored this far downrange, this lost beyond the perimeter. For all practical purposes we are surrounded. So of course, Rangers are going to attack. I made coffee, hoping it won't be my last.

Now, the warts and all like I told you I would.

It's time to tell the story of Portugon, the Purple Abyss, and Sanya. This is my confession and if you judge me and find me wanting… well, so do I.

This story is about *Fado*. Which is the Portuguese word, and now Portugonian word, for *Fate*. It's a form of singing.

Music. It's survived the ten thousand years since we disappeared and reappeared.

The songs we once knew, the ones we sang, old and new, have become their *very* old songs, sung so much down through the centuries that no one now has the faintest memory of who wrote them or the times they were about. Or, in most cases, the original lyrics. But the melodies survived to pass the time in comfort, and there is probably now some tradition in singing certain ones during certain events. Life, death, marriage. Sorrows.

Like I said, the lyrics have changed. And the meanings. *Oh Susanna* is still around, but I don't really understand what it's now about. *Here we go round the mulberry bush*, you'd be surprised what that's about.

I'll be honest. Tarragon broke me. I've been dead ever since Autumn, Last of Autumn, would no longer look at me anymore. See me.

Just like that medusa we blew to smithereens had wanted to be seen.

I understood her more now than ever. The medusa. More with each passing moment now that it didn't get better with Last of Autumn.

Just Autumn.

There's no one to argue with me, but with a battle an hour away, I'll indulge myself and say her name inside my head, and a little to the night, just as it once was said to me, and to me alone.

I threw myself into Ranger School after Tarragon. And we know how that turned out. Threw myself into the pump as we trained for what was coming. I worked tirelessly to get us over the mountains, down through the Ogre Wall. Trying to master the things I needed to know in Ranger

School, and would need in the here and now of what we would be facing.

Trying to be the Ranger she said I was.

If we couldn't be together, then I could at least be that. You know?

But that was a lie even I didn't believe.

Or at least that's what I was thinking.

We made Portugon and I was happy and sad to see it though I didn't show it to anyone, on my face that is. I just worked like they did, the Rangers around me, and got stoic about the whole thing. About Autumn, about the long pump we were facing. About the end of things. All things.

I stopped writing this account. And that should have been a warning sign that I was slipping away.

In time, I told myself, I'd get over it. Right? Isn't that how it goes? Give it time, you'll get over it.

We located ourselves, as I have told in this account already, down by the docks of that greatest of the western port cities of the Cities of Men. We ran security, acquired, planned, got in the with the locals who ran the docks without ever formally meeting anyone in government, that we knew of, which was a big part of my work, and settled in to load ships and get on with the pump.

But in the evenings...

In the quiet as I watched the harbor and thought about the boat we'd both dreamed of... the dream of the Cities of Men... it was hard to forget what had been lost.

I can tell you this. Silence is hard. Real hard. When you're alone.

It was the Portugonian sailors who took me to bars across the cities when the day and the work was done. Food.

Hanging meats. Cheeses. Olives. Wine. Beer. Then further on one night when I told them we had to hear music.

I wanted music.

We would hear it.

I'd been seeing Autumn all night, from the early evening on the paseo and in the faces of the women in these places we went to for more drink and the music of forgetting. Shades of her in every one of them.

Shades of the thing we could have been.

I remember thinking after one beer too many that maybe if I could just close my eyes and listen to some music, then perhaps I could turn off what I hadn't been able to turn off since Tarragon.

The memories of us that never were.

Didn't happen. Got worse in fact. Like it does.

The Purple Abyss is the bar where the whores are. There is a singer. An old whore. She sings *Fado*. It is the music of the hardships of life. And is best described by the word *longing*.

In the Purple Abyss there were songs I recognized. Songs that were old when I was young, and some that weren't. All sung in the style of *Fado*.

For a moment, after all the weeks since Tarragon, since the end of us, I was able to forget. And lose myself.

In the losing of myself I found… something. Someone. Some little thing I shouldn't have found. Some soul that needed saving by a tarnished knight who hadn't been able to save himself.

There was this one song, and I liked it, that the old whore who wore black and sang the sad and familiar songs every night, sang.

"That Was Then, This Is Now."

But in Portugonian.

I knew the words. Knew from its stylings that it had to be from the times we came from long ago. And the title, the chorus—*That was then, this is now*—that resonated for me.

Because that's what needed to happen.

The past, Autumn and I, that was then. And what I would do next... well, that was now.

It was my third night back at the Purple Abyss. Much of Portugon in those rougher quarters had heard of the Rangers being there about the city before moving on to something dangerous.

"*Rangiers*" was how they pronounced it. Pronounced us. Like *estrangiers*. Soft, and almost romantic.

But none had ever come here to the Purple Abyss, and the sailors who had first introduced me to the place stopped going, and so, on that third night, it was just me. Even though I knew it was a bit of a dangerous place, it seemed... darkly friendly enough. To me at least.

There was an anonymity in that, and I needed it. Away from the Rangers, away from the sailors, I was just the friendly stranger who liked the singing and the beer. The linguist student I had once been before I went off on an adventure and got my heart broken.

Feeling sorry for myself much? Yeah. I accuse me. I was guilty without prejudice. So don't think I'm making excuses.

What happened, it's all on me. I entered the fatal little drama playing out in that bar and got everyone killed.

I'll be honest. I had a little fatalism going on at that moment. I'd faced enough death recently that I thought...

No, I don't know what I was thinking. I still don't know. But I'd gotten into two fights, had held my own in both, and had been rewarded with drinks and the adoration of a wounded dark little bird.

It was a dark place.

An end-of-the-road kinda place.

Which suited me just fine after a few beers and a little respect. That was the mood I was in now since Tarragon. In hindsight... not a great plan, Talker. I see that. I have clarity here at four thirty in the morning as we get ready to go deal death, or meet it. There's a cold honest clarity about how you arrived at the point where you're carrying an assault pack full of high-ex. And that's now. So just in case... let me tell you everything about me so that no one thinks, no Ranger thinks, anything misty about me when I'm gone. I'm flawed. Really flawed.

The plan was canked. She was the queen to the king now. Last of Autumn. The plan... had been, was supposed to be, different. The plan was *us*.

I would have run away with her. In a boat to the Cities of Men.

I drank more than I should have that night and tried to ignore, at first, the stares of the doe-eyed wounded-bird girl in the shadows. The pale shadow of the girl I loved.

She wasn't Autumn. She could have been. A pale imitation. I'll be honest about that tonight, or rather this morning, with just an hour to go before we move to the LOA.

Line of Advance.

All of us—yeah, even the linguist who's carrying enough explosives to make a small crater—will be fighting out there on the bridge. And we've got to push through to reach the bridge before that, house to house, clearing out the orcs along the way and moving fast so we don't get rolled up by the orcs up there on the cliff.

It feels dangerous out there in the dark morning.

Got to.

And… I have a bad feeling. That's why I'm confessing. But then again I've always had bad feelings and I've made it this far.

This has to come out so you can think whatever you want of me going forward and perhaps never read what I've written down in this account ever again. And then maybe I can go on.

I'll leave it here with my gear. Don't want it getting blown to smithereens.

She had a scar, the dark little wounded-bird whore, where some pimp had cut her badly in the past.

But she was still… beautiful in a damaged way. She needed protecting. She needed a protector.

She wasn't gone. Jaded, or hard. Even that first night you felt like… she made you feel like… you were loved. And that you could love her back if you wanted to.

Drunk, I spent the night with her. And at times I thought she was someone else in the shadows.

In the gray morning of Portugon I retreated from her, promising never to go back to the Abyss again. But hey, I did. Don't we all.

I did. And I did for two weeks.

By the end of it there was Busto. Her pimp made it clear I could have her, buy her if I was so inclined. I was enraged about that. The *buying*. But we, Sanya and I, had whispered about it in the lateness of the night, lying in each other's arms.

Pretending that we could have dreams like... other people who'd had dreams.

She said that she would run away with me and that we could go to Navarre and no one would know us there. We'd start over and be someone else.

She didn't understand that I had a pump. The Rangers were going to get their hit on Sût the Undying. They needed me. Needed me to do my language trick.

She didn't understand that. She just hoped that I was the one who would take her away. But she agreed that I had to go as I watched tears fall from her too-big eyes. Dark eyes that had been hurt so many times you didn't want to know the number. She understood being abandoned.

In those eyes I could see that was normal. For her.

So I said yes. We would run.

But I wasn't buying her from another man.

She told me Busto was dangerous. That she would pay the fee herself and then we could go.

I told her no. Then said stuff about freedom that had once made sense in a world that wasn't this one anymore.

The Ruin is a different place. There are slaves here. There are masters.

I don't know if there's freedom.

But... it's needed. What had the sergeant major said after we took the FOB? Something about someone throwing up a prayer for help. And the universe sending Rangers.

I know that now. It's needed very much. Freedom.

She said we could just run, and in my drunken state I was reckless enough, *cavalier* enough might be the right word, like I was some high and mighty being that was above these petty human struggles of pimp and hooker, that we could run and no one ever would stop us. That I was some kind of lightbringer to a dark world.

In the afternoon of the evening we were to run, I paid out Ranger gold for a room on the other side of town in some quiet tavern out of the way and sent word to her to meet me there with all her possessions.

We would leave in the dead of night.

I saddled the horse and told the Rangers I was just going for a ride and that I would be back. But I was leaving. I was leaving the men who had called me one of their own though I never deserved it.

Warts and all.

Warts and all.

Warts and all, Talker.

I told ya.

We met in the afternoon, and she told me, after we had embraced and I was suddenly in full realization of what I was about to do, she went through her things babbling about what kind of life we would have, and what kind of woman she would be to me, all good things, and then she froze. A small scream erupted from her delicate lips. Part of the scar ran through her top lip. She was frantic and desperate instantly as she told me she'd forgotten her Iago. She was inconsolable instantly. Sobbing as though she had committed some great sin that could never ever be forgiven.

That's what she called the idol. *Iago.*

Her local god from whatever village she'd been cast out of, sold from, forgotten by.

I told her I'd get her a new one.

She wept.

Let me say this. She was a wounded bird. A fragile thing. But there was a strength in her. She was a survivor. And my guess, if just from the scar, was that she had been through some pretty horrible things. Very horrible things.

She had survived.

And if life, or the universe, could just give her a break… she could've shown them.

"Iago has never forsaken me," she babbled, weeping to the point of hyperventilating. "He has heard my prayers, Talk-ir, and brought you to me," she said, throwing herself on the floor.

I'll go, I told her. *I'll go back to the Abyss and get your idol.*

"Busto. Busto will know if you take it. He'll know I am gone forever, and he'll want his money and then we must pay!"

There was a part of me that wondered if this was a con. I was… angry. I swore and told her I would go, get my weapons at the tavern the Rangers were using for a base, and come back with the idol soon.

I stormed out.

The last time I saw here she had tears in her eyes and she was smiling that I would do what I had told her I would do. Smiling that I would be the hero she had prayed to her god for.

In that moment, even as I raged, the look in her eyes told me that finally, for her, all the good things she had prayed for to that piece of stone, were coming true.

All the good she'd ever hoped for, prayed for, and had never found, was in me.

Someday every girl dreams her prince will come.

It's just that Autumn's prince was someone else.

Sanya was what life would have called a loser. A delicate, fragile girl sold into slavery. Praying to a lifeless carved rock that a prince would come and carry her away from the prison her life was at the Purple Abyss. And where other whores might have dreamed that and never believed it, she believed that it would happen. For her, every day was a chance that it might.

Today you might get to ride an elephant.

Instead of a hero, she got me.

Back at the Ranger CP tavern Kurtz got a hold of me and put me on detail loading *Sofia*. I loaded until dawn and then ran out the back door of the tavern to the Purple Abyss, praying, praying when you don't believe that she hadn't gone herself to get that stupid idol.

But idols are powerful things.

The place was empty and the door was locked.

I went to the inn I'd put her up in.

She wasn't there, but her stuff was.

It wasn't a con, and two days later they found her body down by the river. She was cut up badly. Her throat slashed as she stared up at the sky with those limpid eyes, asking for help. Begging to be saved so that she could make it to me. So that she could save me. Clutching her tiny god she'd gone back for. Staring up at the gray sky and never seeing again.

Two nights later, the night before we left Portugon on the pump, I walked into the Purple Abyss.

No carbine. No secondary.

Just *Coldfire* strapped to my hip.

Busto and three others were sitting at our table and the looks on their faces were pure stone as they watched me go to the bar.

Jao, who had served me happily in all the nights I had come there, laid out a dirty cracked cup quickly and then tersely whispered, "Leave now, *Rangier*."

I swiped the glass and emptied it in one go.

"No," I croaked. And then again, if just to tell myself what I was here about. "No."

I turned and put my arms against the bar, leaning back like some gunfighter from another age who did this all the time.

The old whore who wore black began to sing. *That was then, this is now.* Her solemn eyes imploring me to leave right now, and live.

She'd sung it before, and because I knew Portuguese I knew the words. I'd even sung them to Sanya in the night after the nightmares she had. Waiting for the dawn to come, and the darkness to finally relent.

But does it ever?

Busto smiled.

Then stood.

"If this is the way you must have it, *Rangier*," announced Busto, low and slow, full of pimp menace. "But... she was just a whore. And no one cares for whores, do they? So have another drink on me. And then go away, *Rangier*. Go away and live."

Busto's two sidekicks stood and started to walk toward me.

I remember laughing sickly, almost like a stray dog with a cough, as I drew *Coldfire* and thrust it into the first one who thought rushing me would destabilize my intentions.

In seconds it was chaos.

And in seconds it was over.

There were three cuts.

And one for me in the middle of it all.

The first one got it right through the heart and I heard him inhale and gasp in horror at the sudden ice that filled his heart when the blade called *Coldfire* found him.

Boot to the chest I pulled the blade free and slashed desperately to get thug two. The blade seemed to fly through the air, caught him in the neck and then he was dead, falling to the ground into a crouch to gurgle while Busto and I circled for the final exchange.

You don't get to be head pimp in the worst bar in the city without being good with a knife, and Busto's first move was so lightning-fast I didn't feel the deep cut he gave me until he was dancing away from me like a bullfighter.

That was the cut. The one Santago would need to sew closed. The one that would haunt me all through the battle in Atlantea.

Every time it did I told myself I deserved it. I had been unfaithful.

To what? I could almost hear Santago asking me in the morning fog as I babbled insanely and drank the hot white liquor he gave me for pain for the sewing work that needed to be done before I reported back to the ships for the hop into the dangerous east.

"For what, Talk-ir?" he said through gritted teeth holding thread while he worked.

I don't know that I answered the old man then. I was pretty drunk.

But for letting her down, is the answer I would have given at the time. She had gone back to get the idol, thinking I had abandoned her. Yet another disappointment in a life that was nothing but for a forgotten girl called Sanya whom no one would remember.

She had believed in love, once.

And I was it.

And when the darkness beyond the afternoon had come, and I had not returned because Kurtz had me on duty, she had gone back for the stone herself, the idol, the charm and nothing more, that had listened to all her tears through every pain and humiliation as she waited for a Prince Charming to arrive.

And I had betrayed my... brothers.

The Rangers. That's what they called me.

Hey, brother. It's all good.

Rangers.

Rangiers.

I was leaving them. I was going to.

I lunged at Busto, slashing low and batting his weaving knife aside as I disemboweled him right there. He danced away, screaming and crying at once because he instantly knew it was a bad cut and that he was surely dead.

He was dead. I'd seen enough wounds to know you weren't getting out of that one. Guts slithering out onto the floor of the dirty tavern as he dropped his pimp's knife and someone screamed. The status quo had been upset. He was whimpering on his knees as I stood there in the silence, panting and finding none of the revenge I'd come for.

Or Autumn.

The old whore looking at me. She'd stop singing. She was old and dressed in black. She stood, humming the tune, and crossed the floor and stood before me. Her old dark eyes bored straight into me, seeing everything I really was, everything I really wasn't.

"You never listened," she spoke in a voice more ruined than Santago's. "Only heard what you wanted to. Just the line that made you sad and brave, soldier. Just as all your kind must be when it comes time to die. But the line that comes after is the one you should have heard. *Let me prove my love, I'll show you how.* You never listened. Men and soldiers never do."

Her thin lips pressed together. Dark eyes driving straight into my heart. "Go," she said. "This is over now. I will say the prayers for her and spend the brass to see that she is buried. Go. And never come back, soldier. Prove your love in the battle you will die in. Wherever she is... she will know then, soldier. Perhaps that is your only chance now at salvation."

I turned, walking, stumbling really, from the bar. At the door she said one more thing, loud enough for me to hear.

"That was then, Ranger, and this is now. But you should have listened to the line. The truth was there. Life was there."

I made it outside and fell against the alley wall, noticed for the first time the blood coming from the wound in my side. It was everywhere and slick. I saw the cut and groaned because it looked real bad. I leaned against the dirty wall, holding my blade.

And Santago was there, helping me away.

When no one else in the Rangers or along the docks knew what was going on, the old sailor did. He had been there. Had seen enough knife fights over whores. Seen enough young and stupid love to know that sometimes you'll lie to even yourself and pretend that you're doing something noble when really...

Really you're just trying to selfishly forget.

The one that you love.

I'm sorry, little girl. Sanya. I never loved you. I just wanted to save someone. And I didn't do that at all.

One day, when I'm gone, the Rangers will read this. And they'll know who I really was.

Warts and all.

Until then, I'll never let them down. I will never leave them. But they will know that, once, I almost did.

CHAPTER TWENTY-FOUR

THE battle's over. Talker's gone. This is Tanner. I think you know who I am. But Talker's gone. My best friend is gone now.

CHAPTER TWENTY-FIVE

TANNER here.

I... I am not good at this writin' stuff down. But my friend is dead... so... I guess it's my job now.

In the three days since... I've tried to find out what happened to my friend in those last moments of the battle against the genie.

Everyone I talk to, who was with him, tells me he was a straight-up hero that morning. He Rangered hard enough that Kurtz, who hasn't said much since, seems, at points when he's not getting the weapons teams ready for the hump out of here, to be as lost as I feel now.

So...

Here's how the battle went down.

Sorry about my grammar and stuff. Like I said, I ain't no writer. But maybe I'll get better. I read a lot of books. There's a lotta time being a soldier to read books. And we pass around the sci-fi books about dudes all jacked up in-side Iron Man armor croakin' aliens.

So I read those.

Maybe that'll help me to do Talker's job now. Talker said it was important. Getting it all down. I read his stuff. He was all over the place. Talked about coffee way too much.

I'll cut that out. Coffee's coffee. Dunno what else to say about that.

Now dip… dip is life. Dip and Miller High Life is about as good as it gets for sure.

Nuff said.

When we came into the bay and anchored at that big freaky head, captain dividing us into two forces to hold the line there, make sure the smaj's element could link up with us if they got back into the fight, that was a big old fight against the orcs in the boats.

Those guys were rough. They were tough monkeys. I thought the 240s were gonna be enough to unlive them good and proper. Cept they had spellcasters on their boats throwin all kinds of stuff at us. Swarms of biting bugs, like swarms that blotted out the skies and left big old welts and made you feel like your raw nerves had just touched an electric fence. And hurling fireballs and lightning bolts at us.

The 240s sank several of their ships as they came at us. The orcs just swam through the water to come for us while more of their ships kept coming around the cape and makin straight for us to get their fight on.

All told, we fought about twenty ships before the smaj showed up with the other galley end of day.

Then we had two big battles in the middle of the night. The orcs in boats used the fog to get close to us for the attack and so we were exchanging broadsides fire with 240s, indirect grenade launchers, primaries, hell even secondaries, and their bows and big emplaced bows someone calls *ballistay*. Those shot big flaming arrows and I got stuck on duty putting those rounds out when they planted themselves in our two ships. We had a team for this. The orcs were trying to light the ships on fire at the bow, so we'd start taking on water or have to abandon ship.

I don't know what we were gonna do then. Climb out on the big old weird head and fight from there?

Knowing Kurtz, yeah probly.

We'd fight in the water even though it was filled with sharks and those other weirder things down there in the dark.

The smaj's element came in and drove off the final attack by the end of the day. Sergeant Kurtz had done an excellent job of holding our ship against an overwhelming number of ships and orcs. Give that man an Army Commendation Medal. Our galley was all burnt up in places and the deck was littered with expended brass.

But no serious casualties.

Problem was, we couldn't make it into the bay because of all the shipwrecks and fog. We'd have to wait until morning.

I know what I need to write. But I ain't ready. I ain't ready to write the Talker part yet. Lemme have a smoke and think about this. Plus my hand hurts from writing so much. Right in the spot where I punched a wall and found the stud when my ex-wife sold all my TA-50 at the off-post pawn shop for meth.

I didn't know she had a meth problem. Pump after pump'll do that to a stripper.

Okay, I'm back from the smoke. We're leaving in a few hours. Smaj is taking the other boat back to Portugon to get more supplies from the Forge. The squad of Rangers at the FOB will be bringing it from Hawthorn.

It's cold here at night in the desert. That last of summer is gone now. The days are shorter. Feels like when you were a kid at back-to-school times and you can't pretend it's summer anymore. Right around the time change, y'know? When you have to accept winter's coming and that's the way it's gonna be until the end of spring.

Unless you're from California. Cali got it good all year around from what I hear.

Sometimes I think I shoulda just gone there. But I like being a Ranger, don't get me wrong. I'm surprised they let me keep doing it. They were getting ready to kick me out before this all happened. Tabbed and all. I should be a team leader, according to Sergeants Chris and Joe. Instead, I keep getting in trouble.

They said one of the agencies would pick me up for some secret squirrel work. But I think I was just gonna go to California and maybe try to be a stunt man in the movies, or on TV. I ain't bad looking if you don't mind the scars.

Maybe meet an actress.

And then I remember that was all ten thousand years ago. And that actress, she's long gone now. Hollywood's gone too probably.

So I'm glad I'm here.

We tied off the smaj's galley and fought the next two battles in the middle of the night. They boarded us on the last one and took *Sofia,* which was half ready to sink. We were gonna transfer cargo in the morning and we would have let the orcs have it, but since they took it about ten at night we had to counterattack and clear it.

I led a fire team to take the cargo hold while the weapons team stayed on the orc Viking ships with black sails circling us in the fog.

That was some shooting down in there. As tight as close quarters battle gets.

Freaky too.

The orcs were like pirates, but tribal too. Lots of em had shrunken head necklaces. Carried big knives, bigger than Jackson over in Third Herd's Bowie knife. You had to lay the late on em fast or they'd stick you. I got one right in the side. A knife.

But I don't bleed anymore.

I'm special.

Talker told you about me. I read that part.

Damn. I was trying not to think about him. I know I gotta write all this down and I keep hearing him, waiting for him to show up with a coffee in his hand, telling me excitedly about the freaky stuff he's just gotten up to here in this weird world the locals call the Ruin.

Talker was new.

I think all us Rangers liked that about him. New and shiny. He was excited about what we, the regiment, were doing in ways we aren't always... *allowed* to show it.

Not that there are any rules against being Super Duper Ranger. It's just, we keep it low key.

Don't wanna be SEALs or nothing, eh?

But we liked how much Talker dug the action of being a Ranger. It is pretty cool.

Now that's gone. He's gone. And we all feel it.

I just laughed.

I don't laugh much anymore.

Not since I changed after getting killed by that Joker Chick I'm looking for.

You wanna know about death?

I learned from reading Talker's stuff that it's okay to just start talking about something else.

Both Brumm and I have been dead. Brumm got killed by orcs and the chief resurrected him. After I came back, when no one was around, he came over to me and asked, "Hey Tanner, when you were, uh… dead and all. You meet anyone?"

I told Brumm I didn't. To me it was just like being asleep. But in a nightmare kinda way that was a mystery you were about to figure out. And then I was so angry about getting killed so cheap-like by a chick doing ninja stuff while looking like the Joker's girlfriend, Harley what's her face, that I got angry about sleeping, and I just got back up from the dead. I just did. Pretty weird.

I accept that I'm dead now. I have some business to finish.

And when that's done, I'll go back to the nightmare cause I've been headed there all along. I'm fine with that. But I gotta settle Joker Girl for that one.

Know what I mean?

I told Brumm, "No. Didn't meet anyone, man."

He looked off out in the forest for a long minute. Said nothing and then went off to do Brumm stuff.

In his defense, he doesn't talk much.

I guess since I'm the writer now, get used to the phrase, *In his defense.* I learned it from a JAG officer during one of my UCMJ actions and it's stuck with me ever since. That and *mitigating circumstances.*

I don't know why.

I just learned em and now I use em a lot.

I think I coulda been a pretty good lawyer.

I understand criminals. For reasons none of the Rangers need to know about and no, I ain't confessing here.

So by that time we had comm with the ground force commander, and the smaj told us the plan to assault the beach at first light and clear the new insertion point. Then link up with main force and attack "a heavy."

We had no idea what a heavy was going to be via the smaj's frago.

That means fragmentary order.

Talker said he tried to explain things in the account in case anyone who wasn't military read it someday.

So. There. I did.

I think I'm bad at this and my hand hurts again.

Okay.

So about that time in the battle, just after dawn, we started in through the bay, weapons teams ready to support from the ship while assaulters took the beach, secured the path up to the citadel, and effected linkup with the other support element setting up a crossfire from the bridge.

What I've heard from the boys with Sergeant Joe is that Talker fought house to house in the last couple of hours when they crossed the LOA and entered the buildings in the district east of the bridge and the big old inlet that cuts the whole place in half.

Command Team calls that the Mouth of Madness.

Freaky huh?

Talker.

Man.

He was on point that morning. He hung with Joe and his boys and they are killers.

They embody LGOPs. That's *Little Groups of Paratroopers*. It's a thing for airborne units. Sort of a last stand to ruin the enemy's day when things go to hell in a handbasket and the mission's sideways.

In other words, small groups of pissed-off 19-year-old paratroopers, armed to the teeth and with a serious lack of adult or command supervision, getting lethally creative and then hey... Anything goes. As they say.

Some smart general once put it like this. "March to the sound of the guns and kill anyone who ain't dressed like you."

Joe's boys are the living breathing practical application of killer 19-year-olds being run by a guy who's forgot more about Rangering then most Rangers will ever learn.

Kurtz is a purist.

Joe is a practicalist.

Even Kurtz acknowledges Joe's wisdom. He just wishes Joe would be a little more... Ranger... about it.

Joe's squads devastated their lane on the move to the bridge, with Talker bringing up the rear and carrying explosives to det the bridge.

The problem for the Rangers was they couldn't leave anyone in their rear. So the Ranger squads were clearing both sides of the street, tossing frags in, and shooting anyone inside the building leading to the bridge, while at the same time fighting large concentrations of orcs in running street battles as they pushed the enemy back to the bridge.

In these situations, Talker held rear security and at times engaged in street fighting as the Rangers clearing the building got attacked from the street.

Suarez tells me Talker even smoked a large four-armed orc who appeared out of nowhere and tried to smoke the breaching team just as they'd gone into the building and got into a firefight with hajis inside.

It was chaos in all directions and Talker held cohesion and hung with the fire teams to get it done.

The huge four-armed orc guy was supported by orcs with flaming oil who at that point were lobbing their "grenades" into every building the Rangers would go into. The smaller ones, little like Jabba, were all over the rooftop and the snipers were clearing them off as fast as possible while the Rangers advanced block to block.

This was fifteen minutes after dawn. The whole squad would have gotten cooked in there, in that building, but Talker grabbed a stretcher canvas, unfolded it, and started beating the flames out, while carrying an assault pack full of explosives mind you, and yelling for the team to get out of there.

They did, then Talker backed off and the Rangers let the building burn they would have just been killed in.

Suarez told me, "Man, if it wouldn't been for Talker, that old mud and wood structure would have turned into an oven all over us quick."

I talked to Suarez about it. Wrote down what he said. Like an interview. It was weird, but I'm trying to do this right. For Talker's sake.

Suarez told me Talker had two arrows sticking out of his assault pack right at that moment, he'd disregarded incoming so much to put out the flames.

They'd tried to shoot him in the back while he was saving the fire team.

By that time, we in the galleys were closing on the beach. We could see what the "heavy" was now. It was like a giant dust devil just twisting and throwing debris away from itself. It was growing taller by the second as we approached.

At first sight, it had a giant emotional DO NOT DIS-TURB sign hung out on it as far as I and everyone else was concerned.

What were we gonna do? Shoot it?

I had two jobs. Me and the fire team I was leading. Get the old wizard on shore. Then go get Kennedy from the bridge and link those two up so they could do their thing against what we were being told was some kind of genie.

Both ships beached while the Rangers on land, supported by snipers, took the far end of the bridge.

Dixon was hit bad by orc sniper fire and the medics had to pull him back. That was when Talker stepped forward and took his place on the fire team Sergeant Joe needed to work the bridge.

The orcs knew they couldn't lose the bridge.

If half of what I heard about my friend is true… then yeah, he straight up Rangered as they took the bridge. Shooting, moving, and communicating, with much violence of action, they took that end of the bridge and held it while other lanes were cleared.

Two things happened at that point. The orcs trapped on that side of the river were slaughtered. The orcs on the bridge ran for the other side, giving Joe's teams a chance to consolidate and get ready to set the explosives on the bridge.

The fire teams pushed forward, and Talker was held back with Joe and a few others to assist Sergeant Kang with the demo work.

Meanwhile, my fire team is shooting its way on shore, under fire from catapults, with the old wizard saying things like, "Fear not, Rangers, I shall cast this spell to protect you," and, "Zounds… look at the size of that thing!"

He didn't really say *Zounds*. But it was like that.

I had no idea if his magic did anything.

I was busy killing orcs coming at us in waves, rushing down through the sands, screaming like nutjobs and trying to hack us to pieces.

My team held cohesion and we made the plaza at the top, leaving dead orcs in our way like ya do.

The Rangers escorting Kennedy made the plaza in front of the citadel and signaled they were ready to effect linkup between our two wizards.

The Dust Devil Genie was huge now. Taller than the enormous citadel that was already huge. It dominated this place.

I saw the captain leading an assault force through the catapults, shooting down the orcs working them and setting the catapults on fire with incendiaries.

It was too much madness for six thirty in the morning. Trust me.

My hand hurts but I can't stop now. Not now. I just need to push through.

From what I understand… this is what happened.

Sergeant Joe and Talker were forward along the bridge, Joe working the knots on the det cords while Talker managed the hi-ex from his assault pack.

The other Ranger with them, Torres, good guy, pulling security.

Kennedy and the wizard start attacking the dust devil genie with… magic, I guess. That stuff's a mystery to me. Way above my paygrade.

Now, the dead, I can tell ya all about that and maybe I will after I get this worst part down and out of me.

But then again, maybe I'll never write again. Don't like it much right now.

So, whatever Kennedy and the old wizard were doing, it drove the genie dust devil nuts instantly. It started screaming.

Yeah. It did. And that was a gut check, let me tell you.

The winds went to hurricane force in fight gear. And trust me, I been in one of those.

Like you couldn't move at all.

So, the genie thing tries to get away from the power ray magic beams Kennedy and Vandahar are shooting at it, while the old wizard speaks like the announcer at a rock concert above the howling genie storm saying all these crazy strange magic words that only Talker would understand.

Then the genie goes straight for the bridge to bust outta there I guess. It's so powerful, it's tearing up paving stones as it moves. Ripping columns that must have stood there for ten thousand years to pieces. Everything it touches explodes and is carried away by its own force, sucked into the storm above. The genie is exploding through the terrain to reach the bridge to get away from Kennedy and the old wizard.

Torres tells me Joe told them to run at that point once they noticed it was headed right at them. That the giant swirling magical tornado thing coming at them, the genie, it was like out of a special effects movie that was like the big bigga biggest movie of the summer.

It was flat out freaky, and Torres is not given to exaggerating like some of us do.

Joe was probably going to det the bridge once the thing got on. Try and drop it into the Mouth of Madness would be my guess.

Because it didn't look, at that point to me, hanging onto a stone wall and trying not to get hurled out to sea like the orcs all around us were, like Kennedy and Vandahar were doing anything to hurt it.

If anything, it looked like they were just pissing it off.

Torres and Talker did as they were told and ran for the far end of the bridge, especially because Talker had the explosives that hadn't been placed yet. Then they turned and saw the bridge collapse where they had just been. They watched as Sergeant Joe looked at them, shrugged, and then went into the Mouth of Madness as the bridge went down around him. He'd detted it.

I've looked at that water. It's like a waterfall disappearing into a mountain at the far side of the city.

It's rapids on crack.

Vandahar, and I've asked him, says no one knows where it goes and that it's certain death. It's just the sea flooding into a desert the people of now call the End of the World.

"No one ever returns from there," said the old wizard.

The genie went in too, just after Joe did. The thing thrashed and churned the water something fierce, exploding in every direction as it died.

No one thinks Joe survived.

No one thinks Talker survived.

In the seconds after Joe and the genie went in, Talker did something.

He stopped as the bridge collapsed in the portions they'd just run across to get away from the killer whirlwind thing.

Torres told me, "Talker just stopped, shucked that assault pack and his gear. Then he looked at me and said, 'Rangers never go alone.'"

Then he jumped to his death, going in like he was gonna save Sergeant Joe. Who had already been sucked under the surface of that hurricane.

They were the only ones near enough to Sergeant Joe.

No one thinks anyone, the genie, or Joe, or Talker, could survive a waterfall that disappears into an underground cavern, gets sucked over rocks and chasms beneath the ground like a jet engine, then shoots out into a desert no one ever returns from a hundred miles to the south probably.

I've gone to what remains of the bridge. Even Thor wouldn't surf that nightmare.

The Mouth of Madness is certain death.

EPILOGUE

TANNER here. We're leaving in the morning.

Last night I stood and watched the Mouth. My mind tells me there's no way my friend survived. And we'll never find the bodies.

We're back on mission.

But I see the dead now. That's what happened to me when I came back from the other side. I see them as ghosts. Sometimes sad. Mourning over some wrong.

I see that a lot here among the ruins of this place.

But sometimes they're happy.

They look at me and smile, then go off wandering over the beach and sea grass, disappearing into the ocean.

There are strange ghosts here.

There is the smell of death here.

I don't know if Talker is dead. Reason and facts would tell me he and Sergeant Joe are dead. No one could have survived what they fell into.

I smell nothing but death from the Mouth of Madness. And something worse.

But…

I don't smell Talker. Or Joe.

And I should.

I'm a dead thing now on a trail of vengeance.

The Rangers need to get back on mission. We ain't got time to go looking for their bodies.

But we also never leave anyone behind.

Late last night the smaj came to me.

"Know what you're gonna do, PFC Tanner. I can read it plain as day, boy."

Me: "I have no idea to what you are referring, Sergeant Major."

"Yeah…" he says and just looks at me like the stone-cold killer he is. "Best get to it tonight before we go and start looking for you. Be gone before the NCOs start pitching a fit at me about accountability."

"What about the captain?" I asked.

"Had to stop him from going himself, son. And he's done that before. He's got medals that are classified for doing stuff like that."

I couldn't smell them. Talker or Joe. And I smell the dead. See em, too. They come and stand around me, asking me to right the wrongs that ended their lives if I'll just listen to their stories.

But the Rangers need me and so I just tell them to hush now.

The dead think I'm some kinda… *sheriff*… for them.

I don't know what I am, but I know I am becoming that thing. Whatever it is. And it's getting hard to put it off.

"What if they're dead, Sergeant Major?"

He looked off toward the east and the dark night there. Where we were headed to get our hit on some ancient pharaoh that's been giving the Ruin a hard time, for some time. *Someone prayed for help*, Talker told me the smaj said once. And someone answered and sent us in.

Rangers. Why not?

Okay.

"Then they're dead, PFC," answered the granite monument to soldiers everywhere that was my sergeant major. The only law I ever understood and feared. "You just make sure they go out on their shield, PFC Tanner. And that we didn't leave them behind for the vultures and the buzzards to pick on them wherever you find em. And if someone has to pay…"

He walked away into the shadows, checking the watch. Watching the night. Ready for whatever came next.

"Then you make sure they pay the full price, whoever they are."

The End

ALSO BY JASON ANSPACH & NICK COLE

Galaxy's Edge: Legionnaire
Galaxy's Edge: Savage Wars
Galaxy's Edge: Requiem For Medusa
Galaxy's Edge: Order of the Centurion

ALSO BY JASON ANSPACH

Wayward Galaxy
King's League
'til Death

ALSO BY NICK COLE

American Wasteland:
The Complete Wasteland Trilogy
SodaPop Soldier
Strange Company

Made in the USA
Middletown, DE
06 July 2023

34640743R00159